RUINS EXCAVATION

EDITED BY ERIC T· REYNOLDS WITH ROSE REYNOLDS & EMMELINE WOLFE

HADLEY
RILLE
BOOKS

RUINS EXCAVATION

Cover art © Vishnu Kumar, Bowie15 | Dreamstime.com
Cover Design © Heather McDougal

ISBN-13 978-0-9892631-6-0
Published simultaneously in the United States of America and the United Kingdom by
Hadley Rille Books
c/o Eric T. Reynolds, Publisher
PO Box 25466
Overland Park, KS 66225 USA

www.hrbpress.com

To John & Patty Finn

Contents

FOREWORD

BY NISI SHAWL

/Hearts of carnelian. Hearts of bitumen. Hearts of Aztec gold. The hearts of these stories' heroines pulse to the beat of discovery, the rhythm of knowledge. Sometimes that knowledge is completely new, but more often it is old, lost for centuries to dust and whispers.

The task of reclaiming the knowledge of the past—a past in some cases corresponding to our present and future—falls to women within these pages. With brush and rifle and bioengineered bugs, with psychometry and spreadsheets, this anthology's imagined archaeologists excavate secrets hidden in the depths of the earth and the depths of their own selves. As women are often trained to do they look down—though not necessarily in meekness. They calculate. They observe. They share.

Who hasn't wanted to dig for buried treasure? Picking up this book is the next best thing to picking up a map and trowel. Whether outsiders to the cultures whose riches they seek or their undisputed heirs, the heroines of *Ruins Excavation* stand in for all of us as they explore sites of legend: respectfully, carefully, and wonderfully—that is, with hearts full of wonder.

INTRODUCTION

BY ERIC T. REYNOLDS, ROSE REYNOLDS & EMMELINE WOLFE

Archaeological ruins serve as gateways to other cultures, to other times and places. In 2013, we issued a call for submissions to authors to write a science fiction or fantasy story set in or about ruins with a protagonist who is a woman of color archaeologist. The women who excavate the ruins in these stories explore cultures from across the checkerboard of humanity and encounter unexpected presences (not necessarily human) as they work to not only add pieces to the human jigsaw puzzle of life, but also demonstrate who and where we are in our place within the Cosmos.

—ETR, RR ,& EW
Overland Park & Lawrence, Kansas
August 2015

COVER HER GHOST WITH A FEATHERED CAPE

BY JENNIFER CROW

RUST-RED DUST SIFTED DOWN as Lucia Alvarez shook the screen, revealing bits of pottery, stark white with black geometric figures. Sacred pottery, broken when the last people to inhabit this place walked away, their ritual places burning behind them. Lucia liked to think of her own ancestors traveling with them, priests and priestesses out of the southern lands, bearing tales of ferocious gods and wealth beyond dreaming. The people of the Colorado watershed, the ones later settlers called Anasazi, had far-flung trade relationships, even as far south as Mayan territory, and her research helped establish those links.

She imagined envoys arriving, resplendent in their tropical furs and feathers. They'd have walked up wide roads marked with towers and beacon fires, or perhaps been carried by servants they'd captured. Would they have brought warriors, too, or come with economic hegemony in mind?

A quick gulp from her canteen and the warm metallic tang of the water washed away the grit that coated her tongue and teeth. She ignored the buzzing at the base of her skull that told her someone was trying to reach her. Layers of time blanketed her, the shimmering heat pressed down, and for the moment she could forget everything except her immediate purpose.

"Work is a blessing," she murmured, quoting her grandmother. As a child, she hadn't understood what the words meant, but now she used them to build a wall around her darkest thoughts. A bead of sweat trickled from her hairline, until an impatient brush of her forearm smeared it away. The hard, clear eye of the sun had burnished her brown skin to deep mahogany, and she wished she'd cropped her curly hair short before landing in the back country. Perhaps, when evening came and it was too dark to work, she'd find a knife in her supplies and cut it all off. There was no one here to care if she looked ridiculous.

She sat back on her heels and studied the site. A great kiva's broken walls jutted out of the ground to her right, like a gaping maw. Where she crouched, at one end of a trench, rooms branched off from that central point. Behind her, the ancient builders had constructed their settlement in a shallow cave scooped from the rock by ages of wind and water. More buildings stood guard at the canyon rim, and the signs of gardens and more homes crowded beside the stream in the canyon depths.

The man who'd discovered this place a century earlier had called it 'El Jefe,' the Chief. Lucia thought she'd give it a new name, before she finished her work here. But she wanted to live in it for a time first, feel its soul in her bones. Only then would she understand its innermost, holy self.

She smiled at her own pretention. After only a couple weeks alone, she sounded more like a religion professor than an archaeologist. The best way to tell the story of a people, she'd always believed, was to look at the simple goods and arts that made up their everyday lives. That point of reference formed the foundation of any understanding. Yet how could she deny the deep spiritual base of life in this arid place? Any civilization in the red-stone lands had lived here at the sufferance of their gods.

And after the ecological and social devastation of the twenty-first century, even the few brave souls who'd made the desert their home had vanished. Most had moved to the security of the great cities, all that was left after the collapse of the United States. The rest had died of disease or starvation.

The hum from the implant in her skull grew too insistent to ignore any longer. Lucia tapped it, her teeth gritted.

"*Mother. How could you?*"

"Yolanda. A little loud."

"Because I'm *angry*. I can't believe you'd strand yourself *out there*."

Lucia stifled a sigh and picked up a trowel, scraping gently at a mass of broken pottery to tease out individual shards. "I've found lots of black-on-white ritual pieces. And some lovely polychrome—evidence the people here were trading with settlements to the south."

"You're going to die out there. Mother—" Yolanda's voice broke, and Lucia's heart twinged.

"I was going to die in the city. I chose to come here instead." She dug the tip of the trowel into the dust, grounding herself in the reality of the place. "I love you so much, Yolanda."

"Then come home. Dr. Yazzie said he could send a team for you—"

"He shouldn't have said that. I won't go." She brushed at her eyes, where traitorous tears had formed. "I'm like a cat, *corazon*. I don't want everyone hovering while I fade and expire. I'll just find a quiet place and pull the night around me."

"Stop. Just stop."

"Give your father my regards. Tell him I'm grateful to him for the gift of you." Lucia laid her hand at the nape of her neck, pressing the implant's activator until Yolanda's voice disappeared in static that blurred to silence. She was glad the implant didn't allow video conversations. If she'd seen her daughter's face, she might have weakened.

"This is my place," she murmured. The broken bits of pottery kept her attention until evening crept in. As shadows stretched across the site, she packed up her tools and trudged back to her camp. Late in the day, after hours stooping, the aches grew fierce. Something degenerative, the doctor told her. Genetics and environment, working together to kill her slowly. Experimental drugs slowed the progression down, but the side effects dulled her thoughts. At last she decided to make the most of what time she had. So long as she had strength, she meant to reach into the past and shake free some secrets. Too much had been lost already.

Lucia rubbed at her shoulder, where a bone-deep ache settled. She was pondering what she hoped to accomplish on the morrow when a light sparkling on the canyon rim above caught her attention. A faint tang of wood smoke hung in the air. Curiosity and concern together sent her in search of the source. As night closed in, she pulled a lantern from her pack and wound the crank that powered it.

Even with light, the path was treacherous, loose gravel slipping underfoot and branches scratching at her face. She skidded once, then again. But by then she'd passed the halfway point of the climb, so she decided to keep going rather than try to descend. Rich-scented sage and pungent, stunted creosote brush provided handholds, and at last she pulled herself over the brink. The muscles in her legs trembled, so she lay for a time on stone that still radiated the day's heat.

No storm had rolled through, no lightning strike could have sparked that blaze. Lucia held the lantern high and trudged forward. Anger crawled in the pit of her stomach at the halting pace that was the most she could manage. Somehow she'd convinced herself she'd have the rest of the summer and fall to work. It seemed her body had other plans.

A low mound hid the fire, the shrouded ruins of some long forgotten tower or kiva. When Lucia reached the top, her lantern gleaming on potsherds half-exposed in the dirt, the fire had dimmed, fading to embers. "Hello?" she called, though she knew no one else was out in the wilderness. No one answered, and she laughed at herself.

Still, she couldn't deny the evidence of her eyes. Someone had laid a circle of stones and cleared away the dead brush, someone who had left footprints in the soft sand around the dying blaze. She tried to follow the tracks, but they vanished just outside the sandy hollow. Sudden weariness struck Lucia, so she sat and closed her eyes.

Morning light woke her, spears of light cast across the desert. Though she ached all over, she'd slept solidly. With care she bent and examined the scene. The ashes were cold, already almost buried by drifting sand. If she'd just come across it, she'd have thought the fire had burned decades earlier. The footprints blurred, edges softened by a wind that blew steadily from the west.

Lucia considered the ashes. After a while, she admitted to herself that it wasn't a mystery she could solve, not with the evidence at hand. So she returned to the lower site. To her surprise, when she reached the wide ledge that held the great kiva, she saw that a crack had appeared in the ground.

She eased around its edges, examining potential weak places. Where the sun and the lantern shed light on the darkness, she saw deeper masonry walls, scraps of basketry, signs of a much older settlement beneath the ruins she'd been studying. Impatient, she tapped her implant's switch and asked for a connection to Professor Hosteen Yazzie.

"Lucia! What's happened? Are you well?" He'd insisted that she call if anything went wrong, but it irked her a little that he assumed that was her purpose.

"The most amazing thing. I'll send you video soon, but I had to talk about it with someone." She explained what she'd found. "It looks undisturbed. I'm not planning to go in, not yet."

"If you can't resist, touch as little as possible and document everything." For Yazzie, it was an unprecedented offer of trust. She heard the longing in his voice, but it could be years before the powers in charge of Greater Dallas let him spend another season at the site. That stinginess, the reluctance to let even scholars out on their own, had been behind her clandestine plans to stay behind when Yazzie and the rest went back to the city.

"I'd like to leave it for you. I've more than enough to keep me busy." Even as she spoke, she bent closer to the crack, which at its widest could be spanned with her arm.

"What do you see?" The tone of exasperated patience told her he knew she was leaning as far over the edge as she could without tumbling in head first.

"It's . . . oh my God." The sight knocked the breath from her lungs.

"Lucia! Lucia, what happened?"

A laugh bubbled up. "Yazzie, you won't believe this. A cape. A complete feathered cape. The colors are gorgeous, even after all these years."

He laughed, too. "You've always had Coyote's own luck, haven't you? Get pictures. Protect it."

"Yaz—"

"You must. It's not sealed in any more." An odd note crept into his voice. "Maybe it wanted to be found."

"I'll be *so* careful," she promised. She let him give her instructions, knowing he ached to be there, to secure the cape himself. She'd have felt the same, were their positions reversed.

When she'd signed off, she laid a tarp over the crack and secured it with rocks. Hunger and excitement had made her lightheaded. Before climbing into the lower layer of rooms, she'd need to eat and gather additional supplies.

The path sloped gently toward the stream, where a cottonwood grove sheltered her tent. She lighted the little camp stove that sat on a flat outcropping of rock and warmed water for tea. Protein bars tasted better after a good dunking, she'd found. Calico Wash trickled lazily by as she ate. It ran northwest out of the hills to the Little Colorado, the river at the heart of this wild country.

She opened a bottle of painkillers and shook one into her hand. It had proved a challenge, striking a balance between remaining functional and saving enough of the medicine for a swift and painless death when the time came.

Having swallowed a pill to take care of the lingering aches, she gathered a headset with video gear and a collapsible ladder. Sturdy cases stood in a line, solid enough to withstand years of bad weather, but light enough for her to wrestle up to the main site on her own. When she'd explained her plan to Yazzie, she'd expected him to argue, but instead he'd come through with enough materials to enable her to continue working on her own. Yolanda had always said, "That professor has a crush on you, Mother." Maybe the girl had seen something her mother hadn't.

Though autumn was coming on, the sun still blazed overhead. Lucia tied a bandanna around her forehead to keep the sweat out of her eyes and settled the ladder in the crack. There wasn't much room to wiggle through, and she hoped her efforts wouldn't bring down more of the ceiling in the lower level.

The people had built with great care, even courses of stone decorated with paintings and geometric bas-reliefs, and broken by T-shaped doorways. The floor beneath the ladder sat level, and she clambered down with only slight qualms. Before touching anything, she set up a portable flood light and filmed everything in the room, focusing on the exquisitely preserved feather cape. Few had survived the centuries, so to find a complete one in good condition promised years of study for some lucky archaeologist. "They'll remember I found it," she told herself. "Even if I don't write the papers, they won't forget what I did."

Once she'd filmed and taken still shots, she returned to the surface and retrieved the case. Engineered to provide climate-controlled storage, its heavy latches took some wrestling to undo. When she'd programmed it, she eased the cape off the floor, jaw clenched. She half expected it to disintegrate in her hands, but though she sensed its fragility, it had been constructed to last.

As she moved the cape toward the case, she saw what lay beneath it and froze. The pale curve of a skull and shoulder blades like wings, then the long bones of a skeleton splayed in the dust. A woman, given the shape of the pelvis, and an older one, given the condition of the joints. Lucia sighed and set the cape back down. It hadn't been her intention to disturb a burial. She considered sealing the lower levels again, but she doubted she'd be able to recreate the airtight conditions that had preserved the cape. A mutter of thunder in the distance decided her.

She whispered to the dead woman, "I'm sorry. I can't leave this here to be destroyed."

As she worked, she imagined the wonderful scenes of which the cape had once been a part. When she'd settled the garment in its case, she sighed with relief. A quick check of the case's security and climate systems showed it was fully powered and ready for sealing. For a moment, before closing the lid, she admired the scarlet macaw feathers, the glossy iridescent black of raven pinions, the soft brown of turkey feathers that made up the warm underlayer. It amazed her that someone had crafted the whole thing by hand, and that it had outlived those hands by hundreds of years.

A pang struck her as she closed the lid and snapped the latches. Whatever time remained to her on the site, she felt sure she'd find nothing else as wonderful as this. It would, in a way, be her memorial as well.

As she moved the case to the ladder, a movement above caught her eye, a brief, shadowy flicker. She laughed at herself. Even if her mind tricked her into thinking the shadow had a human shape, it must be one of the animals that occasionally strayed into the canyon, a coyote or bighorn sheep perhaps. Their population had rebounded after humans fled.

Thunder grumbled again, closer. Right after Lucia heard the hushed sound of falling rain, the first droplets spattered the dusty stone floor around her and the crown of her head. She heaved the crate up the ladder, a tricky task for a lone researcher. The ladder shook as she braced herself, lifting the storage case one rung at a time.

A blinding flash, followed at once by a double peal of thunder, shocked her so she almost dropped her burden. At the same time, the clouds released a deluge that created a watery halo around every rock and tree.

Once the case stood on solid ground, Lucia went back for her day pack and tools. The rain made the ladder's rungs cold and slippery in her hands, and water had begun pouring through the broken ceiling into the room below. Lucia considered bringing another case out to protect the skeleton, but her team had decided to rebury skeletons after studying them in situ. In the past, too many of the dead had been carted off to museums as if they were no more than another set of artifacts.

"Farewell," she whispered, raising a hand to salute the long-dead priestess. Storm runoff churned around her boots and flowed into the depths. Rain blurred her vision, but she was determined to find a safe place for the cape. Only when she reached the camp below did it dawn on her that the task might prove difficult, if not impossible. Though it hadn't been raining long, the stream already ran high, the usually clear waters red-brown with mud and choked with tree branches and other debris. Even as she watched, the cottonwood nearest the water groaned and toppled in. The current caught it, twisting it over and over.

The stream seemed to rise from moment to moment as the downpour fed into the churning runoff. The tent snapped free, bright blue material buckling and flapping until the flood swept it away. Frantic, Lucia backpedaled as the stream burgeoned, already licking at her ankles. How had it risen so fast? She recalled tales Yazzie had told, of relatives and neighbors swept away in flash floods, their bodies found weeks later and miles downstream, if at all.

A slab of stone slid down the cliff wall, as big as the wall of a house and far heavier. It crashed first into the upper site, then upended and plunged lower as smaller chunks spalled off its surface. Lucia darted out of the way, but her feet slipped from under her. The impact deafened her, and sent up a fountain of water that all but blinded her. The case slipped out of her grasp as she struggled to regain her footing.

"No!" When she leaped after it, the ground beneath her feet seemed to dissolve, and the torrent swallowed her. Panic followed; she flailed, striving for the surface. Her lungs burned, and she struggled to hold her breath, until the current slammed her into something hard and unyielding. Pain burned from her shoulder to the pit of her stomach. One gasp, and she was choking, her lungs filling with silty water. For an instant she breached the surface, just long enough to see the fallen cottonwood. It had snagged, bare roots trembling with the force of the raging stream.

Lucia fought the current. It tumbled her over and over, sometimes scraping her against the rocky bottom, sometimes thrusting her to the surface. The chill was seeping into her, and damp clothing and hiking boots weighed her down. *I don't want to die,* she realized. *Not now. Not like this.*

She threw herself against the waters, reaching for the cottonwood's roots. When she caught hold of them, her fingers, cramped with cold, scrabbled at the muddy wood. Coughing, her whole body burning with pain, she hauled herself to the trunk of the tree and managed to clamber halfway out of the water.

The snag gave way. The force of it flung her back into the water, and she had to fight again to regain her perch. The cottonwood's progress had an almost stately quality compared to the smaller branches that spun and bobbed around her. The rain slowed, the drumming on her back shifting to a gentle patter.

At last the cottonwood ground against a sandbar, and Lucia lay with her face pressed against the tree's bark. Weak and watery sunlight broke through the clouds, soothing her aches until she thought she might be able to move again.

It was only when she'd reached the shore that she remembered the storage case she'd lost, with its precious cargo. She lay back in the damp sand, her hands pressed to her eyes to dam up the tears. It might be lost, she told herself, but not destroyed. The cases were designed to take a beating and remain airtight.

Exhaustion overtook her.

A crackling sound, at once familiar and unexpected, pulled her back to reality. Hours had passed and the sun was setting, a bloody eye winking in the western mountains. To the east, the last of the storm blackened the horizon. Lucia rubbed at her face, and turned. Another fire burned unexpectedly, its cheerful flames painting the shore. The stones circling it had the look of masonry, sharp-hewn edges only a little smoothed by passing time.

She found her feet and stumbled forward. The heat offered relief for the cold and the pain; she held her hands over the flames and studied them with bemusement as they trembled uncontrollably. Something moved on the far side of the fire. "Who's there?" She circled, cautious.

A shadow bunched against a hunk of sandstone, a shadow that, as she watched, became clearer. It was like watching one of Yolanda's computer art installations, gradually fading into view. At last she could make out the figure's features. An old woman with the fierce visage of a hawk stared at her through the fire.

"Who are you?"

18

The woman made no answer. Her hair was white and thin with age, braided and wrapped in a coil around the crown of her head. She hunched under a blanket—no, it was a cape, a cape of feathers—and watched Lucia with dark eyes that caught and reflected the firelight. Something passed between them, a jolt that rose from the ground and seared Lucia from the soles of her feet to the top of her skull. The woman rose, drawing the cape about her like a bird settling down for the night. As she stepped out of the circle of light, she faded until her shadow barely showed against the background of stone and sand and brush.

"Wait!" Following the stranger broke whatever spell had taken hold of Lucia. Pain rushed back, a raging current that threatened to pull her under once more. She fought it, one step at a time, following the shallow footprints the woman—the ghost—had left along the stream bank. She stumbled across a few little bodies, pack rats and jack rabbits that hadn't been able to outrun the flood. Their empty eyes reminded her how lucky she'd been to escape.

The ghost's prints were clear in the damp sand. They seemed to levitate over snags of debris and large boulders, the path as straight as the stream was crooked. Then, as the sun dropped below the horizon, the tracks veered into a slot canyon Lucia had never seen before. Darkness closed in quickly, as it always did in the canyonlands, and she glanced around for landmarks she'd be able to use to find her way back.

The flood had roared down this narrow passage as well, banking the mass of material it carried into every curve and crevice. One such pile caught her eye; something within had a rectangular shape. She traced its edges with her fingers and almost sobbed in relief. As best she could tell, the artifact case remained sealed.

"Thank you," she said aloud. "I'd never have found it, if it wasn't for you." A glance around showed no sign of the ghost, however. Lucia pulled the case free from its nest of branches and mud. As she did, the base of her skull tingled and shivered. She pressed the implant, and it hummed to life. Professor Yazzie was talking before the connection cleared.

" . . . saw there was a huge storm. Flooding, they said, and I worried—"

"I'm fine," she said. "Well, banged up, and I almost drowned, but I'm all right."

"Lucia—"

"Really," she said. "I've had some very strange experiences, but I've got the cape, and that's all that matters." She shifted the case to get a better grip on it. "Tell Yolanda I'm well."

"I think she'd prefer if you talked to her yourself."

"I will, before . . . Well, before the end. You know. But not yet. She needs a little time to cool down."

"Can you blame her?" It was the tone of his voice, the wry humor, which sent a shock of realization through her. She loved Yazzie, and had almost since the first time they'd met. And now it was too late to tell him.

"No," she said. "If you could try to make her understand?"

"You know I'll do what I can."

And he would. That was Yazzie. "I wish I'd understood earlier. This. Everything."

"Don't we all." From the tone of his voice, she guessed he knew exactly what she meant. "Take care of yourself."

"Will do." She signed off before she had the chance to grow maudlin. She had no idea how far the flood had carried her, but it had seemed to go for miles. She'd need to rest by that fire tonight, before attempting the walk back to the remains of her camp site.

The blaze was already dying when she reached it, but it still threw off enough heat to drive away the worst of the chill. She built a rough windbreak with a tangle of driftwood, and settled down to rest.

By morning she could barely walk, and even the warmth of the sun did little to alleviate it. She wished she hadn't lost the day pack. "But that's water under the bridge. Or down the canyon." She managed to croak out a laugh. She turned upstream and started walking. The journey took most of the day. At times, she had to climb without the case, finding the optimal route through rough terrain before returning for it.

When she at last reached the camp site, she almost passed it by because the stretch which had held her tent and supplies had disappeared completely, the ground torn away by the force of the flood waters. Only the ruins on the higher ledge and at the canyon rim told her she'd found the place she sought.

"Oh, damnation." She dropped the case and pushed the tangled mop of curls off her forehead. She'd lost almost everything. Worst of all, the precious supply of painkillers had vanished downstream, leaving her without an exit strategy.

Lucia sat through the night, watching the stars overhead and shivering, as much from dread as cold. The case bulked at her side, and every so often she patted it, reassuring herself that she hadn't lost it again. Morning light brought a little relief, for she spotted a few bags caught on tree branches that overhung the river. No painkillers, she noted regretfully, but protein bars and water purification tablets. Now paranoid of storms, she dragged them up to the wide ledge that held the ruined settlement, and stashed them deep in the recesses of the cave. Someone tried to reach her as she worked, but she ignored the urgent pulses of the implant.

With each trip down to the stream, she moved more slowly, the pain harder to ignore. After she'd secured the feathered cape, she made one last trip to the devastated camp, and at least found her tattered sleeping bag. Under it lay a plastic bag, torn by the force of the flood but still containing a single bottle of prescription painkillers. She stuffed it into her pocket, wanting it close.

Her sense of relief shamed her. She hated feeling so dependent on a substance outside herself, but the illness and the repercussions of the fight for her life couldn't be ignored. She allowed herself one pill, though she knew it wouldn't be enough to do more than blunt the pain. The rest she had to save, in case matters grew truly desperate.

The tarp she'd set up in the ruins had vanished and the crack had widened, but somehow the ladder had wedged tightly and remained upright. She stooped at the head of it and stared into the depths. A shadow flickered on the far wall, near the spot where she'd found the cape. "Hello," she said.

The ghost stilled. Lucia waited, but it didn't acknowledge her. "I found it. Your cape. It's an important find. It will teach us much about your people."

Your people. My people. Thoughtful, she tapped her lips. She'd never before considered this place her ancestral home. "I wish you could tell your stories to me."

She prepared to store the artifact case deeper in the ruins, but the memory of that patient, silent figure nagged at her. At last, she swung onto the ladder and returned to the deeper layer of the ruins with the case. "See? It's right here."

The ghost took shape in the dim recesses of the room. She watched with sharp, ageless eyes, her translucent form hovering over bones that had been swept into a heap by the flood.

"If I take it out, it'll be ruined." Even as she spoke. Lucia unsnapped the latches of the case. It hissed a little when she opened it. Within lay the cape, its sharp colors only a little dulled by dust. Lucia's hands hovered over it, longing to touch it. A chill breeze touched the back of her neck, and she knew the ghost had joined her. As it waited, she whispered a poem, a prayer she'd learned while studying the mythology of the Pueblo people. Then she lifted the cape out of the crate and carried it across the room. When she shook it out, one scarlet macaw feather drifted to the floor.

She laid the cape over the bones. *Yazzie will understand,* she thought. She wouldn't even have to leave a message. Someday, he'd come back, and see the remnants of the cape, and the skeleton, and know why she'd done it. The chill departed, and with it, the shadowy spirit.

When she'd finished, she climbed out of the ruins. The bottle of painkillers poked uncomfortably into her hip. She stuffed it into the bottom of a bag of supplies she'd retrieved. She might want it someday soon. But not now. Not now.

THE BALL GAME

BY KAOLIN IMAGO FIRE

THE SUN TICKLED SRIVAN'S DEEP brown skin as she walked under the mottled semi-tropical canopy. She hardly cared that the rumors she'd followed into the jungle had left her empty-handed; it had been an inspiring walk, half a day of gentle hiking and communing. The life, the colors, the smells of the semi-tropical forest saturated her with well-being.

A humming of wings had followed her for the last while, deep and rich like everything else around her, a primal comfort note floating through the trees. She hum-uuuum-hummed along, drifting from shade, to sun, and back beneath the abundant vegetation. It cleansed her mind, opened her lungs, filled her legs with fresh blood. She found herself pushing onto a harder path, up past cracked boulders, marching to the odd syncopation of the bird's unique vibrations.

And then she stopped, fingers trailing part-way along a rock outcropping. It seemed only moments had passed, but her calves and thighs burned slightly from the exertion of an extended walk, and her breastbone hurt from the camera bouncing against it. An unnatural relief in the surface of the stone had pulled her from her reverie. Something human? Perhaps, she thought, following the rumors would pay off after all.

A shadow passed over her, and she looked up just in time to catch a black tail with a horizontal white stripe shoot past; reorienting, she found herself looking at her first Horned Guan. It looked liked a squat, narrow egret—only a hundred times more graceful. It was black from head to tail with slight exception—a red crest fluorescing in the sun, pale blue eyes, orange feet, and a bushy white breast. And it was rolling around in the dirt like a chicken—if only chickens could look so lithe and elegant.

Srivan knelt slowly, and moved her hand to her belt-pouch to fetch some mulberries. The bird did not react to her movement, so she picked out three berries and extended them to it in her open palm. As her hand's shadow hit the bird it leapt to its feet and moved several feet back, away from her.

She paused, afraid to startle it further, but it ignored her, returning to its dirt bathing. Srivan adjusted her balance to move one leg closer to it, and reached out again with her hand—and again when her shadow landed on the bird it leaped to its feet and moved several more feet back. Startled by the swiftness of its movement, she fell on her palm that had been holding the mulberries, squishing their red blood along her palm and forearm before she fully caught herself.

Taking a deep breath, she saw that the Horned Guan was again bathing itself in the dirt, just a bit further on. Realizing the rarity of her encounter, she took the camera now dangling on the ground and removed the cap from its lens; she centered the bird in her viewfinder and snapped a dozen shots in quick succession.

Covering the lens with its cap, she sought to approach the bird in a more roundabout manner. It continued to retreat from her—and in a very decided direction, no matter the angle she employed to approach it.

Srivan knew that, while it was usual for them to come down to dirt bathe, Horned Guans were primarily not ground critters. Still, there were recorded cases of their having nests on the ground. She wondered if perhaps this was its attempt to lead her away from its nest. She had the strong suspicion, though, that it was more leading her towards something rather than away. Srivan had a strong suspicion that it had been guiding her here the whole way.

She stood up and walked slowly towards it; the bird stood up and walked directly away from her—moving, they kept pace with each other. She slowly realized she was in a man-made valley, moss-covered rock sloping up evenly a dozen meters to either side of her. This had likely been an arena or a temple—

The bird took to the air, drawing her attention back, and glided up over a sudden drop; Srivan retreated a step, and kneeled down to peer over the edge. The Horned Guan alighted on a scraggly, bone-white shrub sticking out from the cliff just a meter below her. No, not a bone-white shrub—bones, bleached-white bones collected messily in a mostly dried shrub growing out of the wall. And collected in the mess was a perfectly preserved rubber ball maybe twenty-five centimeters in diameter.

She raised her camera and snapped off another dozen shots and a mini-movie in lower resolution to capture the depth and angles of the remains—document, document, document. She wondered if perhaps she should go back and get a crew, but, despite the apparent age of remains, she was worried that the Horned Guan might disturb them past recovery—a small voice in her head counterpointed with wondering whether this bird wasn't just a Mesoamerican will-o-wisp, and how many souls it might have lured to their death. Ignoring that and the sheer distance between her position and the cloud-like canopy of trees below, Srivan took her rope out of her pack, made a catcher's-net with one end, and lowered it over the edge. The bird hopped back and forth on an arm bone, hum-uuuum-humming away.

She managed to get the net around the rubber ball and gently brought the rope taut; taking a deep breath to steady her nerves, then, she slowly reeled it up, hand-over-hand. It was heavy, for something that looked like a basketball dropped in tar—easily three, maybe four kilograms.

The bird took flight, again, then, and began making a ruckus that nearly caused her to drop the rope—or had it snagged on something? It looked like she'd caught the skeleton as well—which should have been bad, should have broken it apart—but the skeleton—

She shook her head, deciding the thin air was playing tricks on her, or perhaps the sun had been too much all at once. The skeleton could not be climbing up her rope—perhaps it was just melded with the ball, and with the wind and the bird, it looked like it was moving. Perhaps that was it. She could let go of the rope and the problem would go away—but it was just a hallucination, nothing to worry about so long as a hallucination didn't convince her to step off the cliff. Nothing to worry about, but why was the rope so hard to pull up, now?

Srivan noticed she was biting her lip, and stopped—clenched her jaw and pulled with increasing force, attempting to dig her heels into the dusty, hard-packed dirt, walking backwards.

When a bone-white claw of a hand was the first thing over the edge, she nearly screamed, nearly dropped everything and ran—but she had to get the ball—the bone was just oddly placed, that was all, and to hell with it! She pulled hard, then, and fell backwards with the rope as the skeleton pulled itself up onto solid ground. Then she screamed, dropping the rope.

The skeleton was holding the ball in one hand and a curved dagger in the other. Srivan screamed again, scrambling backwards, trying to get her footing but not conscious enough to stop pushing herself over her hands.

A thick milky substance was pooling out of the ground, worming its way around the skeleton's bones, up its legs, around the hips, tickling its ribcage and gunning along its arm for the ball. Srivan turned, finding her hands under her, finally, pushing up to run—

Her face plowed a thin furrow in the dust, chin first; she heard her head bounce, and then something else—the ball; the skeleton had just pegged her in the back with the ball. Was it playing, or attacking? Could it even tell the difference? She gained her feet again, turned to see its intent—the now-white ball was arcing through the air back to the skeleton's waiting hands. She ran, angling for higher ground, taking the sloped stone walls that defined the arena.

Thirty meters up, the stone plateaued. The skeleton was climbing the incline slowly, ball held gently, swinging the dagger back and forth as it went. The trail of natural rubber followed it, coming out of the ground like blood from an ancient wound that had never truly healed.

Srivan cast around for inspiration—here, under thick canopy, was an intricately worked stone chair. Its patterns had faded, but she presumed the priest or king had sat there, presiding over the game, thousands of years ago. Or perhaps that chair had been reserved for the gods the game was played in honor of. She swept her hands over it, hoping for some sort of catch, some lever, something hidden that would save her—but she found nothing.

Walking around the throne, then, she examined the trees that sheltered it. They were rubber trees of varying age, untapped—but for one. Scars riddled one large rubber tree, older than any rubber tree had right to be; the scars walked from waist-height up for two meters, diagonally sliced upwards from where it was directly behind the throne, all the way around the meter and a half of each hemicircumference where the cuts met again. Below this, then, just behind the throne, there had been buckets for catching the latex flowing out.

She heard the Horned Guan screech behind her, and jumped away, turning around—it was worrying the skeleton, swooping down and around it. The skeleton had the ball tucked under one arm and was swiping at the bird, in turn, with the dagger. But despite distraction, the skeleton was still advancing on her position.

Looking down for some sort of weapon, her camera caught her eye—she had to take some photos, if it wasn't just a hallucination. Raising the camera, though, she realized the skeleton had stopped paying attention to the bird; without letting go of the ball, it bounced it against her skull. Her camera flew around her neck, burning her neck with the friction, and nearly choking her. She flew a full meter in the air, landing awkwardly on a wrist, an elbow, and a fore-arm, tumbling from there onto her side and again trying to scramble away.

Her left eye didn't want to fully open, and there was a shrill-pitched noise dogging her consciousness. She wanted to just **lie** down, let her wounds sort themselves out. There wasn't any skeleton, after all. She'd just fallen down. Or maybe she'd just rested against a tree for a nap—perhaps this was just a nightmare, and maybe some rodent had thrown a nut at her.

Or maybe she really was being dragged down the stone by a remnant of a culture hundreds of years gone, thousands of years old. Was there really a Horned Guan sitting on her chest? A dagger at her neck?

Surely she had fallen, or pricked herself on an ancient poison—the Aztecs were notorious for their use of psychoactive substances. A Horned Guan couldn't possibly have a dagger at her neck.

She opened her eyes as wide as she could and craned her neck up to see—yes, she was being dragged down the slope, across the ground—sure enough, the skeleton seemed like it was going to take her back over the edge with it. That made sense in the big scheme of things, if you started believing in walking skeletons and the like. But what was the deal with the bird?

She heard it humming again, hum-uuuum-humming, and she had the urge to close her eyes, to sleep, to dream. To dream its dream?

She closed her eyes.

The sun was shining brightly, no clouds in the sky. She could hear hundreds, maybe thousands, of people cheering from the stands. Heavy rhythmic beats were joined by ball-play; she flinched from a foot coming down on her face, but it went through her. Finally, something not real that remained not real!

The sun moved, the scene shifted; she was watching from above as the winners of the game climbed to the throne, to be awarded sacrifice to the gods. A priest dressed as Quetzalcoatl stood to welcome them, a priestess on either side holding fresh maize stalks. This was to be a birth, a rebirth—transcendence.

The lead player, with an orange helmet, black feathered arm-dressings, and a white leather breastplate took a vase in his hands and drank; milk drooled slowly down the sides of his lips, and as he handed the vase back to the priest he blinked, shook his head, and licked his lips as if he couldn't feel them.

Her flesh was melting in the sun, melting from inside, curling, twirling, twisting—she felt the beat of the tree, its blood and her blood and something else, blood of the gods, the sky, the sea; there was pressure at her neck and somehow she knew it was the dagger, the very dagger just now at her neck, and she opened her eyes. The bird was still riding her chest but the dagger had fallen so it was indeed pressed against her neck. She could still feel the liquid rubber swimming around in her belly.

Srivan closed her eyes again, trying to make sense of her sensations.

A crack of thunder broke the sky red, no clouds in sight but the ringing in her ears growing stronger. The priest, Quetzalcoatl, jerked sideways as if played by an epileptic puppeteer. Red, deep red, pooled out of a small crater in his side. There was shouting, clamoring, but her own flesh was still melting, perpetually melting and mixing, and the sacred vase was broken—its own blood melting and mixing with that of the priest. The priestesses were on their knees, wailing for mercy for whatever they'd done—she didn't know, they didn't know.

She turned around and the sky was orange, yellow, red, blue, green—it swam with life and texture. A pain was slowly burning its way up her back, along her shoulders, but that was the other world, the unreal world that shouldn't exist. Dreams were easier, they could mean anything, be explained by anything. She didn't want to think about the other world. Here, there were fierce metal men with pale faces riding large dogs, slashing down players and spectators alike with silvered weapons that sliced through wood as well as flesh, leather little obstacle.

She reached for her camera to record the absurdity but remembered it was in the other world; drawing back, she saw her hands, melting, melting but not falling off—infinitely pliable flesh around the static bones. A moment of disbelief, and then true fear, panic, and she'd taken flight—literally, the ground receded under her and then she was watching herself—her selves—watching the bones on the ground and watching the bird watching the bones. Watching the massacre unfold. Hundreds, thousands of bodies were seized by the armored invaders and tossed over the cliff. The bird watched, gliding above, scared and confused. Winds for which it had no understanding tickled its feathers, but it flew on instinct, flew high and above.

Then the sun was gone, the hare on the moon completely eaten, the only light was pricks of orange and red like stars on the ground; she swooped lower, and lower still, and an anger like none she had known filled her, suffused her. She flew closer and closer and then all was calm. A shout arose near the cliff, and she flew there, knowing what she would find—a skeleton, bone-white already, climbing up the cliff, throwing its rubber ball at the invaders and dragging them over the edge, one at a time.

The ground filled with latex so that none could escape—stuck in their tracks they were easy fodder for the skeleton's burning hatred.

Then she was again awake, staring again into the eyes of the bird, the dagger sawing gently against her already-raw neck.

She took the dagger, presented it to the bird as she had with the mulberries. It stood there, on her chest, calm, detached, as if nothing was happening. And she sliced the dagger, dull as it ought to be, across the neck of the Horned Guan, and the dagger sliced through like cheese. Blood seeped gently out of the bird's neck, onto her arms, onto her chest, down her neck and into the latex that soaked the ground.

She was no longer moving. Her feet burned from a sudden fire and she tried to pull back but they were tangled in flesh, tangled in blood rising up from the ground; the skeleton was becoming whole, unmelting before her eyes in an orgy of biological goo. She kicked, and pulled, then slashed at it with the dagger still in her hand—at the touch of the dagger, the flesh withdrew. Her feet dropped, and she scampered back to crouch low, dagger ready. She took one step back, then another, but everywhere she stepped there was already flesh, amorphous, writhing, and she couldn't run far enough, fast enough, but she tried—she ran, and ran, and when she cleared the ball field the ground was dry, dusty dirt.

Srivan knelt on the ground, brought the dust to her lips, and kissed it. She spread out in the dust, and rolled in it, and the heat from the sun brought her comfort. A greater warmth blazed from behind her and she turned around to see the flesh combusting, writhing, drying, flaking—freed into the sky as ash and disappearing before it again touched the ground. The years had caught up with it, anger finally accepted, resolved, and released through the flesh—soul and body combined to wipe the massacre clean. Justice, as it were, was done.

Srivan lay back in the dust, thought of flying; she raised her wings, and basked dreamlessly in the blessings of the sun as the wind lifted her high.

THE ALUX'S CAVE

BY JAMIE LACKEY

MECATL CROUCHED ON THE CAVE FLOOR and examined the ruins of a *kahtal axul*. Mayan farmers had built the tiny houses in their fields to curry favor with the mischievous *aluxob*, but she'd never heard of one in a cave.

She studied it, torn between her archeologist's training, which urged her to take a few pictures then destroy it systematically to study it, and her respect for her ancestor's traditions, which make her fingers itch to repair the tumbled-down walls. It had been constructed with great care—the walls were thicker than other *kahtal axul* that she'd studied, and it was at least twice as large as any of the others she'd seen.

She pulled her camera out of her pocket.

"What are you doing?" a soft voice asked in Mayan. Mecatl turned, expecting to find a child, but she was alone in the cave.

"Hello?"

"What do you want with my home?"

According to myth, *aluxob* were invisible unless they chose to be seen. Goosebumps raced up Mecatl's arms. Deep down, she's always believed the stories—that was why she'd studied archeology in the first place. "I wanted to take some pictures."

"Why?" A tiny Mayan woman, clad in a long skirt and a simple huipil appeared on the tiny house's doorstep. "My home is in ruins." She touched the tumbled stones.

"Why is your home in a cave instead of a field?" Mecatl asked.

The *alux* shrugged. "I just don't like fields. Too hot, too dusty."

"Who built your house for you?" Mecatl asked.

The *alux* frowned up at her. "That's not really any of your business."

"Oh," Mecatl said, stung. "I'm sorry."

"Why do you want to know?"

Mecatl had spent her whole life making up stories about the past. She loved tales about things that had happened long ago. Her curiosity about the tiny woman and her home was gnawing through her insides. She shrugged and tried to sound casual. "I'm just curious."

"If you bring me a worthy gift, I will tell you the story."

* * *

Mecatl purchased a lump of copal incense and pulled her favorite alpaca scarf out of the closet. It was bright and warm, and she hoped it was worthy. She went back to the cave at dawn. She crept inside, clutching her offerings. "Hello?"

The tiny woman appeared before her. "What have you brought me?"

Mecatl gave her the incense first. The *alux* sniffed it and smiled. "Izel loved the smell of copal."

"Is he the one who built your home?"

She nodded. "I brought him and his family luck, and he built my home here, out of the sun." She curled a lock of black hair around a finger. "He was a good man. Kind and strong and clever. He visited me every day, and sang to me. He told me I was beautiful.

"But after seven years, his family decided that I had to be trapped in my home so that I couldn't turn to mischief. They placed heavy stones outside the doors. Izel never came back after that. I never heard his voice again. By the time I managed to escape, he was long dead."

Mecatl shivered. "I'm sorry."

The *alux* grinned up at her. It was not a friendly expression. "I have been alone for a long time," she said. "I've decided that I don't like it." She vanished.

Mecatl ran toward the cave entrance. Too late, she saw the stones that had been carefully arranged, ready to fall and block the opening.

A single rock shifted, then the whole pile tumbled down with a roar like thunder.

Complete darkness surrounded her. She pulled her cell phone out of her pocket, but the screen stayed black.

She hadn't told anyone about the cave—no one knew where she was, and it would be days before anyone even noticed she was missing.

Light flickered from deeper in the cave, and the scent of copal smoke curled around her.

"ll die—trapped in here," Mecatl said, picking her way toward the light, testing each step and holding her hands in front of her. "I need food and water."

"You will feel no hunger or thirst as my guest," the *alux* said.

Mecatl's mind raced. Her car was a good mile's hike away, and no one would be able to track her by the time anyone thought to look. But the *alux* couldn't know that. "People will come looking for me. Soon."

"They won't find you. They won't even see the cave opening."

Mecatl had imagined magic as a wonderful thing—she'd never imagined how powerless she'd feel if it was used against her.

"You are mine," the *alux* said. "Now and forever. The way Izel should have been."

"Is that why you had him build your house in this cave?"

"Yes."

Mecatl took a deep breath. There had to be a way out of this—she'd find another exit or clear the rockslide.

"Now, you will sing for me."

"What? No."

Pain cascaded through her whole body. She fell to the damp cave floor, writhing till it passed.

"Sing," the *alux* commanded.

Mecatl sang.

Time passed in a blur. She didn't need to eat or drink, so her body produced no waste. She sang till she was hoarse, then the *alux* let her sleep. She used her scarf for a thin pillow, thankful that she hadn't given it away.

The *alux* woke her with pain when she wanted more songs. Whenever Mecatl woke on her own, she stayed perfectly still and concentrated on the touch of air against her skin. She felt for the tiniest draft, the smallest change in air pressure. She dreamed of the smell of rain and the feel of sunlight.

"Do you think Izel knew what you had planned for him?" Mecatl asked after a long night of singing. Her throat burned. "Did he cry when his parents locked you away, or was he relieved?"

"Be quiet," the *alux* said.

"Did you care about him at all when you were planning this hell for him? Or was he just a convenient victim, like me?"

Pain spiked through her, and Mecatl passed out.

When she woke, she heard the *alux* weeping. She was burning more of her copal incense, and the tiny flame seemed almost like daylight to Mecatl's light-deprived eyes. She fought back any guilt and crawled silently toward the mouth of the cave. She loaded rocks into her shirt and carried them toward the *kahtal axul.*

Izel's care had served the small structure well. There were only a few places where the walls had crumbled. Mecatl covered the doors with

33

large rocks and filled any of the other holes with small ones, hoping against hope that whatever magic had sealed the *alux* inside before would work again. The rocks blocked out the flickering firelight, plunging the cave back into complete darkness.

The sobs stopped, replaced by angry screams. "What are you doing! Let me out!"

A wave of hunger drove Mecatl to her knees.

It had worked, but she didn't have a lot of time to escape the cave. She felt her way back toward the entrance and started shifting rocks.

Archeology had given her patience, but her whole body ached as she moved one stone, then another and another.

"You'll starve before you escape," the *alux* said. "Let me out, and I'll set you free."

"I don't believe you," Mecatl said.

"I understand that you don't trust me, but I give you my word that I'll help you leave if you release me."

Mecatl kept moving rocks one by one.

"Please, I can't be trapped here again. I'll do anything—grant you any boon. Just name it," the *alux* pleaded.

Hunger tore at Mecatl, and her throat burned. Swallowing was difficult. She wondered how long it had been since she'd had anything to eat or drink. If she kept digging, she might not have the strength to drag herself back to the *kahtal axul.* She grunted and kept digging.

"This wouldn't have been a hell for Izel. He loved me."

The raw pain in the *alux*'s voice almost moved Mecatl to pity. But if the creature was lying, she'd never get another chance to escape. She'd never heard any myths about an *alux*'s word being binding.

"You're not even a very good singer," the *alux* said. "Please, I'll be trapped if you die out there."

"Is the cave still hidden?" Mecatl rasped. Talking hurt.

"Of course it is! And if you don't let us out, no one will ever find it again!"

Mecatl didn't believe her. She imagined future archeologists finding her bones, puzzling out her life and death.

"Please," the *alux* begged. "Please don't leave me trapped here, not again. Please."

Mecatl wanted to trust her—wanted to free her and ask for a boon—maybe gold or ancient secrets that she could use to make a name for herself—and she didn't want to die of thirst in this cave. She almost turned away, but then she heard something from the other side of the rockslide—it was faint, but she could hear the patter of raindrops. Rocks scattered under her fingertips, and faint, gray daylight filtered in through a tiny hole. It was blinding after so long in darkness, and hope bolstered Mecatl's flagging strength.

She pulled herself through the narrow opening and let the rain fall onto her tongue.

After a week of bed rest and soup, she went back to the cave. She and her best friend, Emetaly, cleared most of the rocks. "I'm going in for a sec, just wait here," Mecatl said. "Promise me not to come inside."

Emetaly arched an eyebrow. "Don't go in the creepy cave where you almost died? That sounds like a great idea, maybe you'd like to try it?"

"I'll be right back." Mecatl slipped into the cave. She folded her scarf and set it next to the *kahtal axul.* "I don't need a boon. Just don't trap anyone else in here, okay? Izel is gone, and no one else is going to replace him." She rolled the rock that blocked the door away.

Then, she ran back into the sunlight.

THE RED QUEEN

BY GERRI LEEN

LORENA MURCIA DE VEGA WALKED UNDER THE ARCHWAY of the covered walkway in Antigua's plaza, enjoying the crisp air of the Guatemalan highlands after having spent a few days in Palenque. The humidity was less, the air easier to breathe, the lovely colonial town spread out around her.

She cut across the Parque Central to get to the School for the Preservation of Indigenous Culture, nodding to an old woman in her elaborately woven huipil and skirt. The old woman smiled at her, then held out a scarf from the pile next to her.

The scarf was a lovely mix of red and turquoise, probably woven by this woman on the backstrap loom so many of the Maya used. And no doubt intended to enhance Lorena's current wardrobe of dull colors: khaki pants and a white t-shirt with dark brown hiking boots. The life of an archeologist was one of dust and mud. It was no place for fashion or vanity. She handed the scarf back to the woman, shook her head with an apologetic smile, and kept going.

At the door to the school, several teens were sitting, drinking *Coca Cola* and laughing. They looked at her without much curiosity. She blended in here. Her parents were Mexican who had moved to the States when her mother was pregnant; her father had been invited to consult on a project on the Aztecs at Arizona State and ended up on staff. Lorena had been born in Arizona, but she'd spent her formative years on site, studying her father's beloved Aztecs, then "slumming" it, as her father had called it, working for a family friend in San Lorenzo learning about the Olmecs, and then visiting Palenque for the first time, and falling in love like most fifteen-year-old girls tended to do.

Only she hadn't fallen in love with a person, but with a culture, a world, an empire. The Maya: a string of city-states that more closely resembled Renaissance Italy than the Aztec Empire her father loved so well. A people once thought peaceful stargazers who, it turned out, lived in a continual state of war. Their obsession with time not one of worship, but an unrelenting need to label things and record history, to place events in context—even if it had taken the experts working on the Maya ruins centuries to decipher them and learn that context.

Palenque had stolen her heart and she'd never looked back, studying, securing internships and fellowships, and finally securing her own place at the University of Pennsylvania. Her father ribbed her continually. "The Maya. Torturers. Chocolate addicts." Their running jokes so old they made her mother roll her eyes and murmur a well-worn comment about the Aztecs not being immune to cacao, either.

Lorena would taunt her father with, "And how long did it take the Aztecs to fall? The Maya weren't subdued until 1697."

"Because the Maya had already destroyed themselves. Bands of guerillas, fighting the Spanish in the darkness, disappearing back into the jungle. Just like the Viet Cong."

"And who won that war, hmmmm?"

They'd laugh and stop the argument, and he'd tell her his latest finds, and she'd tell him how much progress she'd made on finding the piece of evidence needed to conclusively identify Palenque's Red Queen.

Which inevitably was a short conversation if she didn't fill it in with other things found at the site by people who weren't her. Oh, sure, she'd found residences and other buildings buried in the rubble, ceramics and even some jade. But the one thing she sought eluded her.

She was searching for the tomb of the ruler who had come after Pacal, the great king found entombed in Palenque's largest building, the Temple of the Inscriptions. The Red Queen had been found in a tomb in Temple XIII, the building just to the west of Pacal's pyramid. No glyphs had identified her, but Lorena ascribed to the view that the remains were those of Pacal's wife, Tzakbu Ajaw. However, until someone found the tomb of one of his sons who ruled after him, and checked the mitochondrial DNA to see if there was a match, the Red Queen's identity would remain a mystery. As Tzakbu Ajaw's younger son had been captured in war and it was not certain his remains were even in Palenque, Lorena was on a search for the older son, Kan B'alam II.

There were other theories on who the Red Queen might be, but Lorena was sure that the gorgeous pyramid built so close to the great king's was his wife's, that he loved her, that he wanted her near him in death but honored her too much to bury her *with* him, perhaps to be mistaken for a servant when she arrived in Xibalba, the Maya underworld. She'd been buried with honor. She'd been buried a queen. Beloved *and* respected.

Lorena's father often told her that her penchant for the romantic would be her downfall. But she thought he was more worried for her heart than her professional reputation. He was just like her, a romantic at his core, and had been fortunate to find a woman who loved him enough to spend her life at digs, living without the conveniences of the modern world she belonged to. Lorena had thought she'd found that, too, had been surprised when the person who had gone wherever Lorena wanted for so long had chosen something different this time.

She took a deep breath as she walked into the school. The director was smoking in the inner courtyard and blinked as he saw her. "Doctor Murcia?"

"Hello, Doctor Vásquez. I'm sorry to intrude."

"It is a pleasure to have such a distinguished visitor here. Surely you have not abandoned Palenque?"

"No, I'm back there this season. Excavating."

"In search of your tomb?"

She nodded. "Is Shelly here?"

"Doctor Lawrence is teaching a class. They are almost finished. Come, I will take you, and we will observe. It gives me such pleasure watching Maya children learn to read the glyphs."

The Spanish had robbed the Maya of that. Viewing the Maya writing as satanic, they had burned untold numbers of the bark books that were now known as codices. Their purge so effective there were only four known codices left and those dated from the Postclassic era. The Spanish also ensured the writings would not be recreated by killing those who were caught writing the glyphs and forcing the children to learn to write the European way.

The language—or languages, rather: there were around thirty languages in the Mayan group—endured. But the ability to connect the spoken word with the beautifully rendered glyphs was lost.

Until now. In schools like this, where experts gave a people back their birthright.

Vásquez stubbed his cigarette in a pot filled with sand, then led her down to a classroom. They crept in, sat in the back, and it took Shelly a moment to see Lorena there. Shelly stammered for a beat or two, then found her groove again and kept going.

"Is she on staff?" Lorena murmured to Vásquez.

"Why? Do you need an epigrapher?"

"I do."

"And she is the only one that will do? I was hoping she would stay here permanently."

Lorena smiled, one side of her mouth going up more than the other—Shelly had always called that her annoyingly smug smile. Any new excavation had the potential to increase what was known of the classic Maya system of writing by revealing new symbols in the carvings and murals. Lorena knew that Shelly would never settle for teaching what was known when the chance to find new glyphs was dangled in front of her. "Perhaps she will turn me down and stay here."

"And perhaps the sun will rise out of Xibalba." He smiled gently, and turned back to observe.

When the class ended and the students had filed out, Shelly came over to where they were standing. "Lor. Is it the dry season again already?"

Lorena nodded, looking away before she could get lost in Shelly's accusing gray-blue eyes. "Thank you, Doctor Vásquez."

"Call me Luis. It only seems fair since you'll be taking away my favorite expert." He left them alone.

"Poor Luis," Shelly said. "I'm not the only one who'll be leaving. A lot of us are looking forward to getting back to a dig."

"You're happy we'll be working together again?" Lorena knew she should keep the hopefulness out of her voice. It didn't help her do it, though.

"I'm looking forward to the dig. Not particularly to working with you. I'm sick of all the reasons you couldn't spend the rainy season here, like we'd planned."

"You know why. Was I supposed to turn Penn down?" The university had run a lecture series she was invited to speak at—on multiple topics.

"And I'm sure your lecture series kept you very warm at night." Shelly seemed content to let the bite hang in the air before she said, "Or did it? Did you meet someone?"

"No." Lorena took a deep breath. Shelly always made her feel so alive, but she could do this, too: make her feel that no matter what she said, it would be the wrong thing. "And then I went to Angkor."

"It was the rainy season in Cambodia, too, Lor. It's not as if you were there to work." She leaned against a desk, and her expression changed to one that Lorena found easier to deal with. "So, Palenque again, I assume?"

Lorena nodded.

"The quest for the Red Queen's identity." Shelly's laugh was half amused, half bitter. "Nothing changes." Before Lorena could answer, Shelly stood and said, "I'll see you at the site in a week. I have things to do here." Her look changed, got a little mean. "People to say goodbye to."

The comment shouldn't have hurt. It did anyway.

Lorena walked up the steps of the Temple of the Inscriptions. She took the climb slowly, imagining the process one of the Palenque rulers would have gone through as he walked, each step taking him closer to the skies, to where the gods were. He became sacred and divine as he moved up—the sky was far from the depths of Xibalba, where the common dead went. Tourists might climb these steps at will, pretending they were Maya elite, but when the buildings were in use, common folk wouldn't have dared. They wouldn't have milled on the ball court, either. That was sacred ground, routinely trod now by sneakered feet.

She wished the tourists weren't here. They got in the way. They asked annoying questions. She'd never been the...marketer her father and even Shelly were. She understood that tourist dollars were key to keeping the governments of Mexico, Guatemala, Belize, and Honduras interested in preserving the ruins and funding further research on the Maya, but she didn't have to like it.

She turned just shy of the top of the temple and sat down, to the side so she wouldn't block any other climbers. The vista of Palenque spread out in front of her. The lush lawns. The other buildings, some excavated, some no more than tree-covered humps. This was what the ruler saw, this breathtaking expanse, as he transformed in full view of his people. They watched him become divine by ascending, by offering his own blood to the gods.

She smiled, remembering how the males in the audience had cringed during her lectures on Maya rituals, and even crossed their legs when she'd explained that while the wife of the ruler was expected to pierce her tongue for sacred rituals, the king's target of choice was the foreskin, stuck through with a stingray barb or obsidian knife, the blood collected on bark paper, then carried out by the king and burned, the blood-infused smoke rising to the sky—and the gods.

"Never tire of this, do you?"

She smiled at the familiar voice of the young hydrologist who'd started working in Palenque last year. "Hello, Jake. Communing with Pacal?"

"Or his final resting place anyway." Jake Nelson walked down the short distance from the top and sat next to her. "Whatcha doing?"

"Thinking about the rulers and divinity." She decided to not talk about penis piercings. "The importance of these stairways."

He patted the stone step. "Permanent. Even yet." He leaned back. "I took your advice. Traveled around the region this summer, saw some of the smaller sites."

"Where'd you go?"

"Xunantunich, Coba, Sayil, Mayapan. They were amazing."

"I know. Manageable cities. Like Mesa."

"It was weird, though. I noticed the pyramid at Xunantunich is different—it doesn't have a central staircase past the midway point. But the guide said that since it's from the late Postclassic, they decided to dig in, see what it was constructed on. The older version had the central stair."

Most tourists didn't realize the Maya had built buildings on top of buildings, much like in Jake's hometown, where modern Seattle sat atop an underground city. She'd visited the Underground when she'd been at a conference at the University of Washington, had been struck by how similar it was to the Maya ruins they encountered, buildings constructed over existing older ones, rubble filling the gap—and preserving what lay below.

"The guide could tell you the older version had a stair but not why?" She grinned at him. "Let me guess. The guide was a lovely young woman who liked Nordic types?"

He laughed and nodded sheepishly.

"Tell me you at least got dinner if you didn't follow up on such an important academic question? As your mentor, I am concerned about your priorities." She tried to look stern, but it was nearly impossible.

"A. Your not my mentor, B. You'd have been distracted, too, and C. I got several dinners." His grin turned less sheepish, more satisfied.

"I don't need details." She laughed and leaned back. "That pyramid is interesting. It was built very, very late, when things were changing radically. That region was one of the last to be populated with large urban areas, but even so, the kings were in trouble. And their population very likely had come from these interior cities, had seen it all before. The fall of their cities—of their kings and everything that had probably seemed so permanent."

"The fall—not one thing but a perfect storm that hit in different areas with different intensity. Drought, food shortages, increased warfare, overpopulation, habitat destruction." The passion in his voice was clear—he might be new at this, might be more interested in water than stone, but he loved the Maya as much as Lorena did. He patted the stone step they were sitting on. "These things didn't build themselves. They needed trees to roll rock. Trees to burn to make the limestone for the friezes. Everything went to hell."

"Exactly. It seems that by the end, the people weren't willing to take it on faith that the king was divine. Suddenly they needed magic. So the builders put hidden staircases on the side and in the back."

"Clever. Now you see me, now you don't. Oh wait, here I am. A god." He leaned back. "Oh, to be a time traveler. To watch it happen."

She laughed. "You'd hardly blend." Jake's blonde hair and bright blue eyes would have marked him as a high value prisoner. He'd have been sacrificed before he could watch much of anything.

Tortured possibly, too. The Maya were brutal. They scalped their captives, burned prisoners alive. The Postclassic Maya in Yucatan and Belize threw sacrifices into cenotes, even their own children at the end, when the drought came—children being the most precious thing they could give: sacrificing their future to ensure they would survive the present. Hardly a quick death if you were thrown into a cenote unbound and without the ceremonial drugs. You'd swim until you couldn't anymore, unable to climb up the steep, slick walls of the cenote, and then you'd sink, down and down to the rain god Chac, who still didn't send rain.

Given the myriad tortuous and slow ways the Maya had of killing, having your still-beating heart torn out of your chest sounded downright humane—at least it would be a relatively quick death.

"So...no Shelly this year?"

"She's coming. Had some things to finish up."

"I wasn't sure. With the cache being found..."

She frowned. "What cache?"

"You've been buried in rubble, haven't you?" He stretched his legs out. "Camp's abuzz. Big cache of codices discovered this morning in Belize."

"You're kidding."

"I'm not. My advisor always said that's where they'd be found and he was right."

She thought of what a temptation that would be for Shelly. "Postclassic like the other codices?"

"Some are saying Classic."

"Wow." She looked back out at the view, could tell he was looking at her but didn't turn to meet his eyes.

"Is 'Wow' the word you really mean? I stopped to see you in Antigua. Only Shelly was there. And not alone."

She looked over at him. "I know. I got some invitations I didn't feel like I should turn down."

"Way you two were talking at the end of last season, I didn't think anything could keep you from going with her."

She felt the same pang of guilt she'd felt when she'd called Shelly to tell her she'd be delayed—over and over again. "One of the invites was to go to Angkor for a television special comparing ruins around the world. I was *chosen* to go. I think my dad was impressed."

"When are you going to stop trying to impress him and just do what you love with a clear conscience? You didn't pick the Aztecs. End of story."

"The Aztecs are his life. They were supposed to be mine. He used to tell me how it would be when the two of us would work together. I was just a kid."

"Exactly. You were just a kid. You didn't know what you wanted. You didn't even know about the Red Queen." He winked at her. "No way he was going to get you back after you came to this place." He sighed—a happy sounding sigh—and pointed out to the plaza. "It's so special, even for the Maya. They didn't just erect these buildings—they designed the entire place. Terraformed it. Subterranean aqueducts and drainage tunnels. Reclaimed the land."

She nodded. This was his specialty. Urban design and water management. And he had plenty to work with because Palenque never ran out of water, being perfectly situated between many streams and rivers. But the Maya had to tame the land first. Had to make a place for humans. They diverted water, they even seemed to grasp water pressure, had water systems that rivaled the Romans. Small pools and possibly even fountains in the palace.

Most Maya had been forced to rely on the cenotes to get them through the dry season, but Palenque never ran out of water, surrounded as it was by so many rivers. But the ground was inhospitable—uneven and prone to flooding and erosion. How the early inhabitants fixed that problem still amazed experts.

Jake pointed over to the Otulum Bridge. "This place must have seemed like a paradise to visitors. So much water."

"And still it fell."

"Well, even paradise sucks if you're undergoing constant war and food shortages. The people voted with their feet. Is a king still a ruler if he has no subjects?"

"Clearly not. They left this place. Let the jungle have it back." She patted the solid limestone under her hand. "But the jungle couldn't hide it forever." She stood. "I love talking to you, but I need to get back to the dig. Was just taking a little break."

"Only you would think climbing a pyramid was taking a break." He closed his eyes. "I'm going to enjoy the sun. Wait for some tourists to come by."

She laughed as she left him and walked back to her site. Jake loved to pretend to be just another tourist. Loved to see how much people really knew about the Maya. Waited for the inevitable bizarre theories like aliens, lost tribes of Israel, or Atlantis.

44

The Maya were people. Nothing mystical about that. Once you had the context, understanding followed.

The problem was that even yet so little of the context was known. But a cache of codices? The implications for everyone's understanding and research direction were huge.

Shelly hadn't sent any messages since they'd talked in Antigua. Lorena hoped that meant she was still coming, not that she was suddenly headed to Belize.

Lorena stood back and watched as the local shaman performed a ritual to ward off the aluxes—trickster spirits that usually dwelt in caves but might be found also in the tunnel she was slowly making. It made the men who were digging feel better, and truth to tell it made her feel better, too.

And it was probably just coincidence that she'd been unable to get a decent shot with Jake's micro camera whenever they lowered it into the opening. That they'd had two buckets of rubble somehow "slip" off the ropes and go tumbling back into the hole.

She'd been through this before. Most Mayanists had. It wasn't logical. It wasn't scientific. And it certainly wasn't anything you'd put in a paper. But the fact was that it didn't hurt to put any angry aluxes at ease with a little respect.

She heard a breathy laugh behind her, then, "You're still doing this?"

"I still am." She could feel herself relaxing. Shelly was here. Finally. "What took you so long?" She hoped Shelly hadn't been saying goodbye to whomever she'd been with in Antigua this whole time.

"I went to Belize."

"Oh?"

"Fifty-seven codices."

"I heard."

"Well, I've seen them, Lor. My God, they're stunning. The cave was dry, so they're well preserved. Someone must have stuck them down there when the Spanish were burning all the books. Most are Postclassic—that area tends toward that—but some aren't. It looks like some might have come in from Tikal and Calakmul as people moved to the coasts."

"It's exciting."

"Yes. It is."

Lorena turned to her. "A tomb is, too, though. And we may have found one."

"You say that every season, hon'."

"This time, I think we really have. And we have Jake's new camera to help us." She saw the shaman was finishing up. "We can get back to work now." She nodded to the shaman then turned back to Shelly. "I'm really glad you're here."

"Are you?"

"We're a team, Shelly. I can't do this without you."

"That's what I told myself. When I left Belize." She looked down. "Don't prove me wrong. Not again."

"I won't." She eased Shelly away from the dig site, toward where she'd pitched her tent. "Come on. Let's get you settled."

"You didn't show up all summer, Lor. Your calls got shorter and the time between them got longer. You don't get to 'get me settled.' I'm not just moving into your tent."

"It's the only one I've got."

"I figured—God knows if you even realize how manipulative that is. I borrowed one from Tammy."

Lorena felt a flash of jealousy. Shelly had always thought Tammy was cute, and it bothered Lorena, even if she knew it was illogical: Tammy was straight and madly in love with her fiancé.

"I have a cot, too, so I'm all set." Shelly pulled her in for a quick and not very close hug, then let her go. "I know you're dying to get back to work. Nothing for me to do, yet, right?"

"Right."

"Well, then, I'll set up and go hang out at Temple XIII, reacquaint myself with the Red Queen's tomb for a while. Maybe I'll see something I haven't before. Some remnant of a glyph. It's hard to believe they'd go to all that trouble and not identify her."

"Okay." Lorena felt a little adrift. She'd expected...what? A tearful reunion? After abandoning Shelly all summer?

Shelly seemed to sense her unease. She leaned in, kissed her cheek lightly. "I have missed you."

"Me, too. You're my rock."

It was the wrong thing to say; Shelly's expression grew tighter. "No, Lorena. I'm really not."

Lorena watched her walk away from the Cross Group where the dig was set up—the three buildings of the group were the crowning architectural achievement of Kan B'alam II—Lorena's personal white whale.

Shelly didn't turn back, just headed around the corner toward Temple XIII where Fanny López first found the Red Queen in 1994—a discovery often credited to her advisor Arnoldo González Cruz, since she was a member of his team. The skeleton had been carefully tended:

covered in toxic cinnabar to keep thieves away. The Red Queen had been buried with a death mask made from nearly three hundred pieces of malachite, and over a thousand pieces of other costly items, jade primarily, were found buried with her.

This was a person to be reckoned with. A woman honored in a way not generally seen in a culture where males ruled. And yet, there were no glyphs in her tomb or elsewhere on the temple to identify her. Why bury her and not identify her? Had the Maya wanted her identity to be a mystery?

But there had been ceramics in the tomb, and ceramics were items that changed with the years, marking the age of a site with a great deal of precision.

Others before Lorena had done the work of ruling out who the Red Queen could not be. Bone experts estimated that the she had been between fifty and sixty years old when she died, and that the skeleton had not been moved from one site to another, as was often done. The cinnabar had leeched into her bones and made carbon dating impossible, but she had been buried with two sacrifices—a young boy who'd been decapitated and a teenage girl who'd had her heart ripped out—and they had not been painted with cinnabar and could be carbon dated.

Yohl Ik Nal, the only queen of Palenque, had been ruled out by the carbon dating results from the sacrificial companions and the era of the ceramics. Mitochondrial DNA between the Red Queen's bones and those of Pacal ruled out her being his mother, Sak K'uk', who'd held power as a regent of sorts when Pacal had been made king at the age of twelve. Strontium isotopes showed the Red Queen was not from Palenque originally. As kings often married to cement alliances, that pointed even more to the Red Queen being Tzakbu Ajaw.

Lorena walked to the hole that was being tunneled out, straight into the earth. Like so many other Maya buildings, this one had been built on older structures. So far it seemed promising.

She'd searched so long and never found a sarcophagus. All sorts of interesting buildings, even skeletal remains. But never a royal burial. Someone had to find Kan B'alam II—why not Lorena?

Shelly's tent glowed from the light within so Lorena coughed gently.

Shelly came to the opening, smiling in a knowing way when she saw the cups Lorena held. "Seriously? Chocolate?"

"With chilies and very little sugar. Just the way you like it. Dark, dark, dark."

"You're the one who got me hooked on this."

Lorena nodded to the bench near the dig site. "Come watch the stars with me." She wanted to get them clear of the cots, wanted them to talk, the way they used to, when things were good.

Shelly followed her and sat down, taking the cup carefully and licking at the froth first. "I bought a molinillo. Never could master it. Made a mess, not foam."

"Takes work. My mom showed me when how when I was a kid. My father sneers at what passes for chocolate in stores." She took a sip of the spicy, bitter drink. "Once upon a time this was only for the elite. And cacao beans were currency. Not only for the Maya. Aztecs, too. Even if my father blames the Maya for that." She didn't know why she was babbling this way. "You know all this. I bore you with cacao stories every time we find a drinking vessel."

Shelly didn't say anything, just alternated between taking sips of her chocolate and staring up at the stars.

Lorena almost started babbling again, and forced herself not to.

Shelly put her cup down on the bench. "I was with someone in Antigua."

"Yeah, I kind of figured that out based on your parting shot when I left."

"She was a nice person."

"Okay." Lorena wasn't sure what Shelly wanted her to say. "Are you still with her?"

"No. You and I—we're a team, right?"

"Right. Always."

"And this summer, it was a...blip. Not a trend. Not what you're going to be like if I don't follow you around like I have every other rainy season?"

"Are you thinking of going back to Antigua?"

Shelly looked at her as if she was an idiot. "Why would I go there when there are codices in Belize?"

"See that's what I don't get, Shelly. They aren't going to let you have the real thing. They'll make copies for everyone, right?"

Shelly nodded.

"So, you get them and you bring them back here. I've decided I'm not going to leave Palenque this rainy season. It'll be a pain to work if it gets muddy, but I'm not leaving the site half dug for looters to have a go at."

"Everything is first person singular with you, Lor. Why don't you ever think in terms of colleagues?" She laughed, a bitter puff of air. "I want to be there. With the others. They consider me worthy of being

48

part of their team. To be part of that synergy as everyone works with these brand new books."

Lorena wasn't sure what to say, felt stung by the rebuke. "Sounds like paradise. Go, then."

"Well, there's a problem. I love you."

Lorena smiled, stunned that Shelly would be so generous. "How is that a problem?"

"I'm not like your mom or Tammy, following their partners around and finding satisfaction in support work. I'm a professional, too, Lor. I deserve my own chance."

"A king's tomb, Shelly. Imagine if the sarcophagus was as richly inscribed as Pacal's. And it's all yours. You don't have to share."

"When did sharing become a bad thing?" Shelly finished her drink and got up. "Thank you for the chocolate. It was perfect."

Lorena was afraid Shelly was really saying that the chocolate was the only thing that was. That loving her didn't necessarily mean coming back to her.

As Shelly's light went off, Lorena sat in the familiar darkness, under a canopy of stars, the hole in the Earth that might finally lead to an answer lying black and silent in front of her.

Lorena stood next to Jake as he navigated his camera into the hole and began to lower it down. A monitor on a chair showed what the lens was seeing.

Shelly stood across from Lorena, watching the monitor, then said suddenly, "Stop. Turn slightly right. No my right. Sorry." She laughed and her laugh turned into a caw of triumph. "You've got something there." It looked like a carving.

It did not look like Kan B'alam II's name glyph. Lorena tried not to be too disappointed. This was the first glyph they'd found. It might not even be talking about the occupant directly, perhaps an enemy defeated in war.

"I'm going to keep descending," Jake said softly, moving the camera down to the point where the men had stopped—at a solid piece of limestone. Decorated, but not in a way that would likely be a king. "Oh yeah." He reached over and patted Lorena on the shoulder.

Lorena again tried to throw off the disappointment. Until Shelly studied it, she couldn't tell from looking. Just because her intuition was telling her that this wasn't the tomb she wanted shouldn't be a reason to mourn. Tombs were rare finds no matter who was in them.

Jake began to pull the camera up. "Congratulations are in order, Doctor." He grinned at her. "But why do you look like your puppy just got run over? That's a tomb—I'm willing to bet on that."

"I know. I think so, too. But I don't think it's Kan B'alam II's. I thought this time I'd found him."

She heard the bitter expulsion of air that served as Shelly's angry laugh. Looking up at her, she said, "What?"

Shelly waited until Jake finished pulling up his micro camera and headed back to his own site, then she turned on Lorena. "I thought we were a team?"

"We are."

"I was here. Jake was here letting us use his camera. And yet you say: '*I'd* found him.' Is the word 'we' even in your vocabulary?"

Lorena wasn't sure what to say. Settled finally for, "It's my tomb."

She could tell that was the worst thing to say.

Shelly stared at her, her head cocked as if Lorena was some kind of creature she couldn't quite figure out. Then she nodded, a movement that managed to be more derisive than supporting. "It certainly is your tomb, Lor."

She walked over, patted Lorena on the shoulder the way Jake had, and walked off.

Lorena sat on the lower steps of Temple XIII, thumbing absently through her notebook as she ate a breakfast bar. Once she dug down farther to the tomb, she should find glyphs and ceramics to date it. And once she reached the body, once it was excavated carefully, everything photographed and cataloged, then the experts in the lab would prepare the skeleton, would send a sample off for DNA testing.

It was exciting, no matter who the inhabitant was, but Lorena was afraid the tomb was not that of Tzakbu Ajaw's son.

She thought of all the covered humps—tombs and temples and houses. So much left to uncover. One of them had to house her king.

"Hey."

Lorena looked up, thinking how last season Shelly would have sat down beside her, snaking her arm around Lorena's waist, voice soft in her ear. Instead she stood on the grass of the plaza, far enough away that Lorena would have to take several steps to cross the distance between them.

Shelly didn't wait for Lorena to say anything. "The cache. In Belize. I'm going."

Lorena tried to bite down the pang of dismay. "We'll find another tomb, Shelly. A king's next time."

"I don't doubt that *you'll* find it eventually, Lor. God knows you want it badly enough. But *we* won't." Shelly looked like she was trying not to cry, shook her head and laughed a little frantically. "You try to make this about love—that Pacal loved the Red Queen enough to give her a tomb of her own, and one so big, right next to his. But it's not about love: it's about ambition.

"I follow you everywhere, Lor. When do you follow me? You couldn't even spend the summer in Antigua with me, and if I asked you to come with me to Belize, what would you say?"

"What do you think I'd say? I have this tomb. I can't leave it."

"Of course you can't." Shelly smiled grimly, as if she'd been expecting exactly that answer. "This isn't about us, and it isn't about Pacal and his great love. This is about you, getting your name up there with that queen's name. You're obsessed—and that's okay because that's how great discoveries are made. But don't lie about it. Don't pretend you aren't ambitious, and that this isn't about you."

"It is about love, Shelly. She was his queen and—"

"And he didn't even identify her. Not one damn glyph. The Maya labeled everything, Lor. This is Pacal's cup. This is Jaguar Bites the Moon's bowl. They were obsessive that way and yet they didn't give her a name—an identity. And that's what drives you nuts. Not that she's loved, but that she's not known. Her name isn't out there—and neither is yours yet. It may never be. You may never be a Stuart or a Coe or a Houston."

Lorena looked away. She hated that what Shelly said was true. Wanted to tell her she was wrong, but they both knew she wasn't.

Shelly took a deep breath. "I love you. I will always love you. But there are fifty-seven codices with my name on them. My name and that of every other epigrapher that matters in our field. I don't want it to be just about me. I want to work with that team—I can't wait to work with that team. You'll find someone to work for you. There'll be plenty of grad students who can do what you need an epigrapher to do."

Lorena nodded, tried to swallow the hurt she felt and managed to do it, but any words she might have said—any argument she might have made—followed the pain down.

"Say something, Lor."

"You'll be great," she managed to get out. "You belong in Belize, with the others."

Shelly waited, as if Lorena might say something more. Might...what? Beg her to stay? She finally sighed and said, "I hope you find her. Your queen. Although what happens once you do?"

Lorena shrugged. She hadn't really gotten that far. Had been chasing the answer for so long, she wasn't sure what she'd do if she proved the Queen's identity.

But it didn't matter. The jungle was full of ruins. Waiting for her or someone like her to find. If they weren't destroyed by development, by resource mining, they'd be there waiting, just like they'd been waiting all this time. Ten centuries. Maybe more.

"I'll miss you." The words were out before Lorena could call them back.

"Not enough to change." Shelly turned and walked away.

Lorena realized Shelly's bags were on the path behind her. She was leaving now?

She wished she was the kind of person who could call Shelly back, who could follow her lover instead of the other way around, make compromises, stop pushing.

But Shelly was right. Those weren't the kind of people who made great discoveries.

She walked higher up the steps so she was able to see Shelly walk out of site, down the path to the parking lot. She could picture how she would stow her bags in a jeep, then climb in. "Let's go," she would say to the driver. Or maybe "Get me the hell out of here."

She wouldn't cry, though. Shelly would not cry until she was alone.

Lorena didn't try to stop the tears, just let them fall, onto her dusty shirt and pants, onto the limestone. She leaned over, pressing her hands onto the surface of the step, imagining she was pushing all the way down, into the tomb itself, where the queen had laid, cinnabar brushed over her.

A queen with no name. Not yet, anyway. "You're worth it," she whispered. "You're worth everything."

The queen didn't answer back. Lorena didn't expect her to.

ONE VILLAGE

BY NEIL O'DONNELL

"MACHU PICCHU HAS all the answers," Jennifer's undergraduate advisor, Francis Sullivan, once told her as he tried vehemently to turn her own studies towards the Inca. Jennifer fought off the urging of her advisor and instead pursued the archaeological study of the Underground Railroad. Still, her advisor continued to pester her about at least visiting Machu Picchu. Now, eight years after obtaining her Ph.D. in Anthropology and a tenured archaeology professor, she finally arrived at the entrance to Machu Picchu. Yet, her visit served no scientific purpose. Jennifer was there to scatter Dr. Sullivan's ashes over the site he so loved.

With her parents recently killed and being one of only a few African-American students at the private college she attended, Dr. Francis Sullivan was one of the few people who seemed to truly care about Jennifer. He had guided her through her undergraduate years and encouraged her on her quest to unravel mysteries revolving the Underground Railroad though he always kidded her about becoming Mesoamerican specialist. Now, the last person she considered family, Francis, was gone, and Jennifer struggled to find a path for the future.

"We're here, Professor Sanford," Jennifer's guide said as their jeep rolled into a space next to a tour bus. You sure you don't want a guide?"

"I'm sure, Enrique. I already have a guide," Jennifer said as she pulled an urn out of the case she'd carried since her journey started in North Carolina. Unlike the large gathering of tourists already at the site, Jennifer donned her normal fieldwork gear: khaki cargo pants, hiking boots, a wide-brimmed hat, and a white, long-sleeved cotton shirt. Many of those she encountered in town mistook her as a guide for the Incan Trail tours as she carried very little with her other than the bag containing Francis's remains.

"Dr. Sullivan was a great man, senora," Enrique said, which caused Jennifer to stop her jostling with the seat belt. Enrique served as Dr. Sullivan's liaison with the Peruvian government and knew the departed as well as Jennifer did. "You take as long as you need and then call me. I'm only thirty minutes away.

"Thank you, Enrique," she said as she exited the jeep and made her way into the ruins Hiram Bingham brought to modern light in 1911. The walk was idyllic as Jennifer maneuvered around the ruins under a clear sky while recalling tidbits of knowledge Francis passed to her over twenty years.

"Incan stonecutters chiseled granite and limestone so that the stones interlocked without any need for mortar and in a way that made these structures highly resistant to earthquakes that frequented the region," Jennifer remembered Francis stating in one lecture as she ventured along one of the site's perimeter stone pathways. True to his words, Jennifer marveled at the precision with which Machu Picchu's stonework was constructed centuries before power saws and drills were invented.

"We still are uncertain of Machu Picchu's purpose, though I support the thesis it was a Royal retreat, which housed a multitude of servants to support the elite in residence," Francis often said in class and at presentations he gave at conferences. Memory of those words returned as Jennifer made her way through the units Francis believed housed servants. Her trek through Manchu Picchu and memories of Francis brought her to a corner servant's dwelling when the sun reached midday. Sunlight streamed in through breaks in the structure's wall, which took Jennifer by surprise. Precisely cut and assembled stone with breaks? Jennifer gently brushed her fingers over the stones and examined the areas where light penetrated. All appeared solid save for minute holes drilled into the stones themselves; there were no breaks in the seams. Jennifer turned about and backed away from the sunrays, and for an instant, a design appeared: an isosceles triangle within a trapezoid. While her memory failed in specifics, Jennifer knew she'd seen the design before.

After walking about for the better part of two hours, Jennifer climbed to a landing overlooking Machu Picchu. There, she poured Francis's remains onto a flat rock and watched as the wind dispersed her mentor's remains over the site.

"Rest in peace, dear Francis," Jennifer said as the pile of ashes floated through the air down towards the Temple of the Sun. For another hour Jennifer sat there, marveling in the view of rich green grass interspersed between the stone dwellings, paths and terraces. Above, a lone condor soared as if to survey its kingdom, a lord of the sky waiting to enact justice.

Her meditation over, Jennifer made her way to the parking area outside of Machu Picchu before calling for Enrique. As promised, he was there in thirty minutes to drive her to the nearby town of Aguas Calientes.

"Your train will arrive in about an hour so you have a little time to visit the shops," Enrique said as they pulled into the town's main thoroughfare. "Just be careful of what you buy. The purveyors are peddling nothing but cheap replicas of Incan pottery and charging an arm and two legs for the smallest pieces." Jennifer remembered similar advice from Francis.

"Thank you for everything, Enrique," she said as she climbed out of the jeep. Then, grabbing her suitcase stored in the jeep's back seat, Jennifer rummaged around amongst her clothes until she found and removed a trowel. "This was Francis's Marshalltown trowel. He wanted you to have this." Enrique accepted the offered tool and seemed mesmerized by it. Tears welling in his eyes, Enrique nodded towards Jennifer before responding.

"You take care of yourself, Jennifer."

"You, too, Enrique," she replied before lifting up her suitcase and walking along on towards the train station. As always, the town was bustling with tourists whose presence over the last century caused irreparable damage to the historic region. Francis remained frustrated that his and UNESCO's efforts to limit visitation and resultant damage seemed futile. For Aguas Calientes, tourism was a boon as evidenced by the flurry of merchants crowding the path towards the train station. Jennifer continuously excused herself from sales pitches for beadwork, pottery, and blankets until she finally was stopped and trapped behind a mob of tourists in front of the train station. In that instant, a black vase caught her attention. She gently lifted the cylindrical vessel and scanned the iconography along its surface. The image of the isosceles triangle within a trapezoid was repeated across the vase's surface.

"What is this?" Jennifer asked the merchant, an older woman wrapped in a shawl displaying a range of brilliant colors.

"Two hundred American," the merchant replied.

"Not how much, what is this?" Jennifer asked again as she pointed to the symbol.

"Two hundred American," the merchant replied again. Jennifer quickly pulled out all her cash.

"One hundred, seventy-seven," Jennifer said after counting her money. The merchant quickly grabbed the money.

"Agreed," the merchant said as she handed over the vase. "The symbol means *Una Aldea, One Village*," the merchant said in flawless English before moving on to another customer.

"One Village," Jennifer repeated as she moved on with the suddenly mobile crowd of tourists. Then, after boarding the Cuzco-bound train, Jennifer passed the hours contemplating the image, searching through her memories for some clues as to its significance. Seated in a rail car with a glass ceiling, Jennifer and her fellow passengers were afforded picturesque views of the Peruvian hinterland. For Jennifer, the mountains, streams and valleys fell to nothing as her eyes focused on the condor, which seemed to fly along with the train as a sentry on patrol.

Two months later, Jennifer's mind was far removed from her time in Peru. Now half way through the semester, she was focused on her seminar course in American Archaeology. Every semester, she used this class to highlight major events in American history as evidenced by archaeological collections. This day was special as she was covering her research on the Underground Railroad.

"Now, there has been some debate regarding the paths taken by slaves to reach cities like Buffalo, where a number of Carolina-region slaves escaped to. In recent decades, it was argued that slaves and abolitionists used quilts to designate actual routes to freedom." Jennifer forwarded to the next slide in her Power Point presentation, which showed one of the hypothetical quilts. "The designs on this quilt were argued to be representative of such quilts where the sequence of patterns displayed informed slaves of which way to go. Honestly, the evidence to support such a hypothesis is lacking. Yet, this poses a great question. How did runaway slaves learn about the actual routes?"

"Word of mouth?" one student guessed quickly, a response which initiated a series of head nods from the other students.

"Exactly!" Jennifer exclaimed as she forwarded the presentation to a slide depicting several rusted pairs of leg and wrist irons. "Most evidence obtained through excavation is in the form of broken shackles and pottery used to feed escaped slaves. Those that led slaves along the railroad, the *Conductors*, kept a tight lip on routes never writing down specifics for fear of slavery proponents finding runaway slaves. Journals written shortly after the Civil War's end highlight the importance of secrecy." Jennifer's next slide showed a journal page from one conductor.

"*We only knew our section of the route and spoke only to the next Conductor about where to meet next time.*" The words barely legible, Jennifer read the passage, which was written by the Conductor who helped her own great, great, great grandfather make it to freedom, a point she enthusiastically shared with the students. Yet, amongst the applause of students, a quick glance at the remainder of the journal's passage transported Jennifer back to Machu Picchu.

"If bounty hunters were close, we fled instead to the Seneca," Jennifer said, reading the last line of the page. Next to the word Seneca was a hard to see symbol, which upon further scrutiny was a triangle within a trapezoid.

Jennifer was in research mode. First she sprinted to the library after class and checked out a number of archaeological and historical treatises on the Seneca during the nineteenth century. Her next stop was to the supermarket to pick up her main staples during research: chili, hard rolls and Pepsi. Once home, with the chili simmering, Jennifer dived into volume after volume searching for any reference to the Seneca's participation with the Underground Railroad. Well into the night she searched, scanning the photos and drawings of pottery and anything else with iconography to no avail. Frustrated by fruitless efforts and buzzed on caffeine, Jennifer grabbed her tablet and retired to her dad's armchair.

"God, I miss you Mom and Dad," Jennifer said as she pulled the afghan off the back of the chair, an afghan her mother had made. Finding comfort and strength, huddled in the chair, Jennifer scanned for museums with Seneca-themed exhibits, which led her to the Buffalo History Museum's online photo gallery. A virtual catalog of the museum's artifact collections, the site held countless photos for Jennifer to scan. Yet, two hours later, not one of the images Jennifer uploaded included a symbol similar to that which now dominated her thoughts.

"So, what next?" Jennifer asked herself aloud as she leaned into the chair's embrace. As with most archaeological discoveries, chance prompted Jennifer's next step. Clicking to the museum's bookstore link in search of a book on Seneca symbolism, Jennifer found for sale contemporary Seneca pottery. The first vessel, fired with a rich blue glaze, was incised with images including a triangle within a trapezoid. Hope returned as Jennifer clicked on the link to the vase.

While no name for the sculptor was provide, nor any information regarding the symbols, a Cattaraugus Reservation address was included with the simple instructions of 'send all inquiries to'. Jennifer did not hesitate as she grabbed her phone and called the airport.

"When is the earliest flight to Buffalo?" Jennifer asked the airport operator as she began pulling together necessities for the trip.

Fifteen hours and hundreds of miles later, Jennifer found herself in a cab entering the Cattaraugus Reservation. While the cabbie used GPS to navigate through the winding roads, Jennifer scanned the landscape: dense, diverse woodlands that covered a mountainous terrain.

"This certainly had to be a difficult journey before the roads were put in," Jennifer said just before the cab struck a pothole concealed by a fresh layer of snow.

"It's not much better with the roads, to be honest," the cabbie replied as he recovered from the near spinout the pothole caused. A few minutes later, their trek ended after the porous, pavement turned to all dirt roads. "This is as far as the cab can go with the snow, miss," the cabbie replied. "Do you want me to leave you here or take you back to town?"

"It's only about another mile," Jennifer said as she handed her fare and a tip to the cabbie. "I can manage the walk."

"Suit yourself," the cabbie replied as he watched his passenger grab her backpack and march on into the snow. Jennifer, after hearing the cab drive away, pulled out her phone and activated her GPS. For a few minutes, the app guided her steps, but it was short-lived as cell reception suddenly died.

"So much for technology," Jennifer said as she walked on even as snow started to fall and the wind picked up. For an hour she walked along the road until the road ended at a dark stained, log cabin. Jennifer suddenly felt silly as she confirmed the sculptor's listed address with the number on the house. *What would she say?* Brushing aside such thoughts, she trudged through the snow to the cabin's door and knocked. The high pitched cry of the growing wind made the cabin seem desolate. Yet, as she waited for someone to answer the door, the scent of a well fed hearth within provided a sense of security. Then, just as she heard someone unlocking the door, a hawk cried out. Turning and looking skyward, Jennifer spotted the raptor as it circled overhead. For a second, memory of the condor at Machu Picchu returned.

"May I help you?" an elderly woman asked, jarring Jennifer's attention away from the hawk overhead. The Seneca woman was several inches shorter than Jennifer and had long, dark brown hair with streaks of white throughout. Yet, the woman stood tall and appeared unbelievably agile as she fully opened the door. "Miss?" the woman asked after Jennifer failed to speak. A new call from the hawk diverted the elderly woman's eyes to the clouds. "Ever vigilant, my friend," the woman said to the hawk.

"I'll wager there's a rodent out there about to be snatched," Jennifer said as she too looked upwards again to watch the hawk circle.

"No, my dear. The hawk was simply watching over you and me. Please come in." Jennifer entered into a great hall after the invitation. Rectangular in design, the hall was fifteen feet by thirty feet, had benches along the entire interior wall, and included multiple display cases packed with assorted ceramic vessels. "Welcome to my studio."

"Studio?" Jennifer asked as she again looked around the space. "Missing some clay and an oven, aren't you?"

"All that's in the back," the woman replied as she closed and locked the entrance. "This is my display area, which is as far as customers go." The woman then walked over to one of the benches and sat before gesturing for Jennifer to follow. "So, do you want to explain why you're at my door with a winter storm warning in effect?" Jennifer had no answer and just stood there, mouth agape. "Please take a seat, miss."

"Thank you," Jessica said as she walked over and sat. "I wasn't aware a storm was coming. I just had some questions about your pottery."

"You archaeologists certainly are impulsive." The woman laughed lightly while shaking her head.

"How did you know?"

"Lake-effect storm on its way and you're here for questions, you were either an archaeologist or a historian."

"And a historian wouldn't venture out in a storm?" Jennifer asked before smiling wryly.

"Actually, I figured archaeologist because a historian wouldn't have been so reckless." The woman smiled wide before she and Jennifer both started laughing. "So what can I do for you?"

"I'm Doctor Jennifer Sanford and wanted to know who made this vessel," Jennifer said as she removed a printout of the vase. "Is this one of yours?"

"Definitely one of mine," the woman said without hesitation, "but I sense you didn't travel out here to ask just that. What do you really want to know?"

"What is the meaning behind this symbol?" Jennifer asked pointing to the design that now served as an obsession. Jennifer noticed the woman's eyes bulge briefly at seeing the image Jennifer pointed out.

"Onskat enondecha," the woman replied. "It means…"

"One Village?" Jennifer asked before the woman could finish.

"Close enough. I didn't realize you were fluent in multiple Iroquoian languages."

"I'm not. Wait, multiple Iroquoian languages?"

"That phrase is a mix of Wendat and Susquehannock dialects, once our sister Iroquoian nations to the north and south. The funny thing is that I've only seen the symbol at an Erie site.

"Erie?" Jennifer asked her confusion only growing.

"The Erie were the Iroquoian nation that actually dwelled here when Europeans first invaded. The Seneca and the rest of the Haudenosaunee nations were forced here later."

"How far away is this site?"

"It's not far, and now is the best time of day to go to see what I think you truly need to see. Come, let me show you."

It took less than twenty minutes to walk through nearby woodlands to reach the site, which sat hidden amongst a barrier of spruce and maple trees. The ground itself was covered with snow, which was growing deeper by the minute as the first wave of the predicted storm had reached the area. Along the way, the woman asked Jennifer questions of her research, family and limited knowledge of One Village. Then, as they encountered a break in the trees, Jennifer's guide stopped.

"The symbol is carved into the rock ahead," the woman said as she agilely maneuvered through the snow until she reached a large fragment of chert roughly the size of a fire hydrant. Once there, she brushed snow off until the telltale symbol of One Village appeared. Jennifer, now speechless, reached out and traced the triangle with her fingertips. Weathered, the symbol's grooves were smooth and the rock surface surprisingly warm. Sensations of touch fell to nothingness as Jennifer's thoughts were flooded with images of diverse people, all slaves, fleeing from shadows: Aborigines, Bantu, Irish, Japanese, Jews, and Native Americans. Men, women and children of all ages, all bruised, scarred and malnourished, appeared like apparitions that walked by and through Jennifer as if she wasn't even there.

"What the hell!" Jennifer exclaimed as she retracted her hand; the apparitions disappeared instantly. Her eyes welled up with tears, Jennifer turned to the woman for an explanation. Like Jennifer, the woman was now crying, clearly impacted by the images.

"You're the first in a long time to answer the call, Jennifer," the woman said as she walked up to the archaeologist."

"Who are you?" Jennifer asked as she looked back down at the rock. "What is this place?"

"It's a gateway for the lost and broken, an exit for those beyond healing." The woman walked on several yards before stopping and looking eastward towards the nearest mountain.

"A gateway to where?" Jennifer asked though she did move any closer.

"A place where all are accepted and all is forgiven. It's one of several gates in this world for the oppressed to find unending freedom." As the woman's words ended, a glimmer of sunlight pierced the cloud cover and bathed a granite slab atop the mountain. The sunlight found breaks in the granite creating an image on the snow cover far below at the woman's feet.   Again, the symbol of One Village appeared before Jennifer. Without hesitation or speaking, Jennifer stepped forward into the light and took the woman's offered hand. In an instant, a structure appeared around the two women. While its foundation resembled the intricate stonework of Incan temples, the roof and companion supports, as well as the arrangement of hearths along the central corridor, appeared similar to Iroquoian longhouses. Jennifer walked to the nearest wall where stone and wood melded in perfection, in a way Jennifer had never seen. An array of symbols was etched into the stonework, which Jennifer tried to decipher.

"Incan, Celtic, Yiddish," Jennifer said aloud as she pointed out the languages she could discern.

"And Bantu, Aztec, Hopewell . . . countless languages for the countless visitors whom have come to one of the gates," the woman said as she walked toward the room's only doorway. Covered by an animal hide, a brilliant light peered through the spaces the hide failed to cover.

"How many gates are there?"

"I know of a few, but I suspect there are many more."

"What lies beyond?" Jennifer asked as she too walked towards the doorway.

"*Onskat enondecha*, my dear sister, and the answers to many of your questions."

"What is it like?"

"I am merely a gatekeeper between the now and One Village. Like the conductors on the Underground Railroad, I know of the part I play alone."

"You've never entered beyond?" Jennifer asked as she brushed the surface of the hide. It was warm to the touch, comforting.

"I have not been summoned further as of yet, but you have or else the guides would never have accompanied you."

"What guides?" Jennifer asked.   Then, as with the sudden appearance of the apparitions, Jennifer recalled the soaring raptors: the condor and the hawk.

"Walk on, dear sister. You'll find your family and friends waiting, at least those of whom have passed to the next stage."

"But why me? What have I done to deserve this?"

"Perhaps nothing, my dear sister," the woman said before grasping Jennifer's hands. "Maybe one of your loved ones in the beyond suffers greatly and needs you. I do know that were you unworthy, you would not have discovered the symbol of One Village nor would you be standing here right now. Remember, I am just here to conduct you along."

For a moment, fear gripped Jennifer, but the warmth of the hide surged through her as if in response. Peace soon reigned in her soul and mind. Without another word, Dr. Jennifer Sanford entered One Village.

WOULD OLYMPUS FALL

BY LOU ANTONELLI

THE LONE HIKER PAUSED TO CATCH HER BREATH. She leaned heavily on her stave, and looked up along the vast talus field between the two mountaintops. She lowered her head as she breathed deeply, and saw a bright red laser target on her chest. She looked up to see a sentry with a high-powered rifle pointed towards her. She raised her hands.

"Where do you think you're going?" asked the sentry.

"I was hired by Randum for the dig," said the hiker. "I'm Doctor Martravia Qualter." She pulled off her woolen hat to expose her short, close-cropped hair.

"Why didn't you catch the last helicopter out of Denver?"

"Because I didn't know it was going to be the *last* helicopter out of Denver," said Martravia.

The guard lowered his rifle and waved her forward. "Come on, I've heard Mr. Randum wondering what happened to you."

They hiked up the trail another 1,000 feet and came upon a well-concealed outpost. "This is the boss's archeologist," the sentry told one of the men. "Take her to the dig."

It was mile up the trail until they reached the main camp, which was concealed behind a berm made of the same gray shattered talus rock that littered the col between the two mountains. Martravia recognized Randum the moment she saw him sitting behind a folding camp table. The "boss" stood as the pair approached.

"Professor, I can't believe you finally made it," he said as he extended his hand. "Welcome to the Spanish Peaks."

"Twin Peaks is more like it," said Martravia with just a hint of a smile.

"This whole thing *is* pretty surreal," said Randum as they shook hands. "I assumed you were killed in the crossfire after I pulled out of Denver."

"No, I hid out in Aurora until I saw a break in the fighting," said Martravia. "Then I snuck into Denver by such a circuitous route that I missed your last transport. I turned right around and set out on foot. I didn't even take a change of clothes."

65

"Smart move, and a good disguise, you don't look like you are worth robbing," said Randum. "You just look like a homeless person."

"Dichter and Sifuentes are too busy trying to divide up the city now that you've left to mess with some homeless black woman with only a stave and sunglasses," said Martravia.

"Good luck to both of them," said Randum. "I didn't leave much behind." He smiled. "Not even you, as it turns out."

"You paid me well for my research and then you got me out of Orlando," said Martravia. "I owe you for that."

"Yes, I hear the fighting in Central Florida has exploded," said Randum.

"Our generation, the generation that made it through The Collapse, is getting old," said Martravia. "The generation that's coming up now grew up uneducated and uncivilized."

"No respect for authority, nobody in charge anymore," said Randum.

"Except for strongmen like you," said Martravia.

Randum pointed up slope. "The treasure hunt is coming along. Want to see?"

Martravia's stomach growled—loudly. Randum chuckled. "How rude of me, sit down, we'll get you a big fat sandwich."

Randum eyed his guest as she greedily tore into a thick beef sandwich retrieved by a sentry. "You know, I was a police captain in Denver before The Collapse."

"Yes, that's why it was one of the best-run and orderly cities," said Martravia. You knew how to keep law and order. What did they call it? *'Community policing'?*"

"I'm glad you remember that," said Randum. "I'm proud how well Denver held together these past 25 years. But I'm almost 75, and I can't hold off young thugs like Dichter and Sifuentes forever."

"Wasn't there an old saying about policemen doing a big heist on their way out to provide for their retirement?" asked Martravia, with a wink.

"You're sharp," said Randum, as he looked up towards the top of the talus field between the two Spanish Peaks. "If we're right about what we'll find up there, I'll have more money than God."

"Let me do my job and make sure you're on the right track," said Martravia as she finished the sandwich.

They talked as they walked up the old Forest Service trail toward the main dig. "I appreciate the break you gave me," she said. "You don't have any skinheads in your gang."

"Things are screwed up enough, it's time to toss away the race card," said Randum. "What's left of us has to pull together, all of us. By the way, you don't look very old. How old were you when Double D Day came?"

"I was only 24, I had graduated from Central Florida State," said Martravia. "I was a probationer with the Florida Historical Commission cataloging artifacts uncovered at excavations on state land."

"You're lucky you got an education before the Double Dip struck," said Randum.

"I got more good out of my field work, because I learned enough botany and ecology to help with farming," said Martravia.

They stopped and paused to catch their breath in the thin, cold air. "So who was the guy who knew about this?" asked Martravia.

"He had been with the federal Bureau of Land Management back when," said Randum. "He was responsible for busting a lot of weed farms and meth labs in federal parks. He tried to lay low for years after the Collapse, because he knew he'd made enemies. As things got rougher, some of his old 'friends' found him hiding in Denver."

Randum turned to Martravia as they continued to hike. "He had stolen the secret file about the lost Spanish Peaks treasure trove as things fell apart and federal offices were looted. He knew he would be able to trade that information some day."

"Many archeologists knew the code of that Aztec map had been cracked in the 1960s," said Martravia. "It was an open secret. Once you knew the picture of the Earth Mother Goddess was a rebus instead of a glyph, it was easy to decipher."

"Yes, Goemer's Butte stood for the papoose on her back," said Randum. "The Spanish named it "La Muneca, 'the doll'. Cuchara means 'spoon'—someone who once saw the map mistook the ceremonial blade she held."

"I'm impressed, you remember it well," said Martravia. "That BLM guy must have explained it well."

"Yes, and I laughed when he said the Indian name for the Spanish Peaks were 'The Breasts of the World'," said Randum.

"*Huajatolla*," said Martravia. "But it all made sense, didn't it? Where the treasure was hidden?"

They stopped again. "So you mean to tell me that there have been people for almost 80 years who knew where Montezuma's Treasure is buried," said Randum, "and nobody did anything about it?"

"The treasure would have been confiscated by the federal government," said Martravia as she stopped and turned to gesture

67

towards the Colorado plains spread out below them. "We are above 10,000 feet, this was all federal land."

"How long did *you* know about the treasure?" asked Randum.

"I didn't—at least I wasn't sure until you sent me a copy of the map. But most Pre-Columbian archeologists knew there was a golden horde out there in the Southwest, somewhere," said Martravia. "There were reputable accounts that Montezuma hid all the Aztec sacred gold as the Spaniards entered his kingdom."

Randum pointed towards a ridge ahead of them further up the talus field. "The dig is up there, behind that berm."

Martravia wiped her brow. "You sure have moved a lot of rock around."

There were sentries at a gap in the berm of jagged rocks. They came to attention as Randum and Martravia passed. Behind them were bulldozers and rock haulers scraping away at the base of the cliff where the saddleback between the two peaks dropped off. Randum pointed with his stave. "I had to have them specially outfitted to run in this thin air."

"I'm impressed," said Martravia. "How did you get the heavy equipment up here?"

"Attacked a Rocky Mountain Rebel outpost at an old U.S. Army base and stole a Chinook," said Randum, with a self-satisfied smile.

Now it was Martravia's turn to point. She aimed her stave halfway up the newly exposed cliff wall. "See those hack marks? That's where Montezuma's workmen hacked off the rocks that dropped down to cover the cave entrance."

"Yeah, it blended right in with the rocks all up and down this talus slope," said Randum. "Now that I knew to look, I've seen some rocks on the ground that have obvious chisel marks."

A man with a hard hat and no rifle walked up to Randum and leaned over to whisper in his ear. Randum smiled and clapped his hands. "They say they've begun to expose the wall that covers the entrance of the cave!"

"Let's go get a closer look," said Martravia. They walked past a bulldozer and up a short slope. At the top were exposed large rectangular building stones. Martravia handed her stave to Randum. "Here, I need to scramble on all fours."

She clambered up the loose rocks until she reached the wall, and peered for a minute before edging her way backwards again. She stood up and brushed her hands on her denims.

"Definitely Aztec masonry," she said to Randum. "No mortar, precisely trimmed, perfect fit."

"Great, we should have it all cleared away in a couple of days," said Randum.

"Sort of a joke, isn't it?" asked Martravia. "Hiding the treasure between the breasts of the world?"

"Time for the old gal to give," said Randum.

"Hey, what happened to that BLM guy?"

"I paid him, and the last I heard he was hiding in an old mine with lots of protection," said Randum. "Let's go back to base camp."

It was bitterly cold after sunset and Martravia drank a cup of hot chocolate. She nodded to her host. "Thanks for the hospitality."

Randum chuckled. "Sorry I couldn't offer you a warm shower."

Martravia laughed. "Now that would have been going overboard!"

Randum looked at his guest and furrowed his brow. "I expect you'll want the rest of the money I promised you?"

Martravia smiled. "Not really. I'll take it in room and board."

Randum raised an eyebrow. "What do you mean by that?"

"I'm an archeologist, remember?" said Martravia, "We know a lot about history. With the collapse of America—like what happened after the fall of Rome—we are reverting to feudalism."

"You want to be my vassal, then?"

"Exactly. You need someone who can identify what you find behind that wall up there." She set down her mug. "You really don't owe me anything else. I would just be grateful not to be a refugee."

Randum held out his hand. The pair shook. "It's a deal," said Randum. "You supply some badly needed brains to this outfit."

Martravia resumed drinking the hot chocolate. "Where do you plan to set up a permanent base of operations?"

"Cuchara for the time being, which is where I've stashed he Chinook, then either LaVeta or Walsenburg," said Random. "Whichever is easier to defend."

"With all the men and equipment you brought from Denver, I can't imagine the locals will give you any crap," said Martravia.

"I'm also not worried about any problems out of Boulder or Trinidad, the universities have control of those cities, and Cheyenne Mountain and the Academy still have control of Colorado Springs, but— and it's a big but—Sifuentes might push Dichter out of Denver."

"You think he would come after you?" asked Martravia.

"If he gets pushed out, he might retreat the same way I came," said Randum. "And try to fall on my rear."

"Think they know you're treasure hunting?"

"I'm sure they do," said Randum. "But they think I'm crazy, and I know I'm not." He sighed. "We both need to get some sleep. I'll come get you in the morning."

Martravia squinted as she saw a man standing at the flap of her tent. Bright early morning sunrise shone in her eyes as he waved a gun in her face. "Hey, you know how to use one of these?" he said.

Martravia had slept in her clothes. She yanked the sleeping bag off. As she stood up, she heard scattered gunfire outside.

"Yes!" she shouted as she held out her arms. The sentry gave the rifle to her. Martravia ran out and followed the man to the berm where other men were lined up and firing towards an unseen enemy.

Randum was in the middle of the line, a Kevlar vest under his down jacket. "It's Dichter," he said. "They tried to sneak up on us."

A sentry three men down from them crumpled with a bullet in his chest. "We have the advantage, shooting down at them," said Randum. "But as the sun rises, it's right in our eyes."

Both sides had machine guns, but accomplished little being shielded by so much rock. An attacker ran towards them and threw a hand grenade as he was shot down. The grenade hit the berm, bounced off the granite and rolled back down the slope, where it detonated.

"How many do they have?" asked Martravia.

"No way of knowing, they're still coming up the slope," said Randum

Martravia looked around to get a lay of the battlefield, then looked at her rifle. "Hey, this is a top-notch sniper rifle."

"It's something else I stole from the Rocky Mountain Rebels," said Randum. "I'm sorry I don't have something more practical."

Randum took a potshot at the enemy line. "Crap, we'll be here forever. We have the high ground, but they're dug in now."

"Your sentries are to be commended for not being surprised," said Martravia. "Mind if I move forward a bit here?"

"Sure, go ahead. What are you looking for?"

Martravia squinted through the sight. "See that man maybe 500 feet down slope from where the rest are all dug in? The one with the red cap?"

Randum peered. "Barely."

Martravia squeezed off a shot. The man in the distance disappeared, as his cap flew up into the air accompanied by a red mist.

"That was Dichter. I saw him in Denver before I snuck out. He was wearing the same stupid red cap."

The gunfire from down slope began to trickle off. There were obvious cries of dismay from the attackers' position. Randum looked at Martravia in amazement.

"I went to college on an ROTC scholarship. I was a Marine sniper in Iraq for two years right out of college before our Armed Forces were withdrawn." she said.

A white flag was being waved from a rifle barrel by one of Dichter's men.

Martravia looked and grimaced. "What you just saw, we used to call a 'Zapruder Shot'".

Martravia handed the rifle to Randum. "Don't look so surprised. You think all archeologists are only good for finding old arrowheads?"

"We're making better time than ever," said Randum. "I've put Dichter's old crew digging out the wall." He smiled.

One of Randum's men came to speak to his boss. Randum nodded. "They've cleared to the base of the wall."

"Let's go then," said Martravia. "I'll check the glyphs."

The wall in the cliff was only 30 feet wide and 20 feet tall. It was enclosed by a heavy lintel on two thick posts. "This almost looks like the entrance to a railroad tunnel," said Martravia as she walked up.

"The writing is on the sides," said Randum.

Martravia looked the glyphs up and down, first one side and then the other. She turned to Randum. "This is it. It's just boilerplate about how great and good a king Montezuma is, and how he will come back and reclaim all this sacred gold after the enemy is driven from the land."

Randum turned to one of his men. "Get the C4."

"Just use enough to loosen these stones," said Martravia. "You don't want to smash up what's inside."

Two men kneeled at the base of the wall with a metal box. Randum motioned for Martravia to step back.

After ten minutes the men indicated the charges were in place and everyone retreated behind the nearby berm. In a minute, there was a loud boom, and a cloud of smoke drifted over them. Martravia peered over the berm. "Damn, that's good work, the wall is all cracked like an eggshell, but not a stone has fallen out of place."

Workers began to attack the loosened stones with crowbars and pickaxes. "Let's see what's inside," said Randum. Some of the blocks were pulled out, and Martravia peered inside with a flashlight.

"What do you see?" asked Randum.

Martravia waved the beam of light around. "Gold. Gold altars, gold chairs, gold statues, gold daggers, gold plates—gold as far as my light shines."

She pulled her head back. "Congrats, you've done it."

Randum whooped as his men cheered.

Martravia stuck her head back in the gap. "What is it?" asked Randum.

Martravia pulled her head back out again. "This isn't a cave, it looks more like a tunnel. The walls are too square and even."

Randum leaned over and whispered in Martravia's ear. "Who gives a fuck? Let's clear out the gold."

Before the Collapse, there had been a ski resort in Cuchara, and Randum now used it as his base, reinforcing a concrete building where the Aztec gold was stored. It took a full two months to carefully empty the "cave" with Martravia inventorying it all.

The "cave" had proven to be 500 feet deep, and as they neared the end, the workers realized there was something strange about the back wall.

"One of the workers struck it with a pickaxe," said Martravia. "We thought it was another wall, but it's not."

"What is it then?" asked Randum.

"It's iron, an enormous iron door," said Martravia.

"You mean there's another chamber back there?"

"Probably," said Martravia. "You still have that supply of C4?"

"Yes."

"Once we get the last of the gold out, it will probably be easier to blast through the adjacent cave wall than directly blast that iron door," said Martravia.

"I didn't know the Aztecs knew how to make iron?"

"They didn't. I think this door is much older than the Aztecs. I suppose the cave the Aztecs filled with gold and sealed up was really an entrance tunnel for whatever is behind that door."

"Who could have built it?"

"Who do you think?" asked Martravia.

* * *

The explosion this time sent a powerful cloud of smoke out of the cave like a cannon shot. The Spanish Peaks echoed and rocks cascaded down the talus field towards the base of the mountains. Randum, Martravia and a handful of workers huddled behind the berm like they had two months earlier when the outer wall was first breached. After 15 minutes one of the demolition experts gave an all clear and the small group advanced into the tunnel. The crack beside the massive iron door showed it was four feet thick. Martravia looked it up and down. "This is a blast door," she said almost to herself.

"What do you mean?" asked Randum.

"Like the door to the entrance of Cheyenne Mountain," Martravia said.

The crack was barely wide enough for a man to push through. Martravia and Randum carried small oxygen tanks as they stepped into the inner chamber.

Their lights illuminated a vast room with rows and rows of metal craft of all shapes and designs, with strange insignia, covered in a light gray dust.

Randum pulled off his mask. "What is this place?"

"Isn't it obvious?" Martravia hissed beneath her mask. "It's a lost military base," she said as she looked around, "abandoned by the Atlanteans. I recognize some of the symbols and designs."

Randum began to gasp. "Let's get out, the air is very stale in here."

They met the others on the other side of the fissure by the blast door, and then went outside into the Colorado sunshine. Randum fell to his knees and breathed the fresh air. He looked up to see Martravia gazing northwards into the distance.

"What are you looking at?" Randum wheezed.

"You can almost see Cheyenne Mountain from here," said Martravia. "It's only 120 miles away."

Randum sucked in his breath and shook his head. "So?"

"You don't get it, do you?" she said. "The old U.S. put its missile command in the heart of the Rockies away from major population centers. The Atlanteans did the same thing. Independently, they came up with bases within 120 miles of each other."

She looked down at Randum. "Maybe thousands of years from now, some barbarian kingdom will hide its treasure in the tunnel leading to the Cheyenne Mountain base."

Randum staggered to his feet. "We can take the old machines out from here and study them, take them out like we did the gold." He stared at his companion. "What's with the look?"

"It just hit me, there must have been a number of bases left behind, hidden in remote places, after the catastrophe that destroyed the ancient civilization," said Martravia. "As time went by, and the people at those bases still clung to some of the old technology, they must have seemed like Gods to the people living below them."

She looked at Randum and nodded. "Yes, they seemed like Gods on high, descending from Olympus, on a cloud—or a contrail. Hurling a thunderbolt—or perhaps a missile."

She turned and looked back towards the entrance tunnel. "We opened up the last base left over from the Atlantean civilization, just now after the collapse of the American civilization."

Randum looked and pointed north. "I will contact the military that's left at Cheyenne." He put his hand on the archeologist's shoulder. "We can combine resources."

"And create another great devastating Army?"

"No, professor, to use the machines to rebuild things faster than ever, and then to make sure the next world civilization doesn't make the same dumb-ass mistakes again."

Martravia looked at him, and laughed. "There, I was so sure I was the smart one."

"You can start an inventory of what's inside there, while I contact Cheyenne," said Randum.

"Sounds like a plan," said Martravia.

"I'll keep at it for as long as I hold up. I'm glad you're here, you're younger," said Randum. "You remember the guy who came to your tent that morning and gave you the gun, when Dichter attacked?"

"Yes? What about him?"

"I originally told him to take you out and shoot you. But I changed my mind when Dichter..."

"Why you..." Martravia stopped. "Aw, fuck. It's in the past. We've got a lot of work to do."

"Right, let's fight the problems instead of each other," said Randum. "Maybe that's one way to bring the world back together, if not for us, maybe the people who come later."

"You think somebody had this conversation once before?" asked Martravia.

"I'm sure they did," said Randum. "I'm sure they did."

SEARCHING FOR PEACE

BY ROB DARNELL

TWENTY YEARS HAVE PASSED since Beatrice was rescued from war-torn Uganda. She'd been fifteen then, she was thirty-five now. Twenty years have passed and she still had nightmares. She still woke every morning to find her pillow soaked from her tears. Twenty years ago Beatrice relocated to the United Kingdom, far from Uganda, but the memories stayed with her.

She hobbled between the pillars of the now roofless structure. Her crutches left deep prints in the finely kept lawn that made the ground within and without the abbey. A warm summer breeze drifted through the arches on either side of her. With the breeze came the smell of the grass, and something else.

She stopped in her tracks and turned her face into the wind. There was the faintest scent of decay. An animal had died not too far off. Just a dead animal, but the smell of it made her think of the cemetery behind the abbey. The cemetery was her reason for being here, or rather what she hoped to find in the cemetery.

She turned back to the tower. Mark Brocklesby was coming toward her. He wore a dark polo shirt with the logo of the Reading Football Club on the left breast. The breeze stirred his shaggy blond hair as he strolled along.

Beatrice reached her crutches to the ground in front of her and hopped forward. She repeated the two motions hurriedly, with determination to meet Mark at a place halfway between them. She had never liked the idea that people might be going an extra distance out of pity for her.

"Sullivan is turning over another grave," Mark said when they were no more than a few feet from each other. "That'll be the third grave we disturbed."

Mark glanced down at her stump. That was something people did on impulse when talking to her, as if checking to make sure their eyes hadn't deceived them. No matter how long people had known her, their eyes were always drawn to the empty air beside her left leg. She'd been fitted with a prosthesis leg years ago, but she'd found the leg uncomfortable and getting used to it required more patience than she was

75

willing to apply. Eventually she'd stopped putting the leg on in the morning. Though she was wearing pants now, the right side was pinned up at her thigh to keep it from dragging on the ground.

Beatrice looked past Mark toward the massive tower. The entrance was wide enough that she had a clear view of the large arch-shaped window in the back wall. She could not see the cemetery that was spread out behind the abbey, but she knew Gary Sullivan and the digging crew were out there with the shovels.

"Do you really think we'll find this stone?" Mark asked.

She started forward and he stepped aside to let her by him. But now she was not in a hurry and hobbled at a reasonable pace. Mark strolled along beside her.

"McClelland was hard pressed about granting that permit," Mark went on. "There never was much evidence that Garrett Royce had been buried with the Stone of Peace."

That was true, but Beatrice was not going to let the lack of evidence stop her from looking. She had pushed for more than a year, enlisting the help of her old professor from the University who had some friends in the government. One of those friends was Kevin McClelland who had granted them permission to dig here, but not without conditions that he expected to be met.

She passed through the arch that was the entrance to the tower. Craning her head back and looking up toward the top of the tower, she saw a square-shaped piece of blue sky. Once a bell had hung at the top of the tower and was sheltered by a roof. But the bell was long gone.

She lowered her gaze and her eyes came to rest on the flat stone monument near where the altar had once been. The monument was the length of a coffin and marked the place where Lady Devorgilla was buried. In the 1500s a larger monument had stood there, but the old monument was destroyed along with the rest of the abbey after the Reformation.

The new monument was created in 1932 and contained surviving pieces from the old monument. Lady Devorgilla had been an admirable woman and she had done much for the people of Scotland. She had also carried her husband's heart with her everywhere she went for the remaining twenty-two years of her life. When she died in 1290, the heart in its casket was buried with her. That was the reason people began calling the abbey Sweetheart Abbey.

Beatrice turned away from the monument and hobbled toward the door in the wall at the side.

"Suppose we find the Stone," Mark said as they exited the church. "Are the people of Uganda going to know what to do with it?"

"That's not the point," Beatrice said. "I want to return the Stone to my home country because that's where it belongs. Whether the Stone serves any purpose or not is another matter."

She stopped and leaned forward on her crutches. The cemetery was spread out in front of her. Gary Sullivan was in the middle of the cemetery with the other two members of the digging crew. The three of them had shovels they were busily digging up a grave.

Kevin McClelland's terms had been simple. They were to dig up only one grave at a time. Immediately after confirming the Stone of Peace was not in the grave, they were to refill the grave and put the grass back. They were also not to dig up any graves that did not have Garrett Royce's name on the tombstone.

The Stone of Peace was a little known legend from seven hundred years ago. Uganda had not been a nation then, but the land was peopled, and the Stone was a symbol of faith and goodwill. According to the legend, in the mid 1400s the Stone was stolen from the tribe that kept it and carried across Africa to Italy. There it was auctioned off to the highest bidder.

The Stone was said to be black marble and carved in the shape of a fist. It was often hung from ropes that were worn around the necks of tribal leaders.

About six years ago Beatrice came across a sales record from the 1400s. The record showed that a Garrett Royce from Scotland had purchased a black marble fist at an auction in Italy. Further research revealed that Royce was a wealthy businessman who lived in Dumfries. The problem was he had a son and a nephew who were also named Garrett. The sales record had not indicated which Garrett Royce had bought the Stone. Fortunately they were all buried here at the abbey.

Beatrice started forward again, making her way into the cemetery. She had to stop every couple paces and change her course to hobble around a tombstone in her path. Mark easily stepped around each tombstone he came upon and continued toward the digging site in an almost straight line.

The man had no idea how lucky he was. He had not grown up in a nation torn to shreds by decades of war. He did not have wounds, either physical or mental, that hindered his ability to find peace in life.

She envied Mark. She often wondered what it was like to live without scars so deep they would never heal. She remembered when her two brothers were taken away from the village with other boys to serve in the Lord's Resistance Army. None of the boys were older than fifteen and the youngest was ten. They had been scared; their fear was readable in their wide-eyed expressions as the flatbed truck drove them away. Beatrice had cried as she watched them go.

She had seen countless acts of cruelty committed by soldiers from both sides of the war. And then there was the day one of her family's goats wandered too far from the rest. Beatrice had run through the tall grass to retrieve the goat and stepped on a landmine.

She blinked. She was leaning on her crutches a few feet from the hole in the ground. Gary Sullivan and Brian Brunner were in the hole scooping out spadefuls of dirt. A discolored headstone with a crack cutting through the name Garrett Royce stood behind the grave. This would be the grave of the son or the nephew, given that the date of birth was two decades after the elder Garrett Royce was born. The letters and numbers engraved in the tombstone's face were misshapen after centuries of battering weather.

Beatrice did not remember crossing the rest of the cemetery to the grave. Her memories of Uganda had distracted her from the current world. But a fraction of her brain had functioned to keep her on with her initial goal, whether she was paying attention or not.

She'd been thirteen when she stepped on the landmine. The deafening blast still sounded in her ears. She remembered hitting the ground as if she'd been flung straight down from Heaven. And then there was the burning pain that engulfed her upper leg. She was screaming and so was her father as he frantically ran to her.

"Miss Mpanga?"

Uganda faded and Beatrice came back to the present. She felt tears welling in her eyes and blinked them away before they rolled down her cheeks. Gary Sullivan was looking up at her from the hole in the ground.

"We hit something," he said.

She gave a single nod and hopped closer to the grave so she could look down into the hole. The two men were standing on nothing but dirt. Gary stabbed his shovel into the soil and she heard the clunk as the shovel's blade collided with something hard. Whatever was under the dirt would not be the lid of a coffin. The coffin would have rotted away long ago. But bones might still remain, and objects that the deceased was buried with.

Gary sat his shovel aside and went down on his knees to dig out the object with his hands. Beatrice hoped they would find the Stone of Peace in this grave. While doing research on Royce, she'd read a journal that was kept by someone who had been at the funeral of one of the three men. There was an entry that said Royce was wearing an odd piece of jewelry around his neck, but the jewelry was not described in further detail.

"It's a skull," Gary said as he brushed away the dirt, revealing a skinless forehead and empty eye sockets. The jaw bone had apparently become disconnected at some point and was nowhere to be found.

"Find its neck," Beatrice said. "And see where it leads."

Gary dug into the dirt just below the head piece. In a matter of minutes he'd cleared away enough dirt to reveal a long, thin piece of bone that could only be the spine.

Beatrice laid her crutches down and dropped into the hole. Together she and Gary uncovered the ribcage. Only after the ribcage was uncovered did they see a thin metallic chain that circled the spine where the neck and shoulders met. The other end of the chain disappeared in the dirt under the ribcage.

Beatrice did not think the Stone of Peace would magically bring peace and healing to her home country. But for her it would serve as a symbol of hope. If she could return the Stone to Uganda and put it on display for the people, perhaps the Stone would at least inspire peace.

She took hold of the chain and pulled. The dirt packed around the chain gave way and in a moment she pulled out the object the chain was attached to.

The object at the end of the chain was not a dark stone carved in the shape of a fist. Instead the object was a metal circle, like a large coin, on which the shape of an eye had been engraved.

Disappointed, Beatrice let the chain fall from her hand. She climbed out of the hole and gathered up her crutches. The sun was setting. A long, wide shadow stretched from the abbey and covered part of the cemetery.

"Fill the grave in," Beatrice said as she headed back to the abbey.

ROB DARNELL

THE FIRST TIME

BY TAMMY A. BRANOM

AMISI ELSAYED CRUMPLED THE LETTER from the Supreme Council of Antiquities in her fist. "Further exploration denied," the archeologist mumbled. "Of course."

Amisi leaned her back against the wall of the treasure-filled tomb embedded into the Giza Plateau. She discovered the crypt and worked in it for months. Golden statues, jewelry, chairs, beds, jars, boxes, and baskets filled the chamber.

After ten years of conducting numerous archaeological surveys and in charge of many important excavations, Amisi realized this tomb held the finest artifacts of their kind. Details in inscriptions and radiocarbon dating of the relics indicated these were of a time prior to the building of the pyramids; all the way back to the First Dynasty.

But, she had found more.

Swiping her boot over the sand covered floor, Amisi knew that beneath her lay a passageway to another, grander tomb. However, Hassan Abdalla, the expedition director assigned to oversee Amisi's work, did not share her enthusiasm when showed ground-penetrating radar pictures of the anomaly. In fact, Hassan was furious.

Amisi gritted her teeth. Full appreciation of the plateau and its secrets could only be born within someone cultured, yet native to the land. Born and raised in Cairo, Amisi grew up amid the bustle of international organizations and world-renowned businesses. She attended al-Azhar University, the world's second-oldest institution of higher learning. She loved her homeland. Yet, here she stood, denied the grandest discovery of all—by a fellow native. And, a man.

Now commanded to leave, Amisi realized too late that her reputation was forfeit. Although she collaborated with the Supreme Council of Antiquities to uncover the site, the Council acted as judge, jury, and executioner over the plateau. Moreover, when discoveries of "unusual" artifacts turned up, they were protected—with lies. Anything contrary to accepted history quickly vanished in inaccurate dating and deceitful cartouches. Hassan was only the latest in a long line of those who had the power to conceal the extraordinary finds of Giza.

Amisi huffed and her brow furrowed. Just that morning, her British friend Paul Jeffers had warned her that something like this might happen. Being a reporter, he had a nose for these things. He knew she needed to act.

"Get proof before it is too late," he told her as he handed her a pocket camera. "You find it, I'll write it."

Amisi flung her backpack over her shoulders. "It's now or never," she said under her breath. She dragged away some artifacts in a cluttered corner and threaded out a hidden rope tied to one of the immense gold statues. No one knew was aware of the hole in the weakest part of the floor—a gap only large enough for Amisi to fit through. Getting on all fours, she shined her flashlight into the blackness below. The gloom devoured the light.

"I won't give up," she said aloud as she adjusted her pack.

Biting her lip, Amisi peered over her shoulder. Disobeying the Council's orders would lead to her arrest. Her skin prickled at the thought of what could come after that. Flogging. Imprisonment. However, she believed beyond any doubt something magnificent waited in the void below.

She tossed the rope into the pit. Again, Amisi peeked back to the tomb doorway, tilting her head, listening for Hassan.

Silence.

Easing herself into the hole, she lowered into tapered walls, her flashlight burning a narrow streak into the dark. Sand and seeping water trickled over her. Dust particles swirled in the gleam as she continued beyond the 150-foot point and well below the known water level.

Planting her feet in oozing mud on the bottom, Amisi guided her light into the black. An archway, embellished with Egyptian characters and ciphers swept in a fluid curve overhead, teasing her with fantasy and imagery. Beyond lay a twisting cavernous pathway.

Amisi continued into the tunnel, creeping along the slippery rock corridor until she ended up at a sheer, vertical wall. A faint glow emanated from a jagged gap in the floor. A ladder disappeared inside the cavity. The only course left led down.

The shaky rungs creaked under her gentle steps downward. Staleness stung her nose and eyes. Her breath fogged in the increasing cold. First one foot, then the other touched the bottom. She spun and squinted into the flashlight's beam at the surroundings.

Amisi emptied her lungs in numb astonishment, her exhale trailing as a ghostly wisp into the soft luminescence.

An entrance to an enormous temple spread before her. Huge pillars towered to a ceiling at least forty feet above. Blue light shimmered amid a mist like the vapor of dry ice, hovering in a thin layer over the floor.

Her heart throbbed in her chest as she passed between mammoth two columns. Panting with excitement, Amisi coughed against the mustiness covering her tongue and stagnant air forging mucus in her throat. Pushing onward, she entered a vast hall stretched deep into foggy grayness and beyond her vision. She directed her flashlight into the shadows. Outstanding hieroglyphs and extraordinary color statues of god-like beings ornamented an enormous passageway. Two rows of majestic pillars erected at 20-foot intervals ascended to twinkling specks of light in the ceiling. Below the colonnade, what appeared to be large rectangular sarcophagi rested atop tiered ledges with canopic jars lined their bases.

Amisi headed to a sarcophagus. Fingers outstretched, she traced the cold, pasty gray encasement. Her brow rutted deep lines across her forehead. The entire casing looked and felt as if molded and imitation, not stone. She knelt and examined the jars and apparatuses at the base.

"This can't be," she told herself.

They were larger than normal canopic jars, but they weren't in a separate area as the Egyptian custom dictated. Amisi rubbed along the lines of the sarcophagus' lid. A jagged edge revealed a broken corner with a small crevice to peek into. She trained her light inside.

Nothing. No body. No mummy.

Suddenly, radiance flooded the temple from tubes resembling incandescent bulbs shaped like lotus flowers. Some lights worked, some didn't.

Hassan appeared in shadow at the pillars like a boogeyman from a closet. "Did you not receive my letter?" His words boomed in the cavernous quiet.

"Hassan!" Amisi called. She hoped to play off her illegal activity. She swallowed a loud gulp. "You found the light switch."

Hassan stepped out from the darkness. "Why are you down here, Ms. Elsayed?"

Amisi scratched her head and glanced around the palace walls. "Well, I. . ." Her jaw slackened and her eyes widened at the sight of the temple in full light. "I wanted to..." Her excuse faded as she took in the sights around her.

The walls were covered with hieroglyphs and reliefs in a multitude of vibrant and undamaged colors. Further inside, more halls split from the main sanctuary as if this had once been the hub of a busy catacomb. Amisi turned slowly, reading the ancient writing. Records of magic and medicine, people and activities, law and labor. Some symbols differed from normal Egyptian script with something she had never seen before. Thirty-two tablets sparkling pure gold and nine sarcophagi bordered a continuous ledge around each pillar. Scattered shards lay in heaps next to two coffins.

Inspecting the sarcophagus next to her, Amisi now clearly saw the vault as not granite and not carved, but a rectangular case of hard, white material. Had she been anywhere else, she may have suspected fiberglass. The lid displayed a flat, 3-dimensional image. Although a bit too pale to be Egyptian, Amisi believed the picture represented the occupant's face.

Lowering herself to one knee, Amisi scrutinized the containers next to the encasement. They were clearly NOT canopic jars. They more resembled oxygen tanks.

Her left eyebrow arched. This was far from a normal Egyptian burial site.

Amisi rubbed the sarcophagus top, revealing a gauge below the inhabitant's picture.

Hassan stepped closer. "It is a temperature indicator."

Amisi's muscles stiffened. Her expression stilled; her face stolid toward the director. She hoped for more.

"Follow me, please, Ms. Elsayed." Hassan scuttled past Amisi and squeezed through an opening at the side and disappeared into the wall.

"Where are you going?"

Hassan didn't answer. Fear bubbled in Amisi's veins, but curiosity compelled her to follow the path the director took. She found a large bronze door opened a few inches. She peeked inside at a small domed room lit with the same type tubes as in the hall.

Hassan stood at a gray podium etched with faces and glyphs. "I understand most of the writing, and, subsequently, who the people are out there."

Amisi moved next to Hassan and eyed the script.

He continued. "It is documentation of what happened to them." He ran his finger along the glyphs. "To those who come...be told our peril...contact...failed...all have fled. Water flows...walls...above. Water has invaded the Great Hall...sealed the doors. We must...before the chamber fills...preserved from a watery death. We pray you shall come for us."

"Apparently, no one came for them," Amisi said.

"No, but the Egyptians found them." Hassan weighed her with a narrow squint.

"The Egyptians?" Amisi cocked her head. "Are you saying these are NOT ancient Egyptians?"

"In here," Hassan stated, motioning around the hall, "are the records of a once great civilization." He pointed to the ceiling exhibiting a map of the heavens—Orion placed foremost in the sky. "The stars' positions indicate a time when the plateau thrived green and lush." He dropped his eyes. "These people awaited their rescue."

Amisi shook her head. "I don't follow."

"Read here." Hassan zeroed in on specific script. Amisi mouthed the words under her breath.

"Do you understand the writing?" Hassan asked.

"Of course. Preparing the body for mummification."

"Read it again. However, this time think within modern technology."

Scowling, Amisi scanned the glyphs once more. "Cool down and washing the body. Preparing the blood and organs. Adding solutions to preserve the body. Wrapping the body. Placing it in its sarcophagus." Amisi sucked in a sharp breath.

"It is a misinterpretation," Hassan stated. "In that time, the people did not comprehend this as life waiting to be restored. They understood it as rebirth after death."

Amisi's jaw hung loose as she took it all in. She swiveled to the director. "These people are cryogenically frozen." Her eyes passed over the reliefs again.. "Particular attention is paid to the heart in the beginning. It must be kept pumping for circulation during the freezing process." She squint at Hassan who stood quietly at her side, his eyes sparkling at the elements on the wall.

"The heart is the soul to the Egyptians," Hassan stated.

Amisi followed over the instructions to another detail. "Here, a hole is drilled into the skull and tubes put in for drainage throughout the freezing. The Egyptians misinterpreted this as brain removal." She reached out, pulled back, and then tapped the wall. "Here, tubing is inserted into the nose. I know this to be a step in the fluid transfer process of cryonics, but it could be misconstrued as a removal procedure, hence extracting the brain through the nose as the Egyptians did." She continued, her fingers gliding lightly over the wall. "Even the sarcophagi the Egyptians created matched the cryostats these people used, including the interred person's image." Amisi gazed in wonder around the hall. "This is an ancient suspension facility."

"Yes." He raised his finger toward the ceiling's center. "And there was home." Diamonds sparkled as stars dotted the domed top forming the constellation Orion. "They are of Zep Tepi; the First Time."

"This must be their language. Some of these symbols I've never seen before."

"It is." Hassan's face traced the writing. "This is all very close to the Egyptian tongue, as if the Egyptians took from this. There are only minor variations."

He looked at Amisi, his eyes glazed as if he were in the midst of wild intoxication. "It is so remarkable—the similarities between the cryogenics and mummification. The suspension begins with washout and perfusion whereby the body and blood are cleaned with a saline solution. The blood is pumped out and replaced with protectant fluid. The Egyptians misunderstood the representations here. They concluded that organs and not only blood needed to be removed. And finally," he indicated one particular passage, "the body is tightly wrapped in layers of protective apparel."

"Just like today." Cold tingling raced over Amisi's skin as the parallels stood clear. "The wrappings, the resin coating, and the shroud that Egyptians applied. It's all here."

"Yes. The rest is simple to see. Tipping the table at one end to allow excess moisture to drip away. The coffin having many layers for added protection covered with a separate, heavy lid, and decorated with a likeness of the person inside."

Creening her neck, Amisi swung her head around to steal another look at the cryostats. She envisioned the people reviving; their white, linen-wrapped bodies stiffly emerging from the solution. She struggled to think of what she might say to these ancient ones.

"Later, the Sphinx was created to stand guard over this place and keep it holy," Hassan added. "They attempted to emulate everything, including the chambers to take their pharaohs to be among the gods themselves. They thought this was how the gods traveled to heaven, or, as far as these people lying here were concerned, to the stars."

Hassan gripped the podium and ran his fingers over one spot. "I just don't understand why this is here." His eyebrows came together in a deep wrinkle. "If I'm correct, this is a date and it is..."

"How long have you known about this?" Amisi interrupted.

"The information has been here as far back in time as anyone can remember." One corner of Hassan's mouth snarled upward.

"This definitely needs more research," Amisi said. "If fully translated, the advances to cryonics would change many lives."

"Yes, but even with the instructions no one in this time can successfully awaken them."

"So, you tried?"

Hassan didn't respond, his face stony, expressionless. The room fell silent like a telephone line gone dead. An icy twinge crawled over Amisi's scalp and she combed her fingers through her thick, black hair. Gulping down her dry ambiguity, Amisi shook off the cascading uneasiness. "Hassan, this is evidence of ancient, intelligent life on earth—of a history before our own." She drew in a deep breath. "Maybe even proof of God."

Hassan shifted on his feet. "Or, that there is no God."

The two stared at each other, their bodies taut, and arms hanging rigid in the ominous silence.

"The truth can never leave this place." Hassan's cheek muscles flexed as he tightened his jaw. "A world without God is unspeakable."

Amisi opened her mouth to continue her protest, but thought better of it. Hassan had probably protected this secret for years or even his entire life. Her words would not change him.

"You were denied further exploration, Ms. Elsayed. You are not to be in here." Hassan's eyes squinted. "Did you think I did not know about the hole in the tomb?" A stony, arrogant smile surfaced as Hassan drew a revolver and aimed it at Amisi. "You are under arrest."

Amisi backed a half step and raised her hands. "Arrest?"

"I found you down here even after you were instructed by the Council to discontinue your excavation. You tried to flee when I attempted to deter you."

Her face scrunched. "I don't understand. Why did you show me this? Why bother to tell me the truth of these things at all?"

The director tipped his head sideways and shrugged. "Because you deserve to know the truth before you die."

Hassan fired. The shot tore into Amisi's shoulder, burning like a hot ember. Amisi twisted back, flopping over the podium. Her blood smeared across the faces of the interred.

Hassan rushed forward and grabbed a fistful of Amisi's hair. Their eyes locked. "You cannot leave here." He put the gun to her head.

Lights sparked to life from underneath Amisi and the tomb shuddered as if an earthquake rumbled the ground. A hum vibrated throughout the crypt. Systems started. Each of the cryostats blinked to life.

Hassan staggered backward, Amisi's hair tearing from his grasp, and the gun cracking onto the floor.

Amisi raised herself from the panel as the director collected himself and stumbled toward her.

Amisi kicked Hassan squarely in his crotch. As he dropped, she dashed from the room, squeezed through the bronze door, and raced into the hall, zigzagging amid the cryostats, checking the dials. The temperatures climbed.

The gods' revival commenced.

Pictures. The word echoed in Amisi's mind. She whipped the backpack off and dug into its depths. Hands trembling, she raised the camera and turned in a circle, each flash illuminating the vibrant colors.

Inside the room, Hassan limped to the podium. Sweat streamed rivers and dripped onto the top as he repeatedly stabbed at the pictures, to no avail. Spit seethed between his teeth as he slammed his fists onto the panel.

The system silenced. The drone quieted. Lights turned to steady beams.

Amisi held her breath, waiting.

Loud scrapes churned in the room. Hassan whipped around to witness the heavy bronze door scratching along the gritty floor—closing. His jaw dropped and he raced for the quickly vanishing gap. He smashed against the door, groaning and shoving. Sweat ran in tears of fear down his lined forehead and across his cheeks.

"Amisi! Help me!" He pressed the side of his face to the closing door. "Amisi!"

She didn't move. She watched as his one eye widened first with fear and then with disdain.

The heavy door continued to close.

"I am more than you will ever be," she said between clenched teeth and ran to the door to help the man who wanted her dead.

A thud and hiss sealed the frame—and Hassan—inside. He pried the edges with his fingers and pounded with his fists, the dull thuds booming in his ears. Amisi did the same on her side.

A whoosh blasted into the room as if on the breath of God.

Amisi stumbled back. She was too late.

Vapors clouded the room, burning Hassan's eyes and throat and stealing his air. Covering his mouth and nose, Hassan hysterically jabbed the podium faces, but nothing happened. He dropped to his knees. "There is God," he wheezed.

Hassan slumped over, dead.

Lights flickered off and on several times at the pedestal and to each chamber, then shut down. A faint mechanical voice spoke in the alien language, but Amisi understood. "Intruder terminated. System restart. Signal activation reset." A low frequency whir inaudible to human ears drifted throughout the temple and along the cavern walls. The ages old sand, limestone, and rock shivered within sound's path

Amisi slowly turned. Sprinkles of dust floated down like snow. The hum intensified, rumbling her body's cells and pulsing in her ears. She tossed the camera in her backpack, ready to get out of the crumpling underground palace, one word exploded in her mind.

Proof.

Pictures weren't enough.

The labyrinth grumbled. Sandy mud slithered a slow stream down Amisi's escape route. She raced to the sarcophagus with the broken lid and grabbed a tank. It ripped from her hand.

It was still attached.

"System restart," the voice blared again. The sound growled low, almost guttural.

Amisi rummaged in her pack for her knife.

"Signal activation reset."

With a smile, she tugged the knife out and flipped it open. Her breaths heaved long wisps into the quickly cooling air as she sawed the line to her prize.

A wet swoosh drew her attention to the ladder. Gallons of silt surged through the hole into the cavern.

She sawed faster, yanking the line as she cut. The quicker she sliced, the more the soupy dirt sloshed around her.

Setting both feet against the tomb and gritting her teeth, Amisi heaved, resorting to wild hacking on the line. The tank broke free, planting Amisi on her backside, and the container into the swirling goop. A river of sludge engulfed it and washed it away.

She slapped the slimy floor in frustration and let out a growl. Muddy drops splattered in all directions.

The drone roared. The wet dirt gurgled in increasing volume.

Without further hesitation, Amisi shoved everything in her backpack and headed for the ladder. Now coated in wet, slimy slush, the rungs slipped in her every grasp. As the muck dumped over her, covering her in a blanket of desert debris, she forced herself upward, each grab, each step, a slow, slippery trial.

Nearing the top, the gritty deluge burped a blast onto her. Her hands lost their grip under the weight and sent her plummeting to the bottom.

Amisi sighed. Failure was not an option. "I will not give up."

Fighting the eddied sediment, Amisi stood and grabbed the ladder again, her knuckles paling with her tightened grip. She boost upward with newfound strength.

Finally cresting the hole, she dragged herself into the cavern, her fingertips burrowing deep into the accumulating grainy deposits. The walls now poured watery sand along the narrow passageway. Grunting, Amisi dug her fingers into the soft walls to haul herself along as the mire deepened over her boots.

At last, she spotted her rope dangling from the tomb above. Her legs ached as she trudged against the mud sucking at her every footstep. At last, her hands wrapped around the cord, and she started shimmying up.

A thrum rumbled from deep beneath her and she peered into the passage below. The walls spewed their pathway closed.

Amisi scrambled up the rope. The thrumming persisted. The floor of the crypt cracked, exploding centuries of dust into the air. Amisi poked her head into the tomb, only to find the artifacts falling to crumbles on the fractured floor. Clawing her way out, she darted through the maze of the disintegrating dig, all the while, it coughed its dirty breath over her.

The low droning continued to follow her, muttering with terrible slowness up and into the plateau above. With a measured moan, the tomb Amisi Elsayed had worked in for months with all its golden statues, jewelry, furniture, jars, and baskets collapsed, sealing the passageway to the grander secrets below.

Giza kept its gods.

Plunging from the cloud of sand, Amisi dropped face first onto the plateau. She rolled over, coughing lungs-full of dust and wheezing in the clearing air.

She sat up and tossed back the flaps of her pack. Gently, she slid the camera from inside and wiped away the dirty layer of mud. With a flick of her finger, she opened the little door to the memory card.

It was unharmed.

As she cradled the camera in one hand, Amisi rummaged in her backpack until she found her cell phone. To her surprise, it was still working. She dialed. The line buzzed and rang through.

Paul's familiar voice answered. "Hello? Amisi?"

She smiled. "Paul, get ready to write."

THIS LOVE REMAINS

BY REBECCA L· BROWN

I do not know him.

I have told them that so many times it almost slips out of my mouth before I look. Here, long before I see the shrivelled flesh which clings to yet another unfamiliar jaw. A sand-smoothed and unlovely cheek – how sure am I that I would recognise him after all this time? That, withered and long-dead, there will be some small fragment left of him. A part of him still held within that withered corpse which I can truly *know*.

I knew him, long ago, in ways I knew no other. Ways which I have known no other since. Some of the details are now lost to me—I do not know now if I bore him children. Whether we grew old together. Instead, I can remember all the little things. The way he smiled. The words we whispered to each other underneath a dark sky weighed down heavy with the heat of Summer.

Dan Parker's forearm brushes mine. The touch, despite the lightness and the speed with which he pulls away, draws on me. Leads me back. Professor Parker shudders, just a little. I forgive him for it. In a way, I understand. Although my flesh is just as firm and smooth as his, I am a dead thing brought to life. His fingers skim across the bone and hide remains of long-dead bodies without a trace of horror, but those things are dead – and stay dead. I... I am re-made; re-woken; re-living. Others have reacted with far more revulsion; openly, not caring if I see them. When I pass them in the street, they draw away as if to touch me is to burn. Sometimes, I watch the protests on the news. Have seen the hatred etched into their faces. By the hand of science I am made again, unnatural and painfully unlovely in those people's eyes. Even here and now, surrounded by Professor Parker's team - such people as have made the past their business – I know that am watched with mixed disgust and curiousity.

Why is she here? they want to know. *What scraps of long-ago has she (or it) remembered?*

I could answer them: I have remembered more than most. Far more than those who, glimpsing some worn relic of the past, see some

93

momentary flash. A fleeting vision from a life that came before. Wishful thinking, some would call it. Dreaming of a former time, the same way that some high-class housewife might announce that in her past life she was Cleopatra. Memory is not a thing of flesh... and yet, despite their doubts, I still remember.

Ah, the things that I remember! Not the way we built or farmed or shaped the pretty faience beads we strung around our necks. The way we *lived* – and living is much more than things. The way we shouted, laughed and cried. The way we loved. For all their clever questions about paints and pottery and kings, I have no answers.

"They found you close to here." A statement, not a question. Even though it was not Parker and his team who found my body, they have read the papers. Done their research long before they sent the invitation to me. I am always welcome at these sites until I get there. Then, I think I am too strange. Too old; too new; both things at once.

I nod. I know, to them, that fifty miles between this site and mine are nothing. Fifty miles of sand takes them less than an hour to cross. The world is smaller now and fifty miles or fifty years is nothing. Once, fifty years was longer than a lifetime. Long enough to make the pretty trinkets that they show me almost alien. So much can change from one year to the next.

"Maybe..." He knows my story, then.

"I doubt it." Parker has the grace to look away. I fight the urge to ask if that is why he brought me here. *How famous would it make you and your team if this were him?* He would deny it. Every one of them denies it. They have hired me as an expert – though I know to some of them that is a joke, like when policemen hire out psychics to help search for long lost bodies. I too am here to talk to ghosts.

Now, they herd me in between the spoil heaps. Loose, dry sand cascades back down the sides, the cores still dark and damp and sticky. Here and there we stop so that they can display to me some prize or other. Not the prize I came to see, of course. The one they brought me here to see. Together, for a little while, we make believe that death is not what brought me here.

"Would you like some tea?" I shake my head. The game has gone on for too long.

"Please, can I see him?" Parker nods. We walk in silence to the tomb.

What if they've found him? What if, this time, when they pull the plastic sheeting back, I recognise his face? My long-lost lover - longer-lost than any other man before or since. It isn't often that a body is preserved as well as mine. Will he be like me? Will they take a sample of his flesh and recreate him? Even if they do, will be remember? There are others like me – hundreds. Less than five percent have any recollection of a life that came before. Even if I can find him – even if they can reanimate him – could I bear for him not to remember me? Would he be someone else who shared my lover's face or else the same man simply with no memory? Impossible to know. No two reanimates have known each other – or else, no two have remembered knowing. We would be unique.

I hesitate. Beside me, Parker is too eager, shifting from one foot onto the other. I lean closer for a better look.

"It isn't him." They'd hoped. They thought they'd found him. Two sites placed so close. *It could be him,* they'd told each other.

"Are you sure? Please, look again."

"I'm sure. It isn't – No." I shake my head. They cover up the body. Peg the sheet back down to keep it safe.

"Can I escourt you to your car, or - ?" Now he knows, he doesn't want me here. Too strange for him to tolerate without the lure of fame to give me glamour. Parker moves away, no longer taking so much care to hide the way he feels about me.

"No. I'll find it. Thank you." I am keen to leave. Keener than they are to get rid of me. I walk back to the car. Tuck both my hands into my pockets so they cannot see my fingers shaking.

"Are you okay?" Luka the driver has become familiar with me. We have worked together now for long enough that he forgets – or else forgets to care – that I am remade. That there is now no trace of newness left to me.

"Yeah. I thinks so." My hands still tremble in my lap long after sand dunes hide the excavation from us.

"It shook you up to see him like that, didn't it?"

"How - ?"

Luka simply shrugs. We drive back to the institute in silence.

Will they take a sample and remake him? Will there be a sample good enough for him to be remade? He looked so dry there, still half-buried underneath the sand. I knew him, though. Perhaps that means there is enough left of him that they'll make him live again. If he is clever – cleverer than I was – he will lie. I wonder sometimes whether all of us remember. If I'd lied, they would have given me some other name. A little money. Sent me out to live. I think I want that for him – that is, if they find that they can give it to him. Better that than this. To live again and be a freak – and if I'd told them it was him, there would be no escape. We would be news. They'd print our faces into every paper.

Let him live, then—or else let him sleep. I'll make an effort not to know what happens one way or the other. Now I've seen him, I have made my choice.

"There's going to be a storm tonight." The sky is clear, thought that means little. Here, the weather is too quick, too changeable, for clear skies to have meaning. Somehow, though, I find that Luka always knows. He says he feels the storm clouds coming.

Tonight, my lovers' face will haunt me. Dreams of dead eyes filled with accusation. Now, I feel the warmth of Luka's hand against my shoulder. Know that I have made a choice. That right and wrong have long since ceased to matter.

The Seam of Life and Death

by Vanessa MacLellan

NANAY, SUMI, GREATEST DISCOVERY of my life.

Professor Aminhan Tiangco hit enter, slipping her instant message along intangible lines across the globe to her mother and oldest sister. Harbored from the cresting Egyptian sun within her canvas tent, Ami returned to her field notes, bearing a smug grin.

"Ami!" a man called from outside. "Come here. We've broken through to the rear room."

Her mother's response from Ami's home town, Makati, Philippines, blinked onto the screen: *I certainly hope you've had the time to contemplate your place in this world, and have re-found your Lord and Savior in Christ.*

Right on its tail, Sumi's message arrived: *What? You found out your cutie grad student has a thing for older women? Not a surprise sis, he'd climb the moon for you.*

Ami shook her head. The women in her family had polar opposite views as to what measured as "the greatest discovery of her life".

Tempting an assault by Biblical verse, she shot off a jab to her mother. *Nanay, I did find god and god is dead.*

Her sister deserved no response. It was a tired track they'd raced around. Ami had a heart of carnelian, too hard to permit any romance. Keith Thorton was a good friend, one she'd do nearly anything for, but date was not one of them.

"Ami!" Keith—sun-bronzed, good-natured and nearly twenty years her junior—tore through her loose tent flap. "Did you hear me calling?" Nothing could mar the way his grin challenged the burning sun.

"You're through?" she asked.

"And seven more inside." His eyebrows rose up and down, up and down, like children hopping over bamboo poles in a tinikling dance.

Ami clicked her laptop closed and tailed Keith through their survey camp, erected east of the Dakhla Oasis at the core of the desert, to the caves thirty yards away, skip-trotting to keep up with his long strides. When she'd first entered the caves, she'd hoped for simple respite from the heat, but after discovering evidence that the caves had been expanded, it hit her with a downright chill. Being a university professor allowed her the luxury to study others' finds, but it was nothing

99

compared to personal discovery in the field. Nothing equaled this feeling.

Nothing.

Illuminated by incandescent lights strung on temporary poles, ancient grime hid reliefs painted in once vivid colors, a mixture of gums, resins and pigments imported from the ocean to the deepest, driest desert. Typically, tomb art set up a relaxing, peaceful life for the deceased. Here, a line of gods—the Ennead and those that came after—battled a wall of swirling black clouds. Each god image brandished a symbol of his or her power: ankh, staff, sistrum, scepter, and from them emitted a golden glow that swelled and challenged the angry storm.

More curious than the face-off of gods and amorphous enemy was the text below the confrontation. Keith had restored two short sections. The Perfect Land—the Egyptian afterlife in the west—was repeated, as was the Adversary. Ami, who loved the poetry of the Egyptian texts from her first *Children's Book of the Dead*, was captivated by one of the legible lines: *Coming forth by day and living after death, the Rising Ones repulse the Dark Devourer, the Shining Ones blind the Darkness, O, Hidden Ones, strike against the Adversary and lead us into the west.*

The team had cleared away the rubble, widening a pathway to the rear where the walls had been chiseled by the hands of men, perhaps thousands of years ago, chip by chip, until a larger series of rooms had been excavated to hold the most precious of cargoes.

Mummies.

Only, these were no ordinary mummies.

Susana Mendez, Ami's other graduate student on the summer survey, stood dumbstruck before the jumbled pile of mummified dead. Dust coated her black braid, aging her by decades. Her deep brown eyes held the wonder of the innocent. Ami didn't blame her. If what they'd found was real...

But how could it be real? The mummies must be fakes, similar to the cat mummies constructed of twigs and cotton wrappings found at Saqqara. They couldn't be authentic.

One atop the other, stashed away like those of the Royal Mummy Caches in the Valley of the Kings. It was possible these mummies, too, were smuggled here to save them from looting. Ami squatted next to the closest mummy. Wrapped in graying flax linen, it was in near perfect condition. The face had been painted, as had the hands. Unusual. But that wasn't the most unusual thing about these mummies. These mummies were not all human mummies.

These mummies had the heads of animals.

* * *

"Chips and shards. That's what I'd said we'd find. Chips and shards."

"Wrong, so wrong, Keith," Susana said. "I know. Look what we found!"

Susana threw back her head and hollered out: "God mummies."

Keith raised a bottle of Italian red in offering; his bush of blond hair looked ready for a bird to move in as the evening breeze toyed with it. Ami lifted her Solo cup and he added another splash, brandishing a grin wide enough to bare eyeteeth. Their gazes caught and she felt that familiar tinge of frustration and regret. His grin dissolved into a warm, resigned laugh. With a grand flourish, he offered the wine to Susana, who gladly accepted.

"Salud!" Susana cheered.

"Mabuhay," Ami had to add.

"Banzai!"

The women laughed at Keith, whose smile had leapt back to life. Even settled in camp chairs, he towered over them, flaunting his Midwest genes. What in the world did he see in a short, middle-aged Filipino woman?

"I never even imagined I'd be a part of such a discovery," Susana said, slouching low in her green canvass chair. The fingers around her wine glass were stained gray with pencil graphite from the day's wall sketching. "Of all the vast desert, we lucked out."

The campfire murmured low between their three chairs, sparks carried up and up by a building wind. The locals she'd hired had returned to their village for the night, muttering about a haboob: a dust laden wind storm.

Ami took a sip, her lips lingering on the plastic rim. "Since my own college days I've surveyed every summer, and I've never landed such a discovery." She barked out a single laugh. "Nobody's made such a discovery."

A pile of 8 x 11 photos and Susana's sketches coated Ami's lap. The reflection from the flickering fire gave them a shadowed liveliness. There was a picture of a cat-headed mummy, another with a jackal head— 'Anubis-animal' Ami footnoted. Hawk. Baboon. And human forms as well.

Dead representatives of one god after another.

"You did it, Ami." Keith squeezed her hand, lingered, then released it, leaving a warm shadow behind. "You've made your name."

Her mother hoped she'd re-find God. Ami might have found something even more fantastic. "You two have earned stars by your names, too. It was a joint—"

"Aminhan Tiangco." Thunderous words cut their conversation. "You have broken the seal. You have awakened the formless *ka*."

Ami peered into the dark veil at the edge of the fire's border. A man stood there, standing tall in a dark business suit. A government spook.

"Who are you?"

He took a step toward the light. Ami stood. Photos fluttered to the ground. The man, his hands as dark as her own, had the head of an aardvark.

The gods of her dreams. Right here. Right before her.

Ami went numb. Though the man wore a tailor-cut suit, he had the head of an animal, and not an aardvark like she'd originally thought, but a Set-animal. An amalgamation of various creatures scientists hadn't quite deciphered.

That meant... this was Set?

Her knees lost strength. Depending on the era and location, Set could represent many things. Defender of Re. God of Storms. The Lord of Chaos. The Usurper.

Keith leapt to his feet. "Jesus, Mary and Joseph," Susana muttered, crossing herself.

Ami knew she wasn't dreaming and she'd only had two glasses of wine; she wasn't about to dupe herself with either lie. It could be a man in a costume—a very good costume—or maybe a Hollywood robot of some sort.... Out here. In the middle of the open desert.

Where they'd just unearthed the mummies of gods.

"Who are you?" Each word bit sharp, Ami channeled her mother's power of command.

"Aminhan Tiangco, the seal is split." The animal-headed man's voice roiled like a building storm, the reverberation echoing within Ami's chest. "Breath has been given to a cycle long in waiting. Behold, the hungry one arises." He looked up into the night sky. "Stand forth, *you* must cease its hunger."

The aardvark mouth rippled and twitched with human speech. This wasn't a Hollywood robotics trick. She closed her eyes, opened them. Set remained.

Set.

The god who committed fratricide in a most gruesome way. A tale that spanned all faiths.

Voice pitched low, she ordered her students: "Go to the truck and leave." Palms and feet cold with sweat, Ami stepped past the sputtering fire, placing herself between her students and the godling before them.

"You must leave; this is a scientific survey."

The wind hissed, a brewing haboob, taking up dust and sand and pelting her with it, culling all other noise. Ami couldn't hear if Keith and Susana had fled. If they'd escaped the Usurper.

I hope they listened. I hope they ran.

The sand buckled, a seismic wave crashing over the earth. Up and down clashed. Ami was dumped onto her back: a turtle on dry land. The desert surged over her body, swamping her hands, legs, and middle. It tightened. A living cocoon of death.

Set was, among other things, the god of the desert.

The sand clawed its way up her chest.

Agaw-buhay, her mother used to say over the sick. At the seam of life and death. Ami felt *agaw-buhay.* Afraid, and at the seam.

"Step away from her, Set."

Straining her neck, straining her eyes, Ami peered behind her.

No.

Armed with one of their critter shotguns, Susana aimed at Set. Keith stood by her side, a length of tire iron clutched in his fists.

"Release her," Keith ordered.

They hadn't run.

"You cannot send me to the two worlds with your weapon."

A boom ripped the air. Set staggered. The sand around Ami constricted as he glanced down at his suit, then looked back up at the three archaeologists.

A shotgun blast to the chest... and he still stood. Adrenalin coursed through her with quicksilver ease. In the distance, the flap of canvas on canvas beat in cadence with her heart. Constructive ideas. *Un*constructive ideas. All had dissolved from her mind. The long snout of the Set-animal pulled back, revealing a tiny set of front teeth. Grit stung her eyes. She couldn't move, could barely breathe. Above her, the stars had disappeared.

Ami lifted her chin, took in a breath, and called out an ancient incantation.

"Lord of the Secret Place." Her voice cracked. Sand pecked at her face. Struggling for breath, she boosted her roar. "Who passed eternity repeatedly, behold that within my presence: the Usurper." Her sand casing squeezed. "Get back, you snake. Take yourself away, for the falcon protects me!"

103

At her prayers, *Nanay* would have called her a *mangkukulam*. A witch. It never occurred to Ami to pray to the old, untouchable God her mother and Susana worshiped in grand cathedrals.

"Isis, Queen of Heaven," Ami cried out, "Mother of magic, aid me!"

"You call out to Isis and Osiris. You think they would work against the Guardian of Re? The Ruler of the Upper Lands?" the mythical man said. "Your prayers have no power to lift them."

The campfire reflected upon the leather of the man's shoes and cast shadows over his nugget eyes. In the near darkness those were the only features she could make out, just the highlights hinted at by the dying fire.

Words tumbled from Ami's lips. "I—I'm sorry the seals were broken. I don't exactly know what that means, but I'll take responsibility. My staff, they—they only did as instructed. Let them be, Set."

"Ami, no," Keith called out behind her.

The animal-headed man stepped closer. "I am not Set. I am but a shadow. Sutah by name." Sutah perked up his long, donkey-tall ears and faced the wind-beaten tents. "It is here. The Darkness across the Desert. The Devourer of the *ka*."

"The Devourer?" He wasn't Set.

Not Set.

"The Adversary descends. You, who opened the way, must smooth the sands to the gate. Come."

Sutah turned toward the cave-tombs. With even strides, he dissolved into the darkness. The sand encasing Ami lost its life and cascaded to the ground. She gulped down air. The fwap fwap fwap of canvas against canvas marched with her desperation.

Keith charged towards her. "Ami, are you okay?" Susana tucked the gun under her arm and jogged behind.

"I'm fine." Ami shook her head, disbelief and fear warring with the golden hopes of her childhood. Batting randomly with her hands, she brushed sand from her body. "You two, run. Get out. If I stay," she held Keith's gaze, "he might let you go."

"What! Why?" Keith grabbed her arm. "The sand—it moved. He tried to kill you with it."

Ami shook her head. "He didn't kill me when he could have. Remember what was written on the wall: the Dark Devourer. Striking out against the Adversary?" Ami thought about the animal-headed mummies lying inside. "I need to know... This is *really* happening. I'm following him. You two..." she gripped Keith's hands, then Susana's, "be safe. Go!"

"Professor," Susana began, but Ami had already left them for the mystery.

"It's myth written on cave walls!" Keith called out, but Ami couldn't stop. Couldn't pass by this moment, this promise that something *more* existed.

The mouth of the cave was a dark hole in the earth. It swallowed her down with only a battery lantern to light her way. She nearly rammed into Sutah where he knelt, head bowed before the cache of mummies. His long snout dipped down. A posture of prayer.

Ami gripped the handle of her lantern with both hands. "Are these really dead gods? Like yourself?"

He stood and looked down at her, his nonexistent brows rising. "Dead? Do the air and void die? They are preserved. To live again. I am but a guardian of the Ennead and their brethren. I am no God."

He wasn't a god. She felt both relieved and disappointed, a sensation she hadn't felt since her last failed relationship, over a decade ago. "So, what is this darkness we have to save them from?"

"The Adversary."

Yeah, she got that. Every great mythology had an adversary. Odd that so often in Egyptian mythos the adversary was Set.

"Not... er, not Set?"

A long tongue snaked out from the aardvark snout and licked along his lips. Ami twisted her grip on the lantern handle. "Not Set. The formless *ka* of the Adversary desires form. If the divinity here is discovered, and the Devourer consumes their *ka*, it shall gain form and gain hunger everlasting and feast on the earth. The cycle ends. Rebirth is ceased. No more living after death."

The *ka*, the spirit of a person, and, apparently, a god. She knew what Sutah was suggesting, but you had to believe in that kind of thing, in gods and souls and rebirth, to allow any of his words meaning.

And here he was, an agent of a god, standing before her. Flesh and blood and *ka*.

His gaze shifted, drawn to the exit. "The darkness has been given no name and has been given no spells." Wind plunged into the cave mouth, disrupting the air pressure within. "It is near."

"Actually, I think it's here," Keith said, stepping into the mummy room with Susana, still armed.

"Keith." Ami struggled to keep her voice low. "Why are you still here?"

"I'm not leaving you," Keith said to Ami, his eyes latched onto Sutah with sullen distrust.

Sutah stood. The shotgun blast had chewed holes in his suit vest. "Time has not deserted us. You, Aminhan Tiangco, broke the seal and must save them. The mummified divinity must be taken to Shinpuh and bathed in the dawn pool."

Susana shook her head. "We can't move the mummies." Her voice edged toward shrill. "We don't have all the pallets. We haven't stabilized them. They might be damaged in the move without the proper equipment."

"I have a feeling these mummies won't be so delicate." Ami glanced at Sutah.

"But, how can you be sure?" Susana demanded. "These mummies are precious." Ami smiled at her. An archaeologist after her own heart.

Sutah blinked his onyx eyes. "I have spoken the words and said the spells. I was to guard them for the age of the reawakening. It is now. The seal has been broken and the divinity shall soon be going forth by day." Susana leaned against the wall; the gun's muzzle dipped toward the ground. Keith's jaw flexed.

"Where is Shinpuh?" Ami asked.

"South of the ruins you call ain Asil, hidden home of the *ka* of Atum."

"Not heard of Shinpuh," Keith said, "but ain Asil is at least thirty minutes on the old road by Jeep."

Ami took a breath and nodded. *"Kapit bisig pa mga arkeologo,"* she muttered in Tagalog. "We need the truck, and the handcart." Ami took stock of the mummified dead, piled up like matchsticks. Not a one was broken or sloughing, as expected of a 5,000 year old mummy tossed in a cave.

She glared back at her assistants, stiff and stalled in thought. "Truck and cart. Get going!"

They jerked to life and shared a look. "You think this is the right thing, Ami?" Keith asked, touching her shoulder.

She clenched her jaw, nodded. "Yes. I do." Then she softened, smiled. "I do."

Outside, the wind held the spicy scent of frankincense. A scream pierced the darkness: high and deadly like a diving falcon. The hairs on Ami's arms stood on end. She sniffed, her nostrils stiff with dust, and leaned into the biting wind. "It's gotten worse." She checked her watch. Sunrise was near five AM and it was now two. Three hours to transport and unload these mummies at the Shinpuh ruins.

One by one, they hauled the dead to the military-styled vehicle, fighting against the angry sandstorm. The last, buried at the bottom of the pile, was a Set mummy. Sutah gazed at the mummy as they unloaded it from the cart. Ami studied the mythological man from an age long dead, not a god, but an agent of a god mummified and now stored in the bed of her truck. "Once we're at Shinpuh, what do we do?" she cried out to Sutah.

"The pool will open the way."

"You can get us to the pool then?"

"It is as you say." Sutah pulled a paper from his inner pocket and handed it to Ami. GPS coordinates.

A suit. GPS. This agent of Set, a modern marvel.

"All right, let's go. Keith, you drive." Her words were nearly ground away by sand hissing against itself. A ton of it beat against the truck, pecking against the canvas canopy. She handed the slip to Keith after he mounted the handcart onto the truck side. She hated the truck. It was huge and she couldn't reach the pedals. "I'll stay with the mummies."

Keith opened his mouth, obvious protest on his lips, but Susana was already moving toward the passenger side, hunched and shielding her face with her arms. Swallowing down anything he might have said, Keith yanked open the door and wrestled to close it against the wind.

Ami hoisted herself into the back, straddling the tailgate and swinging her legs over. Inside the canopy, the air felt dead, as dead as the wall of mummies beside her. Sutah climbed in, his suit immaculate but for the pellet blast. Ami beat her hands against her grungy khakis and sat. Near her knee was a mummy's swaddled arm, near her shoulder, the wrapped feet of Set.

In all her years... All her choices. Leaving home, attending university, jumping on any dig for experience. It all lead to this.

The engine chugged to life. She bounced against the tailgate as they lunged forward. Across from her, sitting in a cross-legged position, the animal-headed man in his suit looked terribly out of place.

"How long have you been here? Watching over them?" Ami asked, putting force behind her words to fight the truck's engine and the howling haboob.

The beady aardvark eyes blinked once, then stared at her as steadily as the gusting wind. "I have been here since the beginning."

Ami nodded, as if what he said explained everything. Which, it didn't. It didn't explain a thing, and she wasn't quite sure what question could blow this shadow from the truth.

Truth. Once so easy to expose with brush and trowel.

The truck rumbled and rocked over the surging desert surface.

"So, the Egyptian gods are real."

His snout dipped. "Of course."

"Why did they go into this sleep?"

107

"For protection. The Adversary was, then, very strong. They have been waiting their passage into the west. "

The truck jumped. Ami collided with the mummy heap. A painted hawk face met her own. Horus, maybe. Isis' son, the golden child. The one who would face off with Set.

Time rocked with the truck for Ami and the Egyptian dead.

With a hop and a shriek of brakes, the truck lurched to a stop. Ami poked her head beyond the truck's cover; the force of the gale nearly sheared it off. Head held low, she tumbled out of the back of the vehicle and dropped the tailgate.

Sutah climbed out, took a few labored steps then fell to his knees, palms planted against the shifting sand. Chin to his chest, his ears thrashed wildly.

"Sutah?" Ami lumbered towards him, fighting the tempest.

Susana appeared in Ami's peripheral vision, leaning into the dust engorged wind. Her mouth moved. Ami shrugged her incomprehension. Susana tried again, stressing her words and gesturing.

Is he okay?

Ami didn't know. She placed her hand gently on Sutah's shoulder.

The long snout pulsed, catching a scent on the air. Ami smelled it too. Frankincense.

"You okay?" Ami called into his ear.

An electrical shock zinged along her arms. Her hairs stood on end. The air had become denser, thicker. A towering windstorm of dry, black cloud.

"Sutah?" she said, his name softly spoken, and therefore silent.

Keith grabbed Ami's arm. She looked up into his alarmed, young face. "This is insane!" he yelled. "What now?"

Susana pointed. In the shadow of darkness they could see the even darker silhouettes of tall columns. "The ruins?" she mouthed.

As the three archaeologists watched, eyes narrowed against the grating dust, sand receded from the stone pillars.

Ami screamed in Susana's ear, "Can you find the pool?"

Hefting a flashlight in her hand, Susana nodded and staggered off, light beam truncated by the storm.

Keith fumbled the cart from the truck's side. Ami offered the agent a glance, then ran to help her student. Keith lowered the handcart to the thrashing dunes, rotating the pipe handle upright, his lips moving and head shaking. The grit in Ami's eyes milked a constant stream of tears as they loaded two mummies onto the cart.

Darting around tumbled stone, arms shielding her face, Susana waved at them, urging them towards her. Keith and Ami pushed; the small wheels sank into the sand. The cart would go nowhere, mired in the soft, churned dust. They'd have to ditch the cart and carry their precious cargo by hand.

Sutah, still kneeling behind the truck, lifted his head, snout aimed high. His ears flopped, beating his skull. The desert sand rolled. Ami grabbed Keith and the cart, steadying herself. Then the ground beneath them firmed out. Sun-baked-mud secure.

Keith stomped upon the hard ground. "How is this happening?"

Susana squatted and ran her fingers over the hard surface. "If he's Set, he can control the desert."

"He is not Set." Keith's exasperated words challenged the storm. "Egyptian gods are mythology." He leaned into the cart and pushed it into the ruins. Ami watched him, shaken by his conviction. The same facts available to him had delivered Ami onto an entirely different path.

The power of denial.

With one hand supporting a mummy, Susana guided the cart around fallen stonework. The remnants of lotus columns marked the edge of an ancient temple, the shafts' artwork ground smooth by the feasting of time. They passed by worn statues of Atum and his entourage of Tefnut and Shu: moisture and air. The dual crown of Upper and Lower Egypt dwarfed Atum's head, a huge icon of his title as the finisher of creation. Ami lost herself in the face of the stone god, Atum's gaze looking forward into forever. A shiver scurried over her body.

Susana pointed and said something Ami lip-read as "pool." She led them along a stone corridor lined with limestone columns, the central shaft carved to look like overlaying leaves. At the end of the corridor was an empty, rounded pool. Rubble filled the bottom: chipped blocks, bits of faces, hands.

Here, within the heart of the ruins, the haboob didn't hold its pervasive power.

"So, we just set the mummies inside of it?" Susana asked, her voice loud within the weakened storm. Ami had no better idea.

Keith's brows bunched and he barked his disbelief. "We're scientists, and this is... this is complete fantasy. This is madness!"

Ami leveled a professorial look at Keith. She didn't blame him for denying the fantastical, even when laid out in flesh and cloth, but it nailed home her conviction that he had never dreamed like she had. The space just below her heart tightened.

"Madness it may be," she said, "but think of what we might learn. Think of the once in a lifetime chance. These ruins, are they even real? We knew nothing about them. Maybe once this is all over, we can return and dig at these coordinates. Even if you can't believe in the mummies, or the," she jerked her chin to where Sutah was kneeling near the truck, "Set man, have faith it will change you in some way."

Keith closed his eyes. "But—"

"What do you see!" Ami cut him off, swallowed. "We're wasting time. Get them in the pool."

Keith's face scrunched up. Then he breathed in deep, once, and again. His shoulders slumped.

Together, Keith and Susana hoisted the first mummy, Keith gripping its shoulders while Susana grabbed the feet. They climbed over the rubble with deliberate steps. Ami watched, her body inexplicably tense. Something wasn't right. There should be water in this pool, and lotus flowers and strawberry trees. Maybe some sacred ibis nearby. Her gaze followed the line of a column. Above them the swirling windstorm seemed poised to pound them into oblivion with its fury.

Time was slipping away.

They raced for more mummies. Sutah still kneeled in the sand, the blackness of his suit matching the void of the world beyond. Six trips later, the dead were laid amidst the debris in the pool. Thick tendrils of corporeal darkness snaked into the ruins, stirring up dust, crackling the air.

Susana scraped at her eyes. "Keith, remember that passage we restored this evening, right before you called for a break and opened the wine?"

Keith's pursed his lips, nodded. "Something about welcoming the way to the west and going forth by day. A different version from the Book of the Dead."

"The Opening of the Mouth ceremony," Susana added.

Above them the wind tore at viper speed.

Keith's eyes narrowed. "That's what we thought, but I don't think it was an Opening of the Mouth, but an Opening of the Way?"

"A way into the west?" Ami suggested. She'd missed those hours of the survey, draining time on necessary paperwork and goading her mother.

"Through the pool." Keith bit his lower lip. "But there was something more. It happened at morning, and there was a chant."

Susana closed her eyes and spoke. "Proceed in peace! For Re in the east of heaven has given you the good path. From slumber, they rise and emerge forth into the Light. Utter together this magic and guide the *ka* through the opening, Like Osiris into the Netherworld." With a gentle rocking of her head, she slowly opened her eyes. They stared at her. "What? I liked the sound of it."

"All right, then... at sunrise, when Re rises in the east, we say that chant. We've got..." Ami checked her watch, eyebrows rising at the imminent sunrise. In this ruin, with no roof shielding from above, it was still as dark as the inside of the mummies' burial cave. "...only about ten minutes."

All three peered at their ceiling of dust and shadow. "I don't think morning is going to arrive today," Keith said with a forced laugh. Neither Ami nor Susana joined him.

"You two wait here. I'm going to see if Sutah has more information." Ami ran back to the truck, hurtling over sand-dusted stone. This wasn't what her mother or sister had planned for her when she'd moved to America for college. Out here, in a place more dangerous than the slums of Quezon City, monsters were about: real mythical demons. Her mother had wanted her to be happy. Her sister had wanted her to find someone as great as her own husband. But as she came upon the aardvark-headed godling, in his modern suit, hands on the ground clenching fistfuls of sand, she knew such a safe and house-bound life would never be for her.

Ami crouched close to the agent. "Sutah, what do we do now?"

His drooping ears twitched, and his head shifted towards her. "Aminhan Tiangco," he said, his bass voice fainter than a whisper, a breath. "Do you believe in the gods?"

Ami narrowed her eyes. What did that matter right now? "As in true divinity, all powerful beings? Sutah, no. I don't. But, obviously you exist, you're something *other* that I can't explain. Listen, I'm willing to do what I can. Even if I don't believe."

"What then, Aminhan Tiangco, can you give them? You cannot give them your belief or your worship. You cannot give them your love. What can you give them?"

Ami considered that. "How about time?"

The waning man's shoulders tightened. "Time?"

"Yes, the gods and the people who've believed in them have been the focus of my entire life. I studied eight years under experts, then became my own expert. They've had my interest and my fascination since I was a little girl. They've had my time. This I gave to them freely."

Sutah seemed to smile, but such expressions were impossible with an aardvark snout. She did see the nod, a simple bobbing of his head. "That is so, Ami. And will you give them more?"

Ami smiled somberly. "They have my life."

"Then come to me, and touch my head and give to me your time."

With ceremonial gravity, she did so.

A rush of dizzy euphoria filled her body: an instant high. She felt numb, a disembodied coat of fluff. She sensed she was touching Sutah's head, and that she was crouching, and it was windy. But the largest, most powerful sensation was the Presence.

The Presence bore on her from all angles.

"The Adversary?" she asked, her lips barely moving. But she knew it was. Knew it must be the darkness. Her bladder felt weak.

I give you my time, she'd said. She hoped they didn't take it all.

If the darkness existed, and this man with an animal-head, then why not the gods? Why not some being that was a bit more than a human. There were more mysteries in this world than anyone could know. Maybe this one slipped in. People saw them and called them gods. Over the centuries stories and myths were birthed about them, while they slumbered there in that cavern, waiting for their own passage into the west.

"Go now," Sutah said. "Join the spell."

Ami removed her hand, nearly fell. Fighting the dominion of gravity, she forced herself upright. Exhausted. She felt worse now than she had during those months of dissertation writing: snatches of sleep, bad eating habits, reading until her eyes felt chalky and dry. Stumbling, joints impregnated with a deep ache, she turned from Sutah and retraced her steps along the firm sand.

Around her, the ages slipped away. The columns and steps no longer bore the worn face of time. The carvings were pure, pristine like anything you'd find in a well-tended park. The closer she drew to the pool, the brighter the paints, the colors. The years, they had gone. Had been washed away like the grit and grime. Statues stood tall and intact; the walls were lively with an artist's delicate touch of brush and pride.

Keith and Susana stood on the edge of the pool, the flashlight beam dancing across clear, shimmering water. Above, a window of weak light dawned through a break in the swirling haboob. God rays, *Nanay* called them. Susana's lips moved and as Ami approached, the clear tones of her chant rose from beyond the reach of the storm's din, Keith's deeper timbre filling in the places where she took a breath.

"Utter together this magic and guide the *ka* through the opening, Like Osiris into the Netherworld." Susana caught sight of Ami. "It's morning. You should see this. The pool...! Come quick, the mummies. They're... coming to life!"

Keith looked pale, but he nodded, eyebrows crawling up his forehead as if to escape this proclamation.

As she pushed free from the shadows, their joy and amazement collapsed into shock and then seamlessly transformed into dismay.

112

"Ami, what happened to you?" Keith ran up to her, reaching out. A frown took control of his expression, twisting his lips, scrunching his nose. His arms dropped dead to his sides as warped dawnlight kissed his sun-bleached hair.

"You've gotten old."

She laughed—brittle and breathless. "I've always been old, Keith." An epoch weighted on her voice.

He shook his head sadly. "Ami." Just her name.

"It was my choice," she said. And it was. "How are the mummies?"

Susana plastered a smile on her face, one reserved for those *agaw-buhay*. "They're rising. Come," she took Ami by the arm, "look."

They walked her to the pool's edge. From the stairs that disappeared into the glimmering pool, linen wrapped figures stepped away, dripping with water. Horus, and Bast, and Isis, and others. The dawn light caressed the water, casting a kaleidoscope of pinks and pale blues over their off-white wrappings.

Ami's breath caught. Alive. The god-mummies were coming to life.

The haboob swooped and howled, the sound muffled, far away, as if smothered by fifteen layers of cotton.

There was magic about these mummies, first in soaked linens, then naked as the linens sloughed off like a dead skin, moving and walking and living like the ghosts of dreams long ago given up as fancy, but once a life raft to a vision of a life wholly worth living. Each was whole, no scars indicating hollowed out insides of a ritual that would set them forever into a perpetual state of *going forth*. As they emerged from the pool, each one stopped and nodded, first to Keith and Susana, and finally to Ami, a tired, small form flanked by youth and power. Ami felt her students' tension, but also their amazement and wonder. She felt her own too. A smile cracked her face. These were children's dreams. This was her dream.

The last mummy emerged from the pool, the Set mummy. Along his abdomen a line scarred his flesh. He stopped before Ami and bowed.

Ami bowed back.

The long snout of the set-animal lifted in a gesture she'd so easily become accustomed to. "Aminhan Tiangco, you have given to us your time, and though you did not realize it, you have given to us your devotion and your love."

Susana squeezed her hand. Ami squeezed in return, her fingers aching with the force.

Sutah crossed the temple grounds and stood with his naked counterpart. "We walk into the west, to begin our own rebirth and to assure the rebirth of the ages."

"Yes, I know," Ami said. "I was told."

The two Sets faced each other. One step, another. Sutah walked into the revived god. Merged. Where there were two, only one remained. Set's scar vanished; nothing marred the brown, Egyptian skin. "The formless *ka* sought form," Set said. "You opened the way and we now pass through, beyond the Adversary's reach. You have little time left." He sounded sad, but maybe it was her own projection. "And we welcome you to come with us."

Ami's heart fluttered. She slapped her fist to her chest. Was she dying? Right now? Having a heart attack? But, she had no time for that.

To go with the gods into rebirth.

But didn't their success promise rebirth for them all?

"Thank you, Set, but I shall stay here and live out my days. I have too much to do to waste any of them. I want to write about this. Document it. It could be important."

Set bowed again. "It was good it was you, Aminhan Tiangco. You will be welcome in the Perfect Land when you are ready for your rest." Set joined the procession. One by one, the gods faced west, stepped forward and vanished, swallowed by a halo of light.

They were alone.

"Ami, are you okay?" Keith asked.

Ami nodded. She lifted her hands to the light, old and wrinkled, the skin spotted. She'd made her choices, and she promised herself she'd never regret any of them. "I am." Her voice wavered. Around them, the haboob no longer blew.

Keith fidgeted; he tilted his head back, clenched his fists and screamed. Susana dipped her chin; squeezed her eyes shut.

"Ami, they did this to you." His voice broke. "They made you old. They took your life." Pain and frustration quivered in his gaze.

"I'm sorry, Keith. I'm so sorry." So sorry I couldn't love you the way you loved me. Sorrow chiseled her carnelian heart. "I know you feel robbed."

His jaw clenched, the muscles flexing. He took up her hands and held them. Child-sized hands cradled in his large ones. "You never promised me anything." Broken illusions cut deep. Keith pressed his lips together and laughed, bitterly. He squeezed his eyes shut and opened them: stormy with unshed tears. "I'll help you. Until... I'll help you."

Dreams and choices. The weave of her world. Every choice earned an outcome. Every outcome held a future. Long ago, she'd made her choices and held no regrets. Not her unmarried life. Not her all-encompassing job. Not even her stolen years. Not a one.

Except the broken heart before her.

Ami stood on the seam. Life and death on either side.

.

TO TOUCH THE PAST

BY MEMORY SCARLETT

CHETNA WOVE HER FINGERS AROUND THE POTSHERD and let the warm comfort of someone else's memories flood her mind. This particular artifact wouldn't hold its charge much longer, but for now she revelled in the demanding life of an oil merchant who'd died fifteen centuries ago.

A trickle of modern pain seeped through the rigors of an ancient businessman's endless toils. Familial expectations; maternal disappointment. *Damn.*

Chetna was too much of a professional to fling the potsherd away. She laid it gently on her desk and donned her gloves before she returned it to its specimen bag with equal care.

Another item contaminated by her own insecurities. Psychometry could be such a bitch.

Ines bounced through the door without bothering to knock, her whole body vibrating with joy. Her enthusiasm melted away the moment she saw the specimen bag. "Your mother again?" she asked.

"My mother again. She won't shut up about Yashmini's oh-so perfect life." Chetna adopted her mother's Indo-Canadian accent. "'Your sister has such a successful gynecology practice, Chetna, but she does not let her two beautiful children suffer. She is an ideal daughter, wife, and mother. We are all so very proud of her. You must come back to Canada and let us find you a husband so you may also achieve wonderful things.' Yeah. Because there's so much Classical archeology to do in the middle of Manitoba."

"Plus, the husband."

"Him, too."

"Well..." Ines perched on the edge of Chetna's desk. "It's not a solution to every last woe you've ever felt, but I might have something to cheer you up. What would you say to an excavation at the Trevini Villa?"

"I'd say yes, yes, yes, if you've found a way to convince Angel Trevini to let us in."

"God did that for us. Angel Trevini passed away late last year and left everything to her granddaughter, Maria. Who approached me half an hour ago and asked if the Caelian Museum would be at all interested in excavating her property. Turns out, she's curious about her ancestors' footprint on history."

"I doubt the people who lived in the original villa were her ancestors."

"If it gets us through the door, I'm happy to let her believe it a while longer. Meanwhile, you and I get to learn as much as possible about Rome's most mysterious archaeological site. And I do mean as much as possible."

Which was Chetna's cue to let her psychometry run wild. "We can't publish anything I pick up."

"As if that's ever mattered. If you can give us a lead, I'll direct our energies to things we *can* use."

They'd done it before, to great effect. "In that case, I'll keep the gloves off. Some of the time, at least."

Ines winked. "Besides," she said, "I think you'll *want* to touch everything in sight once you hear the real reason Maria's so keen to have us there."

Maria Trevini bore all the trademarks of a young Italian with money to burn: expensive haircut; tailored sheath dress; shoes with a price tag that would've annihilated Chetna's monthly paycheque. "It's so lovely to see you again, Ines," she said, her accent pure prep school graduate, "and so kind of you to organize the dig this quickly. I look forward to meeting the rest of your team."

As if Ines had come alone. Chetna offered up a silent prayer that Maria's indifference had more to do with Chetna's practical cargo pants and sweater than with her ethnic heritage. Some Italians could be awfully intolerant of foreigners, particularly brown ones.

Ines, diplomatic as always, rolled right over Maria. "You're in luck. Let me introduce Chetna Kapur, my second in command. Chetna specializes in archaic mysticism and Roman magic, so I thought she might benefit from hearing your family's story from your own lips."

"Oh?" Maria perked up a little at that. "In that case, I'll ring for a pot of tea."

Once a bland-faced servant had poured them each a cup of Darjeeling, Maria began. "My family has occupied this estate for centuries, and in all that time, we've allowed no one to interfere with the eastern structure. My great-grandfather was so concerned with our privacy that he encouraged the Italian government to write a special proviso, just for us, to ensure we need never let archaeologists on the property."

Chetna bristled at that. *Go on and deny the world whatever we could learn from this place, why don't you.* "You see, Ms Kapur—" Maria's voice dropped an octave "—our villa is haunted."

Ines wiggled her eyebrows behind Maria's back. Damn her, both for keeping this a secret and for considering it a draw. In nearly twenty years of research, excavation, and psychometric practice, Chetna had never encountered the slightest hint of ghostly activity. And Ines knew it. "...I see," she said.

"Oh, don't worry, I don't believe it either." Maria's laugh rang false. "According to my grandmother, a Roman general walks the halls each night. My ancestors kept the ruined portion of the villa in its original state out of deference to his legend.

"I, however, am far more interested in establishing his antecedents. Our records for the villa only go back to the sixteenth century, so we know very little about the people who lived here in ancient times. I hope your dig will help me determine the true story behind my family's alleged ghost."

It was a flimsy reason to undertake a scientific inquiry, but Chetna would grasp any excuse to excavate the most celebrated ruin on the Caelian hill. "All right. You must know we can't guarantee particular results, but we should be able to sketch in at least a rough picture."

Maria smiled, smug. "Of course you will."

Chetna refused to let herself scowl. If the dig got her mind off her mother, it would be worth any amount of annoyance.

As much as she loved archeology, Chetna had always loathed its deliberate pace. If only there was a way to speed up the process of uncovering buried treasure without risking damage to the very artifacts she hoped to preserve.

The surveys and archival research alone took weeks. Despite Maria's assurances as to the site's untouched nature, Ines's initial sweep told them the fifteenth century villa in which Maria lived had significant overlap its ancient equivalent. The peristyle and a portion of the house's rear quarters were uncovered; the rest had been built over long ago. What had once been a fabulously large house was now a residence of decent size, complete with a ruin-studded garden.

"We're probably standing somewhere above what used to be the upper floor, too," Chetna told Maria during an early consultation.

Maria blinked. "But it's at street level."

Was this woman really Italian? "I'm surprised it's even that close to the surface. Soil builds up around old structures over time. Haven't you ever heard about the ancient villas we've discovered right underneath modern buildings? The Caelian is full of them."

"Oh. I had no idea." Maria blushed. "I'm afraid I don't know very much about Roman history. I was raised in Switzerland and nobody there thought it was important."

"I could recommend some articles, if you like."

Chetna intended the offer as a subtle jab, but Maria grasped her hand with genuine glee. "That would be wonderful! I really should know about these things if I intend to stay in Italy. Thank you, thank you, thank you!"

Chetna spent the evening composing a reading list and poring over survey results with Ines.

By the end of the night, they had a rough map of the peristyle's outlines, and with it an idea of where the most interesting rooms were likely to be. "No shrines, I don't think," Ines said. "Sorry."

"Hey, we can't expect everything we uncover to match our particular interests. It's—" Chetna broke off as her computer trilled the familiar notes of an incoming Skype call.

Ines pushed her chair back. "I can duck out if you want."

"No. I'm working. She's got to respect that." Chetna clicked 'decline' and typed her mother a quick apology before she logged out. "Sorry. I shouldn't even have had it open."

"It your regular time, isn't it?"

"Yeah, but it's not set in stone. Besides, I don't think I could handle any recriminations right now." Chetna shook her head. "Indian mothers."

"I think it's just mothers, full stop. The stories I could tell you about my mother..." Ines whistled. "Let's just say there's a good reason I never get into it. So, if you don't object, I think we want to put the first trenches here, here, and here. . ."

A week into the dig, after a slew of stones, a wealth of crumbed masonry that yielded little information to her bare hands, and two abbreviated Skype calls with a mother who couldn't understand the value of her daughter's work, Chetna made her first important find: a copper hand mirror, dull with the grime of centuries.

The moment she'd finished photographing its position, Chetna peeled her gloves away and sandwiched the mirror between her palms.

Slowly, a young woman solidified in her mind's eye. A daughter of the house, second born, frustrated with her lot. The girl had often looked into the mirror as she thought of her older sister's perfection and her own substandard prospects. No one wanted a wife who was better at growing plants than managing slaves. The flowers she convinced to flourish around the edges of the peristyle meant nothing to anyone other than herself.

Chetna laid the mirror down and slid her glove back on as quickly as she could. It was too much like her own situation with Yashmini.

Ines noticed her unease and scurried over. "What did you find?" she whispered. "Was this Roman general an especially bloody sort?"

"I didn't pick up anything about him. It's this mirror. It belonged to a girl." Chetna described the situation as dispassionately as she could.

"Oh, sweetie. I'm sorry."

Chetna shrugged. "I guess some things are universal. Can we drop it?"

Ines's curt nod was answer enough. "This girl never even thought about a general? Her father, maybe?"

Chetna combed through the ancillary memories she'd gleaned from the mirror. "I mostly felt the sister, but there was a father in the background somewhere. I get the impression he was a lawyer, though. There was nothing military about any of it."

"That doesn't seem to lend much credence to the family ghost." Ines laid a hand on Chetna's shoulder. "Thank you. Do you need a minute?"

"No. I'd rather keep working; see if I can uncover anything else about this girl and her sister. And I guess I need to find something publishable while I'm at it so Maria won't feel like we're a complete waste of space."

From the comfort of the patio table her servants had positioned on the edge of the site, Maria regarded them with slightly narrowed eyes.

The picture that emerged over the next two weeks was domestic in the extreme.

One of the students discovered what appeared to be a household infirmary and stillroom, all but intact beneath the dirt—a major find. Ines encouraged the young woman to coauthor a paper with her, while Chetna ducked into the specimen shed after hours and handled each fractured jar of herbs and unguents. She received a torrent of slave memories, peppered with long hours and hard work for a family unwilling to admit its unpaid labourers were real people. Not even the man in charge of their physical wellbeing received more than a cursory measure of respect. The family considered it his own fault he'd fallen into slavery.

By Roman standards, they were right, but historical context didn't lessen Chetna's horror. Reading about such realities was one thing; experiencing them through a slave's memories, another.

From her own trench, she gleaned a little more of the family's life. The eldest girl had often handled a small perfume pot that somehow made it through the centuries with its base intact. Her memories were full of admiration for the peristyle her sister tended so well, tinged here and there with uncertainty for the future. Would her parents find her a good husband? Would her father's legal practice continue to thrive? What if there was a grain shortage? Or an earthquake?

"Worrywart," Chetna muttered.

The perfume pot also held the memories of the slave who had most often attended the girl at her toilette. In this woman's eyes, the eldest daughter was no more capable of taking care of herself than was a pampered pet. Never in her life had she brushed her own hair or donned her own jewelry. The slave thought her all but useless should any of the crises she feared come to pass. Fine stitchery and a good singing voice held little meaning outside the privileged world of a Roman matron.

Chetna wasn't sure whether this amused or saddened her.

"It's probably a little of both," she said to Ines at their nightly debriefing in the specimen shed. "The younger sister thought the elder was so poised and accomplished, but she was just a person who lived how she was told she had to live, same as anyone might."

"Hmm," Ines said. She poked Chetna's arm. "Maybe like Yashmini?"

"Yashmini is nothing like this girl. She's a *prominent gynecologist*, for fuck's sake."

It was a struggle, but they finally managed to get their laughter under control. "Really, though," Chetna said. "I haven't picked up anything abnormal from the stuff I've touched. These were everyday people who did everyday things that we now find extraordinary simply because they happened so long ago. If the memories I've gleaned are anything to go by, the father wasn't even an especially famous lawyer. I doubt we'd be able to find much about him in the historical record."

"Could the general have been an uncle or a grandfather or someone?"

"At this point, I doubt there was a general. Nobody I've read seems the slightest bit martial. Everyone lived their lives within the confines of Rome."

A panic-inducing cough sounded from just outside the shed. "I'm sorry to interrupt," Maria said, "but I've noticed the two of you whispering to one another since the dig began, and now I feel I to ask what you're always talking about."

Ines's wide eyes and slack jaw no doubt mirrored Chetna's own. If Maria told anyone what she had overheard, it would destroy their personal credibility, if not the Caelian Museum's standing within the archaeological community.

Maria stepped inside. "It sounded like you practice psychometry," she said, pointing at Chetna. "But that can't be true, can it, because nobody can really read an object's past by touch."

Chetna's mind raced. "It's a sort of game we play?" she said. "To help us conceptualize the space? That's all."

Maria pressed her lips tightly together, disbelief etched across her every feature. "Is that so."

Goodbye, wonderful career. Mom will be so happy to have be home. Unless... "Okay," Chetna said. "Fine. You caught us out, but I swear we aren't insane. Do you have something you wouldn't mind me handling? A piece of jewelry or a coin? It doesn't have to be yours, but you should know something about it."

Maria's gaze never left Chetna's as she worked a gem-studded bracelet off her wrist. She passed it over with extreme reluctance.

Chetna stripped her gloves away. She pressed the bangle between her palms, soaking in everything it had to offer.

"This was your grandmother's," she said. "You've worn it so often that it's mostly lost her memories, but you've also thought of her so often that she's still a part of it. In her will, she said you were allowed to do what you liked with the rest of her jewelry, but you to keep this piece because it was a bond between the two of you. She used to let you play with it every time you came to visit. You begged her to give it to you, but she said it was too valuable for a child. As you got older, you stopped asking, but she always remembered you'd wanted it. So she made sure it would become yours."

Maria went perfectly still. "There's no way you could know that," she whispered.

Chetna returned the bracelet to its owner. "I don't exactly use the skill in my archaeology," she said instead of answering the other woman's assertion. Might as well get the disclaimer out of the way. "It's more a way to satisfy my curiosity. It helps me answer some of my own questions, even if I can't use what I find when it comes time to share the site with the world."

Maria sat down on the nearest empty chair. "And you've been feeling the things you find around my villa."

123

"Yes. Not on every item we uncover, because it's tiring, but on things that seem interesting. Some of them can tell me an awful lot."

"Enough to debunk my grandmother's ghostly general." Maria leaned forward, earnest. "Please, will you tell me everything you've found? Even the things that aren't strictly relevant? I want to know as much as possible."

In Chetna's experience, such enthusiasm rarely heralded a betrayal on the horizon. Slowly, she outlined her findings for the curious woman.

Most nights thereafter, Maria joined Ines and Chetna in the specimen tent. During the day, she hovered so close to Chetna's trench that the psychometrist relented and invited Maria to watch outright.

"Though this can't be interesting for you," Chetna said. "All I do is make miniscule adjustments to the soil level."

"On the contrary, it's fascinating. You're so precise, and you learn so much from what you do." She sat cross legged just outside the rope that demarcated Chetna's workspace. "I wish I had a purpose in my life, like you do in yours."

"Would you please call my mother and tell her I have a purpose? She's convinced I should go back to Canada and do a degree in computer science or something."

"You're Canadian? I thought..."

Chetna scowled at the ground. "Not everyone with brown skin comes right from India. I was born in Manitoba—that's a province in the centre of the country—and I was twenty-four before I visited India for the first time."

And what a pleasant trip it was, with aunties and uncles throwing their sons at her whenever the opportunity arose. Which it did four or five times a day.

"No, that's not what I meant! It's that you speak Italian so well. I thought you were a local, or at least someone who'd moved here when she was small."

Oh. "Sorry," Chetna said. "It's hard not to be sensitive about these things, what with your Lega Nord and all."

"It's fine. I should have been more specific. And please believe me, we don't all support Lega's anti-immigration policies." Maria rested her elbows on her knees. "Your mother doesn't like you being an archaeologist?"

"She thinks I should've gotten what she considers a professional job the moment I graduated university. None of this mucking around in dirt and writing about the past. And don't you even get her started on the lack of grandchildren."

Maria pulled a face. "It sounds draining."

"I hope it quits when I hit forty. She can't expect me to churn out any kids that close to menopause."

"At least she cares enough to hound you. parents dumped me at a Swiss boarding school when I was eleven and have hardly seen me since. Nana took charge of me every holiday and made sure I got back in time for the start of term."

"Wow. I mean, *wow*. I never imagined."

Maria traced a rough design in the dirt. "Most of the time, I'm completely alone. No parents to speak of, no siblings, no girlfriend, no grandmother anymore." She let out a shaky laugh. "No family ghost anymore, either."

Chetna's resolve hardened. "You might not have a family ghost," she said, "but we're uncovering a family history for you, here and now. You know you'll be privy to everything we find, whether or not we can publish it."

Maria's eyes grew damp. "Thank you," she said. "I realize they aren't my actual family, but learning about these people... it means a great deal. I'm so glad I asked the museum to come here."

Chetna was, too. Rarely had she seen her ability make such a profound impact on another person's life.

It was enough to make her wish she could display it to the world a little more often.

Two months into the dig, the infirmary yielded a corner steeped in sorrow. Illness had struck the villa, and the slave doctor was powerless to check its course. He himself died, only to be replaced by a younger man with little training and no talent.

Neither the elder sister's singing voice nor the younger's horticultural talents could save them from a similar fate.

Chetna touched a hundred items, but found no hint as to the rest of the family. She prayed they'd learn more as they dug deeper; perhaps on the villa's ground floor.

For now, though, the trail was cold.

"I'll bet the survivors abandoned the villa after the illness," Maria said when Chetna shared her findings. "They felt it held too many painful memories, so they vacated the place and built a new one elsewhere on the property. That must be it."

"Maybe," Chetna said, though she wasn't sure that fit with the Roman mindset. It was far more likely the family had died out entirely, leaving the property to new owners.

Or perhaps the earthquake the eldest daughter so feared had struck, burying most of the old villa beneath the ground. A closer examination of the historical record might tell them something on that score.

"It makes you think, doesn't it?" Maria said. "This family, they were utterly ordinary, and now they're gone. They lost one another forever." She bit her lip.

Chetna laid a hand over Maria's. "You could try talking to your parents," she suggested. "Not anything deep; just a phone call or something, to say hello. Or you could invite them to come see the dig, if it wouldn't scandalize them too much."

Maria nodded. "Maybe," she said. "What about you? Does this make you want to keep up your thrice-weekly Skype dates with your mother?"

"To be honest, they've turned into weekly dates." Chetna sighed. "I love her so much, but I can't handle anything more and I don't have the heart to tell her. So I pretend I'm busy all the time. Looking at these people, though, and how soon they lost another, I wonder if I'm wrong to think that way. If I'll end up regretting the whole damned thing."

Maria squeezed her hand. It was enough.

Chetna logged on to Skype that night, though her mother wasn't expecting her. Maybe it was worth reaching out.

She left her status as 'offline' and waited to discover if she had the courage to attempt a call, should her mother's diamond turn green.

THE SPACEMAN'S TOMB

BY SARAH FROST

AZAM PICKED UP THE CLOTH GINGERLY, hoping the motion would attract the shopkeeper's attention. "How old is this?" She asked. If it was half as old as she suspected, then it should have been wrapped in a stacyst membrane, not laid out on a table in the market to be pawed by tourists. She needed to get back to the dig. As the archeologist representing the City of Torq's Antiquities Department, the team from the university would need her to be on-site if they made any major discoveries. Besides, she had the day's supply of snacks.

The shopkeeper noticed her at last, her one hand around an age-spotted ear.

"This cloth. How old?" She repeated.

"Two *hundred,*" the old man said. His eyes drooped back to the crack-faced tablet cradled in his lap.

Azam sighed. Either it was a twenty-first century American original, or it was a modern replica. She swung her bulging satchel around and dug into its pocket. The shopkeeper accepted her money silently, then leaned back into the green shade of his solar awning.

Layer upon layer of translucent solar collector membranes cast the market-street in stifling hot shadows. The great merchant-collectives, like giant ceiba trees, spread their canopies from the highest buildings. Lower canopies vied for whatever light filtered through.

Azam adjusted her scarf where it rested on the bridge of her nose. The streets of her city hummed with life. Dust from the desert turned the sunlight yellow. Azam smiled, watching tourists gawk at a massive beetle-bus loaded down with commuters. She waited on the corner for one of the beetle-buses to slow—their biomechanical engines never let them quite stop—and grabbed one of the tall brown struts that held up the beetle's hollow shell. She welcomed the press of other bodies. The legs of the beetle-bus rumbled across the flagstone streets.

Azam stepped off the bus on a residential street, between high-rise apartments. Walls heavy with flowers gave way to a barrier of black steel grating. Tourists, if any happened by, could look down on broken arches and half-ruined walls of native stone. Azam unlocked the gate and let herself in. She passed the first layer of ruins without a second glance. It was all too recent to interest her.

Azam picked her way down the staircase by the uncanny glow of feral waitomo worms that hung from the ceiling. She passed through an earthwork tunnel so old that it may have been dug by this layer's former inhabitants and not grad students. Azam skirted a pile of specimen boxes and other people's lunches. She set her satchel down on a low pile of detritus that her team had excavated from their level of the ruins.

No one knew how deep the layers of old cities went. Rumor among the students of archeology held that some enterprising civil engineer had once dug all the way down to bedrock only to find it carved with sigils in an unknown language.

Chitinous scaffolding marked the beginning of the dig proper. Florin, the young chimera whom Azam had hired to look after the team's biotech, looked up from the broken cocci-light that lay cradled in her lap. She even smiled, which Azam counted as a minor victory.

"Everyone's waiting for you," Florin called. The flickering light cast a yellow glow on her dark skin. "Old Baba's lit two students' asses on fire for making you go for groceries."

"I needed some fresh air," Azam said. She laughed. "Besides, I found something that will make it up to him

"A sense of humor?"

"What would he do with that?" Azam said. Florin snickered. "He has a sense of humor, he just doesn't bring it on dig s . . ."

"Hey, boss," a man's voice said. Azam spotted Tigger, one of the student volunteers, leaning on the edge of the sunken ramp. "You have to come see this! Oh, hey, Florin," he said as an afterthought. Azam winced behind her veil.

"Do you want to come?" she asked Florin, softly. The tech shook her head and waggled the cocci-light, causing it to flash like a dying firefly. Azam nodded.

Leaving her satchel behind, she followed Tigger down into the dig proper. Past the door, they pushed through a set of fresh membrane-baffles that grew from a cyst on the ceiling. Someone from the dig was thinking ahead; the baffles would ensure a supply of fresh air, keep the dust down, and most importantly, catch any potentially troublesome microorganisms that the team disturbed with their digging.

Cracks in the cement floor showed how thickly the ancient white paint had been applied by the tunnel's long-vanished owners. Black dust, smeared now by passing footsteps, turned the surface of the floor gray.

Azam traced the air above a stripe of faded yellow paint that ran along the wall beside them.

The tunnel made a perfect right-angle turn that reminded Azam of the neat American squares in her quilt of petroleum-fiber fabric. They ducked under a gleaming orange water main that punched through the ceiling in a mess of twisted rebar, and entered the quiet chaos of the active dig site.

A grid of luminescent waitomo worms marked the walls and the floor. Her professor stepped delicately over them on six brush-tipped legs, his own paralyzed appendages tucked underneath him.

"There you are," he called to her, smiling. Other students scuttled behind him. Azam had always thought that Professor Harun Baba deserved to be immortalized like one of those ancient deities—a a multi-armed, multi-legged God of the Dig, with blue-black skin, a face untouched by time, and eyes that could see backward through the millennia. "Come here, come here. This is your specialty, and we have all been waiting."

She followed him past another set of particle membranes and caught her breath. Even with the filtration, the air smelled of dust stirred up by fresh excavation. Azam unfolded a facemask from her pocket and pressed it over her mouth and nose, but that was a hind-brain function. All of her attention focused on the row of metal boxes standing against the far wall.

Classic, she thought. She'd seen them in recreations of American artwork. *Lockers*, the things were called. Layer after layer of paint peeled from their sides, almost obscuring the hinges, the ventilation grilles, the tiny nests of gears that had locked them shut so long ago. Upright and intact and holding . . . what?

She exchanged a look with Harun. He shook his head. "We haven't touched them. I thought you might like the honor."

The original walls were cut off at an angle. Azam imagined the great earthmovers coming through, flattening the old building to make way for new construction, and how close they came to losing the whole site.

They had to cut through the lockers, in the end. The locks had corroded their way into the doors until they were nothing but a solid mass of exotic oxides. Azam had an audience when she began the first cut, but Harun was true to his word—she was the first to see inside.

She pressed the bead of a cutworm against the first locker's door. Leaves of paint shivered free as she pulled the cutworm down. The combination of the worm's enzymes and single point of chemical heat would cut the metal but spare any delicate artifacts behind it. She kept her hands steady while her heart trembled. As she made the last cut, all the gathered archaeologists, student and professional alike, took a breath.

Azam peeled the door back. Beads of half-digested steel clung to her gloves. Someone angled a light into the box. The darkness inside glittered.

"Clothing," she said, for the sake of the other recordings that her colleagues were certainly making. "Black textiles and these . . . these look like boots. Late twenty *irst* century, at least." A groan from the back of the crowd; someone would be revising their pet theories tonight.

Satisfied with her survey of the locker's contents in their original placement, Azam nodded to Manul. He squeezed the bellows of a hepacite, which would preserve any dust that Azam raised when she disturbed the artifacts for further study.

She held her breath and drew the black garment out of its tomb. Gold dust coated her gloves like pollen. Azam swore under her breath. Delicately, she laid the artifact in a tray of inert air. Flashes of color teased her—still so bright, after all this time! She wanted to run her hands down the folds of ancient cloth, examine every inch of it. . .but that would come later. The locker was open, and now that she had disturbed the artifacts inside she needed to get them into a bath of protective gasses as quickly as possible.

A pair of boots, badly decayed. The cover of a book, its pages long gone to dust. Bits of metal. Miraculous things.

She kept an eye on the puddle of black fabric as the rest of the artifacts were packed away for further study under better conditions. She caught a student's arm as he was about to slip the tray with the garment on it into a box. "Can I take a look at that?"

Harun glanced up from the section of the dig that he was supervising. "It will be waiting for you in the lab!"

"But I don't want to wait that long," she whispered. The student heard her. With a smile, he set the tray down on top of its box.

"Just a quick look," he said.

"Bless," she said, smiling. She let her fingers drift just millimeters above the delicate fabric. Clumps of dead nano-scale machines dusted the black surface. They had done their job, keeping the fabric fresh and supple through the long years in the locker. She didn't want to disturb them any more than she had to. She was glad for her mask. Even dead nanomachines could cause lung diseases.

"I think it's a uniform," she said under her breath. She let one gloved finger rest on the shoulder of the presumed uniform. Turning it carefully, she found a circular emblem embroidered with threads that still held their color. A thick scrum of gold dust covered it, evidence that the nano-machines had, at one time, focused their attention on preserving this particular spot. Beneath their bodies, she could make out the complex symbols of the patch. Three red horses rode a streak that symbolized forward motion towards the viewer. Behind them, a set of interconnected ellipses rose over a blue limb of the Earth.

"Is that a flower?" the student said.

"No, it's a representation of an atom." Azam longed to brush the nano-dust away from the patch, to see its bright colors, its fine detail. But the risk was too great that she might damage the ancient threads. *Later, in the lab*, she promised herself. She nodded to the student, who slid the uniform into its box and sealed it inside.

Tigger remembered lunch, which was fortunate because Azam and Harun were preoccupied by the door to the next chamber. It lay behind another brick wall, which Harun insisted meant that it was part of an earlier construction and possibly a totally separate one—as separate as the water line whose condensation posed a constant threat to their newly-uncovered site.

Over lunch, Azam rallied some of the other teachers and no few students to her cause.

"It is the same script," Manul said.

"Which was in use for hundreds of years," Harun pointed out.

"The language, but not this exact script. Those can change from year to year and site to site, but what's on the door matches everything else down here exactly."

"It's the same sort of paint, too," one of the students added.

"You've taken a sample? You've analyzed it?" Harun said. The student folded, shaking her head.

"It looks like the same sort of paint," Azam said.

"Then why was it sealed off?"

"I don't know—why don't we find out?"

"Because," Harun said, mid-chew. Azam looked away until she heard the professor swallow and clear his throat. "We only have a certain amount of time, and that needs to be spent on this area." He gestured at the ancient walls all around them.

"We can document it and come back next season," Manul said.

Azam said, "None of us would be here if we didn't enjoy opening up old doors to see what we can find behind them." Around the circle, the other archeologists nodded in agreement.

Harun finished his lunch and carefully folded up its wrapper. "Fine. We'll take a look. Manul, see if you can work out a translation of the writing on the door." He made a show of frowning at them all, but Azam knew him well enough to hear the excitement in his voice. He wanted to see what was behind the next door as much as any of them. He only wanted to make sure **that** they could justify themselves afterward.

Work began soon after lunch. Harun left, worried about the water line and determined to find someone who could shut it off, or at least admit to knowing where it was. Azam lead the team that would open the great steel door.

Manul shook his head. "Not enough words," he said. "It's some kind of announcement, but it's written in monumental shorthand. I'd need more context." He pointed to one of the symbols on the door, a three-petaled flower painted in garish yellow. "That looks familiar. I think it's a warning of some sort."

Azam nodded. "Masks, everyone."

"Maybe it's cursed," someone said. Nervous giggles. Azam glanced back, silencing them with a raised eyebrow. She gestured to one of the students, who stepped forward to begin work on the hinges with a cutworm.

Anxious hours later, Azam held up a light as she stepped into the chamber. The air stank even through her mask. They would need more ventilation soon. She lifted her light higher, scanning the room, recording everything down to the pattern of dust motes moving in the stale air.

A single, chest-high mass dominated the center of the room. At first it seemed frozen in the act of melting into the floor, but as the light played over it, she realized that it was draped in some kind of cloth. More ancient cloth! Azam smiled behind her mask. She made herself step away and finish her survey of the room.

All around her were panels, trays of buttons, and screens, all painted a uniform shade of bilious gray-green. Painted solid, without gaps. It was all wrong. Azam had seen the few surviving examples of twenty-first century silicon computers. They were all, without exception, covered in symbols. These were blank—blank, and sealed beneath a layer of paint.

What happened here, so long ago?

"You all have to see this," she called over her shoulder.

Her team descended on the new mystery. Within minutes, a new set of membrane-baffles were installed just inside the door. Florin appeared with a fleet of hovering lights and a packet of bright waitomo worms to begin gridding out the new site. Azam made a point of thanking her loudly, where the team could see, but that only earned the young chimera a few grudging nods, followed by a resumption of the social chill that had plagued Florin since her arrival. Azam gritted her teeth and decided not o press the issue. She made a note to mention something to Harun, when he returned.

In the meantime, she enlisted Florin to help with her newest problem. While the rest of the team recorded and began to chip away the first delicate layers of paint, Azam, Florin, and Manul brainstormed ways to lift the shroud off of the room's mysterious central object without destroying the ancient fabric and whatever lay beneath it.

They settled, finally, on a second shroud. An inflated bubble of membrane grown from several stacysts and filled with inert atmosphere might be enough to keep the whole thing from decaying before their eyes, once they cut it open. Azam helped Florin set up more filtration cysts while Manul ran to intercept Harun and explain why they would need a rebreather kit with a helmet for whoever went inside.

Azam massaged the taut skin of the stacyst until it loosened. The gentle give of its flesh under her fingers always reminded her of testing avocados in the market. The cyst needed to go from the consistency of an avocado that would survive for a day or two in the kitchen, to one that was soft enough to eat right away. The cyst was the color of an avocado, too; deep green with chalky veins. She pressed it to the gray-painted floor and counted to five. When she tugged, it stuck fast. Florin was already up to her elbows in her stacyst. Azam moved quickly, before she could gross herself out. It was nicer to think of the cysts as fruit. She split hers open —it squelche—and reached in through the ropes of sticky mucus to grab the roll of modified bugflesh tucked inside.

They sealed the edges of the stacyst membranes together and pressed them carefully to the floor. The cysts of living flesh were genetically identical, and would merge their circulatory systems overnight. By morning, they would harden into a single solid shell, hermetically sealed and inert.

Harun arrived late that evening. Without a word about the dripping water main, he herded his team of groggy archeologists back to their hostel for the night.

Returning to the dig site in the morning, Azam noticed three things.

First, the filter membranes around the shrouded object had not set completely. They were still pliable to the touch. Second, there was no way Manul would be able to fit his gangly body into the suit that he had acquired. Third, Harun was still unnaturally quiet, letting the self-appointed leaders of each small group run free. One of these problems could not wait.

After hours of careful work, one of the teams had cleaned all of the paint off of a presumed keyboard. Azam found the professor examining it, wearing a deeper frown than the simple alphanumeric symbols on the keys deserved.

"Is something wrong?" she asked.

"What do you think of this?" He gestured at the keyboard. Azam added her frown to the collection of frowns regarding the carefully-uncovered machine.

She pointed to the top row of keys. "Well, it's probably twenty-first century. Anything much older than that would have alphanumerics on this row, instead of symbols."

"But why paint over it?"

"I don't know... maybe the paint is a preservative?"

Harun shook his head. "It's the same as the paint on the walls and the floors, the same paint that we found outside—because it's all part of the same complex, congratulations, by the way—and scraping all the paint off would have ruined the machines." He picked up a flake of paint to demonstrate. Squeezed between his fingers, it crumbled to powder that swirled in the slowly circulating air.

By now, that dust was everywhere, having escaped from all their attempts at containment. It made Azam twitch to see a student walk by, tracking the greenish powder across the floor. A special set of boot brushes caught most of it at the threshold, but she suspected that no small amount was contaminating the rest of the dig site.

She resolved to sort it out later. It was time to open the mysterious shrouded thing that loomed in the center of all their work.

Manul helped her put on the suit and rebreather. Florin presented her with a free-floating camera eye. Harun and the rest of the team abandoned their work to watch the screen where the camera would project everything she saw.

She stepped inside the membrane, and they sealed it behind her. She waited while the membranes ate the puff of oxygenated air that had entered with her. Finally, she was alone with the shrouded artifact.

Knife in hand, she began to work. First, she freed the bottom of the shroud from the floor. Flakes of paint clung to it, crumbling at her touch. Then, cringing inwardly, she began the one terrible incision that they had agreed would cause the least damage to the shroud—they hoped—while allowing access to whatever it covered. The thick cloth caught on her blade, resisting, almost like a living thing struggling to keep its secrets. She persisted, and finally the cloth gave way.

It revealed a shell of soot-blackened silvery metal. Steel, Azam guessed, whispering the word for her audience. Aluminum, another common metal of the day, would have melted under the kind of abuse that became more and more evident as she peeled back the shroud. Blocky letters interspersed with glyphs whose meaning she could only guess—she she would quiz Manul later. They all would, poor kid.

The metal twisted. She held up her light, and had to stop herself from flinching away from the row of jagged steel teeth. Some other violence had been worked upon this machine, something worse than whatever had left its surface streaked with char. Azam pushed the shroud back further, and found the skeleton.

It grinned up at her. A shining aluminum gorget held its jaw closed, but mummification had pulled its leathery lips back from its brown teeth. Eyelids sagged over shriveled sockets. It wore a black suit that glittered faintly in the lamplight. For a moment, Azam ceased to breathe. Questions filled her head, but the one that found its way to her lips was, "Who are you?"

The dead could not answer, not on their own. As though pushing through some holy veil, Azam finished the long cut and disrobed the metal vessel and its single occupant.

The team arrived early the next day, Azam first among them, eager to continue their work on the stranger in his or her strange tomb. The shroud was packed away, wrapped in biofilms and inert gasses that would preserve it until it reached a laboratory. They had left the sarcophagus itself encysted in a single membrane, stretched tight and transparent so that everyone could stare into that withered face before retiring to whatever dreams it inspired.

The light was no brighter that morning in the dig underneath the city. Still, everything felt sharper to Azam as she pushed back the filter-membranes that hung over the door. They were oddly stiff under her hands. She felt the first buzzing gnat of dread.

Then she threw out her arms, physically blocking the door. "Masks!" she shouted. Everyone she could see was already wearing theirs, but further back . . . she couldn't be sure. Inside the chamber, the membrane covering the sarcophagus was dead, brown, crumbling down onto the ancient body it should have been protecting.

The press of the crowd eased as everyone made room for Harun. He had a mask and a set of old-fashioned goggles that shimmered greenly, hiding his eyes. Azam let him through, but he, too, stopped at the threshold. Azam watched him as he stared, one spider-leg lifted slightly. She waited, and when he still did not move, she gently took his satchel of tools from him.

"Everyone, please stay here for just a moment," she said. She hardly needed to say anything with Harun blocking the door, but a little politeness now would reduce her headaches later. She sucked in a breath, tasting the familiar sweetness of her fresh mask, and stepped into the room.

It was possible—just barely—that the stacyst had been sick or

135

damaged, and its death was simple bad luck. Her guts churned as she crossed the room. The damaged filter membranes on the door could be a coincidence, too, but she didn't think so.

All the nightmare-tales of poisoned digs paraded through her mind. Had some spore survived the long, dark centuries entombed beneath the city? Had it reawakened within the semi-living flesh of the filter membrane? What would it do to her team? The air under her mask became stifling. The filters were supposed to protect them, but what if . . . ?

Nothing adhered to the corpse or its ragged metal coffin as she ran a pocket hepacite over it, sucking down the flakes of dead stacyst membrane and any other microscopic artifacts that might have survived. A wisp of golden smoke curled up from the corpse's uniform. Dead nano-machines. Could they. . . ?

As she worked, she took in the entirety of the scene. No longer distracted or focused on some small part of the whole, she realized what she was looking at. When the hepacite had consumed the last speck of dead membrane, she sat back and looked at the body in its charred coffin.

"You are a spaceman," she said. The uniform was right—almost military, but not quite. Functional and spare, with no seams to cut into delicate flesh during acceleration. The coffin was his capsule, wrenched open with savage force—to save his life? She reminded herself that she shouldn't assume the gender of the dead; sometimes even genetic testing wasn't enough to tell for sure. The past was tricky that way. But the spaceman was always a spaceman in the stories.

"Azam!" Harun called from the doorway.

"Coming," she said.

The leaders of the dig gathered in a circle in the outermost room. Their students settled around them, their usual boisterousness stunted by fear. Azam waved Florin over to sit beside her.

Harun spoke the words that no one wanted to hear, but everyone could have predicted: "We have to seal the dig."

He faltered. Azam picked up where he left off. "We can't rely on the membranes to keep whatever this is contained. You've all seen why. We'll need the tarps and tape." She pointed to one of the students. "You'll be in charge of sealing the tunnel. Next, we need to send a moth back to the university to let them know what happened." She caught Tigger's eye. "Tigri, that's you. Harun . . ." The professor's eyes were invisible behind his goggles. She started over. "The rest of —" Her voice broke. "The rest of you! Clean this place up. Prepare it like you were shutting down for the season. Make sure nothing gets left out. People *will* come back here, and I don't want them to think we were a bunch of smash-and-grab looters."

They adjourned in remarkable order. Azam wondered if the reality of the situation simply hadn't sunk in yet, for most of them. They were all so young. Maybe that's why Harun was taking it hardest—he was the only one of them old enough to feel his mortality in his gut.

Or maybe they were coping the same way she was. Azam hadn't been on speaking terms with her gut since her first glimpse of the dying filter membrane. She wasn't about to check in with it now.

The moth never came back, but in three hours a white isopod bearing a sealed crate of food and water appeared at their door. The isopod was designed for a one-way trip. Relieved of its burden, it crumbled into folds of empty paper shell, incapable of carrying contagion back to the surface. Only the iridescent lenses of its eyes remained.

Later, Azam found Florin worrying those lenses with the ragged nails of one hand. Her other hand was thrust deep into the guts of a black-shelled analycyst. A swarm of wingless flies clustered around a thumb-sized puddle of blood on the floor, fed by the drips running slowly down Florin's arm. The chimera's eyes stared into the middle distance.

Azam had to call her name twice before she snapped out of her reverie. "Oh, sorry," Florin said. She pulled a stained towel out of her pack and held it cupped under her hand as she drew it from the cyst. She wiped halfheartedly at the blood and mucus that coated her skin, then brought the whole mess down on the flies and their feast.

This is her job, Azam reminded herself. The mosaic of human and nonhuman cells in the chimera's body let her interact with biotech in ways that ordinary humans could only imagine. It wasn't her fault that the result would turn even a strong stomach.

"Well?" Azam said.

"Nothing," Florin said. "No microbes, no viruses. Some spores, but they're sterile. I checked. The whole place is sterile." She shook her head, absently rubbing the marks that the cyst's interface left on her skin. "The filter membrane tissue just died. No infection, nothing, just leftovers from apoptosis."

"A pop. . . ?"

"Cellular self-destruct. Pop, pop, pop. Apoptosis."

"What causes that?"

Florin shrugged. "All sorts of things. I can't narrow it down for you without a lot more data. Or better equipment." She thumped the analycyst.

"You know we can't send anyone out."

"Yeah. Not until we're as dead as your spaceman."

There seemed to be no rhyme or reason to who sickened first. Before any of the people, though, Florin's equipment began to fail. During another interminable round of analysis, a frustrated thump on the carapace of her analycyst split the massive thing open. Half-rotted guts, ichor, and blood spilled across the ancient concrete floor. Florin sat in the middle of the stinking mess, staring at nothing, until Harun crossed the gut-slick and hauled her to her feet. He took her arm and led her out from under the eyes of the rest of the team.

And the tests remained steadfastly, impossibly negative. A fearful ache settled in Azam's bones. Her skin turned raw, then blistered. Most of the team stopped eating. Some vomited miserably. Others stretched out on the ancient floor, gripped by a fevered listlessness. A single thought, whether spoken in whispers or left unsaid, dominated every conversation. They were all going to die.

The next day found Azam sitting in front of the sealed door. She held her patchwork scrap of polyester in her lap. She was careful not to stress the fragile threads that held it together, but the fabric itself was nearly indestructible.

Manul sat down beside her. His handsome olive skin had turned waxy and yellow from the gastrointestinal indignities that plagued them all. Azam said, "They made things to last."

"It's a fine tomb," he agreed. "If we're going to join that spaceman of yours, we could do a lot worse."

"He's not my spaceman," Azam murmured. Her mind drifted on a froth of painkillers. "What does that door say, anyway?"

"Look upon my works, ye mighty, and despair," Manul said. Azam glared at him. "I *don't know*. There's no context. That's not even a word," he said, pointing at the three-petaled flower. "It's an ideogram."

"What does it mean?"

"Danger, keep out. Usually it's on military artifacts."

"Why would the military build a tomb for a spaceman?" She reached up, spreading out her hand to obscure the inscription. Manul shrugged.

It's all sterile, she thought. She closed her eyes, imagining red horses rocketing through low Earth orbit, drawing that strange flower behind them. No, that was wrong. It had been the linked ellipses, hadn't it? The ideogram for atom... Aloud, she said, "Manul? What's this symbol?" With one finger, she traced the strange flower in the dust.

Manul grunted. "An atom," he said. "Usually. Maybe. I don't know. My head hurts. Why—"

She cut him off. "I read a paper about the twenty-first century military. They had a kind of weapon—"usually you see it represented by a mushroom, but sometimes it was a flower. Either like that," she pointed at the drawing in the dust, "or like that." Azam pointed at the symbol on the door. She dropped her hand and forced herself to her feet. A hammerblow of nausea almost drove her back down. "It's not a plague. It's a poison." Manul stared up at her through slitted eyes, his face drawn thin with misery. She wanted to run, to scream. *I might be too late.*It took all of her will just to stay on her feet.

Azam found a moth. She wrote, "Ionizing radiation. Possible contamination with substances producing same." She started to explain that there could not be any biological hazard, but had to stop. The knot of pain in her gut greyed her vision and made her hands tremble. She gave the moth its destination and let it go, then sank back on the floor to wait.

Harun was the last to emerge from the hospital. She waited with him while he settled into his new set of legs, the old ones having been hopelessly contaminated. For the first time in her memory, he looked his age. *As though I look any better,* she thought. The anti-radiation therapies had been hard on all of them. Under her scarf, her hair was finally growing back. The ulcers on her hands had faded to pink pockmarks.

He sighed, at last, and looked up at her, appraising her own recovery with a glance. "Well, now. What have I missed?" He gestured toward the door, then led the way.

"His name was Vale Chang," she said. "We still don't know what happened, exactly. The whole room was contaminated with some kind of particle, mostly in the capsule but also under the paint. I think—it's too early, really, but I think they were trying to cover up the contaminant. Hold it down."

"Maybe. Then we picked off the scab."

She laughed. "That's disgusting."

"And it bled deadly radiation all over us!" He turned neatly on brush-tipped legs, spreading his arms to menace her with waggled fingers. She laughed, relieved to see the professor's sense of humor restored. Relieved, too, that he could make a joke out of the near-disaster. None of the people who had gone down into the spaceman's tomb would ever be completely healthy again, the doctors had told her.

"Oh, look," she said. "I never got a chance to show this to you." From her bag, she withdrew a package sealed within a silvery, semi-transparent membrane. "I insisted that the remediation team bring it up as soon as possible—it didn't belong down there, and I didn't want it to get mixed in with the other artifacts. Besides. . ."

"It's beautiful," Harun said, taking the square of fabric from her. "Where did you find it?"

"Here in the market. It's twenty-first century at least, if not earlier."

"Well," he said, handing it back to her. "We shall see if it can be properly dated. Double-knit polyester." He shook his head. "Some things we humans create really do last forever."

The Delver

By Ransom Noble

Koga twisted a bit of silk out of her pocket and wrapped her hands within it. She didn't like to bring attention to herself, but the fairy paint on her hands screamed magic at anyone who could sense it. To her eyes, her hands still seemed brown on the back and lighter brown on the palms.

Only the silk could mute magic. "I need this for protection." The silk matched whichever creature created it, and the piece in her hands shone a deep green.

"I could have protected you." The dragon sat on the invisible barrier separating the dead zone from the rest of the world.

Her eyes stayed with him. She didn't ask him to join her inside the dead zone. "But would you? You've never seen my work as a danger."

George turned his glittering golden eyes to her. "I would not let you come to harm."

She left it be. "This is the place."

"I know." His head swiveled one way, then the other. "Can't you see the border?"

Koga shook her head. "I only felt it because of the fairies' gift."

The landscape around Koga looked no different than the place she had just left. The trees still grew toward the sky with green leaves appropriate to the season. The long grasses fluttered in the wind. Flowers brought splotches of color. The hills rolled gently as they did everywhere in the midland plains. No one knew what happened here. Once it had been a thriving place, full of magic and life and all the creatures that inhabited everywhere, but something had disrupted the balance here.

Koga's only indication that she had crossed a line into the dead zone lay within the painted stain on her hands. She closed her fists and opened them again. The silk helped, but the itch didn't go away.

"I told you not to do that." The dragon's voice roared in her ears, though she knew he spoke softly for her benefit. "The magic won't wash off your hands. You're marked."

She couldn't help but remember the fairy that breathed over both her hands. He had been black of skin and eyes and hair, almost like a

143

bottle of ink had been dumped over him. Only his fingernails and lips showed anything else, and those places held vermillion. "Thanks, George." Koga let her hands rest near her sides. "I didn't have a choice if I wanted to fix this place."

The dragon raised his spiny head, his words vibrating the ground with earthshaking tremors. "You can't trust those snarking fairies." Spikes lined his back from his head to his tail, all standing upright from his feelings about the fairies. His scales shone yellow-green, not quite golden above the green grasses.

She sighed. "It's a gift."

"It's a curse."

The dragon lowered himself to the earth. He stretched full length, sniffing along the ground and not dragging his feet over the line.

"You know you don't have to come with me." She knew what it meant to have him come with her, but she didn't want to do it alone. All the immortal creatures needed the magic that flowed within the land. Everywhere except this dead zone. If George stayed too long, he wouldn't be the same. He might not recover. He might not survive.

His muscles coiled and he stepped over the boundary. "We have to go in to complete this work you set us on. I will manage as long as I can."

Koga walked farther. She tucked the silk back in her pocket and spread her hands wide over the ground. She thought back to the old metal detectors her people had used to scavenge this land for their precious metals. She wished she had a similar item so George didn't have to do this. Her bag thumped against her side, and she steadied it with her hand.

"There's one here." George hovered his nose above the ground.

She knew he didn't quite smell the magical artifacts, but it was the closest she could imagine. "Can you tell what it is?" Koga spread both hands above the ground, listening and feeling for whatever it might be.

George remained silent. "We must wait until the sun is down."

They sat to watch the sun melt below the horizon. She unpacked food for herself, and George hunted on the other side of the line. The lucky dragon could simply fly off. She needed to remain close to the artifacts. The sun dripped away, and she spread out the tools of her trade in a circle around the spot. George returned. He said nothing as she slowly peeled away layers of soil from whatever had been buried there. Koga kept her eyes on the spot so she wouldn't lose it.

The moon rose, and George spread his wings to block the light. Koga's hands blended into the deep shadows of night. Even the fairies' stain couldn't give her light to work, the artifacts were too sensitive for that.

"What do you think we'll find?"

Koga sighed. "I don't know. The fairies said we'd know what we were looking for once we found it. But this darkness idea of yours isn't going to tell me much."

"Darkness idea? I only do what I know to be right. It's instinct. You can't argue instinct."

She frowned, turned back to her work so George wouldn't notice her disagreement. "What harm could light do?"

George shifted.

Koga realized he no longer stood behind her. She lost track of time easily when she dug at a site.

He stood directly left of her. "The sun's light neutralizes many things, and the moon's glow can activate others. In order to know what truly happened, why the magic stagnates here, we must have it intact. Surely the fairies told you that."

They hadn't. "What else aren't you telling me, George?" Her fingers brushed at the area with her lightest of brushes. She had to be getting close to something. "How do I know how far down I need to go?"

"You're the Delver. You figure it out."

"I'm not a Delver!" Koga snapped her mouth shut. She held her breath, afraid something else would pop out. "I'm not a Delver, George. I'm an archaeologist."

"I fail to see the difference." His head leaned down.

She moved back to stay out of his way. His outline sparkled with the edges of moonlight. She stopped her work to focus on her words. "A Delver destroys its own kind. A Delver works dark magic. A Delver doesn't care about anything but itself!"

Koga didn't know how many kinds of fairies existed. The tiny winged creatures who had sat on her hand and spun out silk had little in common with the half-size dangerously-intelligent sprites who had given her the finished fabric circles. Even those fairies did not cross the Delvers.

Those fairies had told her how to fix the dead zone. *The paint will lead you to the wrongness, the disruption in the magic."*

"But how will I know how to fix it?"

"If you are meant to fix it, you will find the way." The ink-black fairy had handed her the finished silk pieces.

She knew she had to heal the dead zone. Who else would make that work? The blight had appeared before she had gone to college, a strange place where no one could explain the weirdness. It couldn't be ignored.

George breathed over her site. Sparkles landed on sharp edges and a dull glow covered all the surfaces in front of her. Koga could see properly. Her hands created negative spaces in the glow, but at least she had an idea what she was doing. "Thank you."

The brush still moved the glowing embers from George's breath. Her work came easier when she could see.

"I meant no insult. But the Delvers work the dirt and so do you. You have found items within. Can you not see the similarities?"

Something poked out of the dirt. She pushed her brush up and down over the object. It had to be what she searched for.

She did see the similarities, but she didn't want to acknowledge that to George. No one wanted to be a Delver. "I didn't go looking for anything specific. I only want to heal this land and find out what happened here." She didn't have to tell him the rest. She had grown up near here. She wanted her childhood home to be safe.

George sniffed the earth near her hands. "Do not believe everything you hear about the Delvers. They're not all killers." His wings kept the light from her work area. "Their purpose is to bring balance. They have strong convictions and don't let anything stand in their way."

Hoofbeats echoed behind them. Koga stood and whirled to face whatever came.

"No one's supposed to be here, George. It's too dangerous."

"We must assume whatever it is has been affected by the dead zone."

Had they been affected already? Koga couldn't tell. Mental decay came before death, but how would she know? Humans could suffer as much as the immortal creatures in here. "That's why we have to fix this place. So no one else is affected by it."

George stood on all fours, ready to face the threat. He didn't reply.

She remembered the silk and placed a large circle over the item she found. At least it would block the light.

George extended a foreleg and knocked the horse to the ground.

Koga's eyes adjusted to looking away from George's glow on her dig site, and she reassessed. It wasn't a horse - it was a unicorn. The paleness of it shone through the night like it had its own inner glow. The horn spiraled out of the horse's forehead. Its legs scrambled underneath it to stand again. The mane and tail sparkled silver. Her breath caught in her throat.

"Stop it. He isn't worth that kind of adoration."

"But it's a unicorn." Koga held out one hand in awe. She wanted to touch it, to feel the beauty under her hands. She couldn't look away.

The unicorn got to its feet. It aimed itself to Koga, dropped its horn, and charged.

George couldn't move quickly enough to stop it. He reached for the charging unicorn and struck it away from its intended path.

The unicorn knocked Koga to the ground. The slender horn pierced her upper arm. She fell away from the unicorn and her skin ripped from its horn.

George hauled the unicorn off. "No!"

The word rumbled through Koga's head, through her limbs, and the ground shook with force. She spread her arms to keep herself from rolling away. The left arm seared from the elbow down. She didn't have to look to see the damage. Blood seeped down her arm.

The unicorn squared to charge again. It pawed the earth once.

Koga couldn't move. The unicorn's white body shone in the moonlight. She couldn't look away. Her injured arm receded from her mind as the unicorn absorbed all her attention.

George grabbed it with his talons. His wings beat hard, lifting both himself and the unicorn. The unicorn's feet kicked. The wicked horn poked at the dragon's scales. George held tight.

He flew over the hill, over the line, and dropped the unicorn from a dragon's standing head height. He flew back. "You do not have long, Koga, before he returns. Hurry. I do not have hope that he will not re-cross the barrier."

She didn't see the unicorn land. She forced herself to move. She drove the unicorn from her mind. She rolled from her spot on the ground. Hurried to the silk. Used her fingers to lift it from the ground. Her brain slowly worked through that. The silk hadn't moved when George flew. She had to learn what else was different about fairy silk. In the shadow of George and with the light of his glow, she examined the item beneath. The cylindrical object could have been one of her arm bones, except it was more pointed on one end, and black as the night sky.

"It's a unicorn horn," George whispered, which only sent quivers down her back.

"It's black, George. Unicorns aren't black."

"Unicorns don't skewer people, either."

Koga wrapped the horn in the silk and tucked it in her bag. She didn't have a response for that. "What happened to it?" She wrapped another piece of fairy silk around her arm and tied it tight. "How do you know it's a unicorn if it's black?"

"They're in all shades, you know. You see them as white, but I see what they are beneath the surface. Anywhere from white to black, most of them are dull gray hues. They like that image humans paint of them being pristine, so they reinforce those thoughts with magic." George whuffed over Koga's skin. "You're one to talk color."

"That's not the same thing, George." Koga backed out from under the dragon's nose. "I'm mixed-race."

"But in your kind black isn't the color of moonless midnight and white isn't like pearls. The unicorns are the same. They're gray. You're brown."

Koga frowned. She didn't want to think of unicorns like that. She wrapped it in the silk. "I suppose I have to wait to see it in the light. Where's the next one?"

"Cover that fairy paint on your hands, and I'll find it." George breathed out again, covering the landscape with more of his glowing embers.

Koga balled her fists and stuck them within another piece of silk. She held her bag through the silk with her good arm, the wrapped horn sticking out one side. "It doesn't explain what happened to the unicorn."

George touched the ground with his nose, and Koga brushed the earth away from the spot. The object wasn't straight, but more twisted and bent. "This one is different."

"Fairy wingspline." George turned his head away.

"But I thought fairies and unicorns didn't die. The *immortal* creatures, right?"

George snapped his head back to face Koga. "We may not die, but we can be killed. We are almost as fragile as you humans. We simply have another tool at our disposal to create the best possible chance to survive. The unicorn probably had a mate who used to be attached to the horn you wrapped in silk."

"So what happened here?"

George's head ranged back and forth, then he pointed her in another direction. "Someone severed the magic, you know that. That is why it is a dead zone." He tapped another spot on the ground with his nose, then breathed the embers over the surrounding area.

"Severed?"

The dragon curled on the ground. His tail wrapped around him. His eyes half-shut. "Tired. Need a nap."

Koga brushed at the spot before George could really block her work. She covered the area in the silk circle and worked underneath it. She wouldn't be able to find the other spots without him, but at least she could get this one taken care of before the sun rose. Dawn pinked the sky in the distance, and she held the wrapped artifact in her arm. It wasn't a cylinder like the unicorn horn, and it wasn't a bent rod like the fairy wingspline. She would have to ask him when he woke. The round stone wouldn't fit within her knapsack, so she laid it on the ground next to her.

She had to hurry. How long before George would be damaged? That might have happened already. How long before George wouldn't survive?

She held her hands over the ground and searched for another. Her injured arm complained from the movement. She couldn't see, and she couldn't feel despite the fairies' touch, so she tapped George's foreleg with her good arm.

His eyes blinked open and shut again. She tapped him again, and the eyes stayed half-open. His nose sniffed audibly. "You found a dragon's heartstone."

Her eyes fell to the stone. She was afraid to ask if he had known that dragon. "Did I get them all?"

George turned his gaze to her, then his nose searched the scent over the ground. He glared at her hands, and she shoved them deep within a piece of silk. He touched the ground in one more spot. She hurried with her tools. Dawn approached too fast.

He laid his head on his foreclaws. "They're called remnants, you know." His eyes closed to slits. "Magic remnants. Your kind uses them to prolong life and youth and restore vigor."

Koga frowned. "Then what does your kind use them for?"

The dragon didn't say. He watched her brush away the layers of earth.

"You must have someone who's tried." Koga placed the last item, wrapped in silk, into her bag. "Was that a phoenix feather?" She hefted the wrapped heartstone.

The unicorn galloped into their hearing range.

Koga clambered onto George's back. She kept her eyes away from the unicorn; she couldn't get enthralled with it again.

The creature paused when it caught sight of them. He pawed at the ground. His charge aimed for Koga.

George lifted them off the ground with strong wingbeats.

The unicorn followed them. George flew faster than the unicorn could follow. Out, around the barrier, over the forest, and back again to the dig site and the ruin of an altar behind it. He sighed. "I'm sure the unicorn's mate belonged to the horn you found. He would not be so persistent, otherwise."

Koga closed her eyes. "What can we do for the unicorn?"

Smoke sputtered from George's nose. "Nothing. His mate cannot be replaced. He will miss his mate until his existence ends."

She held her knapsack and the heartstone tighter. Ending the life of any immortal creature was sacrilege. The remnants all had that unmistakable weight of wrongness about them. If she couldn't help the unicorn, she would focus on the dead zone. "Losing a feather won't kill a phoenix. Is that remnant equal to the others?" Koga closed her eyes. She could imagine George walking instead of flying far off the ground.

"It will if you lose the right feather." George's landing was tough, harder than it should have been. She had watched him put down light as a cat's step so many times in the past. "Ouch. I need to cross over the barrier again."

"Don't leave me, George. Help me reverse the damage." Koga pulled each artifact, still wrapped in silk, and put them on the altar in the middle of the dead zone. George seemed to want to cross the barrier with greater frequency the longer they stayed. She had to rebuild the altar piece by piece. It took shape with stones and wood in the early morning light. "I just have to make an offering and place them on it, right?"

George favored one of his forelegs. "It doesn't matter what you offer. They cannot return." He looked toward the barrier. "Just a moment? I need to feel the magic around me again."

"But it will release them into the spirit world."

George's half-closed lids shut. A long moment later, they opened again. "Our spirit world is different. We don't have a place to go after we die. That is why we are immortal. We cannot exist once we have been destroyed." George curled around the base of the altar. "Just another nap." His breathing slowed to a point Koga put a hand on his ribs to see if they still moved.

They did, but only a fraction of what they normally did. Koga's hand shook.

The artifacts lay on the altar. She had them still wrapped. She pulled out the memorized passage again, and ran over the words within her mind. So much centered on her efforts.

The hoofbeats signaled the unicorn had returned. The same one, or one she couldn't distinguish from the first. Her arm burned.

Koga turned and unwrapped the unicorn horn. In the sun's pale light, it bleached to white. The unicorn stopped its charge. She dropped it in the bowl of the altar. She unwrapped the phoenix feather, the fairy wingspline, and the dragon heartstone and placed each of them in the bowl. "By the dawn's light, I beseech you, Sun, to render the sacrifice made and allow the magic to again flow here."

The rising sun bleached the remnants. She watched the color leach out and away from the pieces. The whitening objects lost their connection to the creatures they had been. Koga held the thought of what they had been in her head, but it was too much for her. Her eyes blurred. She blinked them several times into focus to draw away the water.

Then Koga put a piece of silk on top and burned it. Did she imagine the release of tension once the fire caught?

The fire held her attention, but too soon it stopped. She worked toward the edge of the altar. She wanted to sleep. She yawned. George's eyes had closed. Koga felt she couldn't stay alert, and she wobbled as she sank to the ground.

When Koga woke, the area looked exactly as it had before. Something within her mind had cleared, and George stood next to her. "I'm not a Delver."

George shook his massive head. "You're not. What did you use for your offering?"

Koga bowed her head. "I gave the remnants freedom."

His head turned side to side. "Then let's go."

The two of them made for the edge of the dead zone. At least the magic had a chance to come back, if they destroyed all the remnants. Koga still felt wobbly from the nap. Her face had been sunburned on one side, something that might not show from her dark skin but she felt with every facial expression. Twenty pieces of silk were all that remained within her knapsack. Koga and George needed food, and shelter, and rest.

At the end of the dead zone, both of them felt better. Something about the barrier still remained. "How long do you think it will take?"

"To clear the barrier? It should be gone by now, but I still feel it."

Koga reached out with her fairy-stained hands. The wound in her arm ached. "I feel it, too."

George and Koga stared at each other. They had to take down that wall.

The wayward unicorn ran through the barrier. It collapsed in a heap on the other side, all bones and nothing to hold them together. The bones disintegrated, leaving only the horn behind.

Koga stopped. "George?"

The dragon breathed onto the barrier. The embers from his breath formed on the barrier and above and below, but did not cross through to the other side.

Her heart rate doubled. They hadn't fixed it; they had only made it worse.

The dragon breathed out fire. "Those snarking fairies."

"So what do we do now that we're stuck in here?"

The dragon padded along the inside of the circle. When she put out her hands, she could feel the barrier itself. It had been activated by her efforts. She could scream, but it would only aggravate George.

He lifted into the air. He flew in a circle, away, along the inside of the barrier.

She sat on the dirt. "How do we get a Delver? They could fix this, right?"

George couldn't hear her. He flew farther out.

She wandered back to the altar. Something else had to be done. Maybe she had to activate it before it came down. George's comment of an offering needled at her. What else did she need to give?

The artifacts lay piled over the altar's bowl. She couldn't see anything wrong with the setup. The fairies had shown her the entire thing in the vision. Koga laid her bare hands over the bowl, fingers spread wide. She let her sorrow show: the tears for the lost creatures, the beauty that had been taken. The fairy stains flared out from her hands. All the artifacts singed to ash. The ashes scattered through the wind.

The dragon landed behind her. His bulk came down hard behind her and shook the ground. "Now what have you done?"

Koga's eyes dried in the wind. "I didn't do anything."

George sniffed the ashes. "The fairies. Always the snarking fairies!"

Koga nodded.

The two of them stared at the altar. "You can't make it work, Koga."

Koga put her hands together. She felt the energies between her fingers. All of it sparked over the altar. The fairy paint on her hands turned to fire. "This isn't normal."

"No, you've been marked by the fairies." George laughed, tendrils of smoke curling out of his nose. "There's nothing normal about that."

"What is this altar for?" Koga walked around it. "Who claims it?"

"Fairies, snarking fairies." George mumbled to himself over her head.

Koga clapped her hands. "Listen to me, George. We have to forget the fairies!"

"It belongs to the fairies. Look at the pattern on the stones. They mark it with their fingers."

She studied it, but she didn't think it would help her understand the markings.

George thumped his tail against the dirt. "You can figure it out. It's going to be a problem."

Koga whirled to face him, leaving the altar at her back. "What is it with you and the fairies? It's getting old."

"Old is what I am. I remember your grandparents, and their grandparents. Beyond that, it's a little fuzzy, I must say."

Koga grinned.

The sun progressed to the zenith. Everything burned hotter. Her hands started to bother her. She stared at her palms. She saw the fairies' marks. They looked a lot like the stone altar.

She couldn't move. She couldn't tell George what she thought about it. She couldn't do anything. The marks flared. George breathed smoke and embers over her hands, but the burning continued. It spread.

George breathed over her again; this time over all of her. "Hold still, Koga. Hold on."

Koga couldn't move, so she couldn't have done anything else.

Up her arms, then somehow it enveloped all of her. Koga shuddered, a coiling within her own skin that didn't quite fit anymore. She fought against it, but the feelings of change continued. Then something flared outside her, and Koga shrunk into herself. Something new happened. Something different. She was different.

George blew fire over her, everywhere.

Koga flinched. She wasn't fireproof. And yet, suddenly, she was. She stood in the middle of the fire. She didn't burn. The fire stayed around her and it energized her. She stared at him, she stared at herself, she took in the world around them. She saw the barrier. And she saw it weakening. "What happened?"

Then she felt the wings unfurl.

"Now you will be a Delver." George bowed his head. "I don't know that you have another choice. I'm sorry."

She snapped her mouth closed. She wanted to ask, but she couldn't.

George pawed the ground and swished his tail. "Snarking fairy!"

Koga groaned. There would be no end to the trouble from George. She lifted herself with the new wings. "Did I have to get shorter, though?"

"It's relative. You were short before."

Koga shook her head. She stared at her hands. No fairy-paint marked her anymore. Just the deep brown of her skin, and where it had been edged with lighter brown had turned indigo. Even her nails had changed to shades of deep blue to purple. Her hair, too short to see if it had changed, stayed out of her wings' reach.

"Let's find your friends." George stood near where the barrier had stood. He still sniffed it deeply, then lightly hopped across. "Oh, the magic! Do you feel it?" He jumped several times, all with only a whisper of wind and no earthquake.

She did. The magic flowed over, around, through her in a way she didn't understand. "I don't know what to do with it."

"You don't know what to do without it."

"But I don't want to be a Delver. I'm an archaeologist. I love my work."

"I told you not to go to the fairies."

"But I had to fix the Dead Zone. They're the ones who know how to heal the land." Koga heard herself whining. "C'mon, George."

"Next time you'll listen to me."

Koga floated over the old barrier, too. The magic flowed openly across the area. The plants on the edges had started to flourish again. The dead zone was no longer dead. "What else, besides a Delver?"

"You'll have to ask the snarking fairies. No one has ever stopped being a Delver."

"Humans don't become fairies."

"And unicorns don't skewer people."

Koga let herself down to the ground. She might not need the rest, somehow, but she had to give herself time to think. She didn't want to just fly away into the unknown without a plan. "I'm not going back to the fairies. I don't want to be a Delver. Or any other kind of fairy." Her arm burned where the unicorn had poked her. Her fingers unwound the silk, uncovered the nearly-healed wound, let the silk dangle.

Her blood coated the fabric. She stuffed it in the front pocket of her knapsack, away from the other pieces of fairy silk. Her arm stopped burning. No trace of the wound remained.

Smoke wisped out of George's nose. "Want has nothing to do with it. You have become a Delver, and you will do what Delvers do."

Koga shuddered. "And what? Destroy you? They hold no creature sacred." She walked to where the unicorn had been. She picked up the horn, a light gray to her eyes with something behind it that might be magic. She wrapped the horn, put it in her knapsack, and slung the bag on her back. Her wings felt fettered. She frowned, moved the pack to her hip. Her wings fluttered free.

George snorted. "The fairies stole my home. I can call them snarking all I want, but they're not all Delvers. You can make it what you will." His talon gestured to her pack. "Already you are keeping remnants from the wrong hands."

She stared at him. She turned in a slow circle, her wings close to her body. The world waited. "All right. Let's go." And she led in a direction away from where they knew the fairies were.

Uno por Cada

by M. C. Chambers

TRUMPETS SOUNDED THROUGH MARISOL'S EAR-BUDS. High, bright brass cascaded downward into vigorous strumming of guitars. Synthesized bass drowned out the rumbles of cars on concrete above..

Dr. Marisol Salvia slid her finger across her nettablet in time with the music. Her fingertips spread wide a photo of a Pre-Columbian shell gorget resting just inches from a chunk of modern concrete. She tapped along with the drumbeat in her ears to label both objects. She slid her finger with the next peal of trumpets to link the image with the rest of Thursday's data and to open a new file for Friday.

She listened to an old playlist from her college days: music from *Las Catrinas Técnicas*, an "all-girl" Mariachi dubstep group out of the University of Arizona. Her cousin, Carlos, had performed with that band (though not a girl, he portrayed one convincingly on stage). Her sister Rosa had designed their fanciful costumes and props, and occasionally traveled and sang with them. They were hot for a time until they became politicized and were kidnapped. Most of the survivors withdrew into *norteamericano* Bluegrass. Rosa became a costume-maker for a puppet-theatre troupe here in St. Louis. Carlos did not survive.

Carlos, Micaela, Natalia...the ensemble that was *Las Catrinas Técnicas* itself...The Day of the Dead approached; Marisol saluted and honored these dear lost.

She hummed as she scrolled through photos and point clouds, checking for data that might relate an item to the Anomalies. Strange; she had been listening to this playlist for almost a decade and had never before noticed the background horns. They blared in offbeat, syncopated rhythms, like an old car horn. The song ended, and the solo vocal introduction to the next song began—*Uno por Cada*, one of her favorites—but the background horn continued. Marisol removed the ear-bud from her left ear. The sound continued from outside—an old car horn. She paused the player, clipped the ear-buds beside the tablet in its case and left her office.

155

Marisol climbed the packed earthen path to the gate of the cyclone fence that guarded the entrance. The site lay under the ruin of Busch Stadium, now collapsed and smothered in silt by the earthquake and flood of '32. Salvage teams seeking steel also found Pre-Columbian Mississippian remains, so archeologists from Washington University took charge. The upheaval of the New Madrid Fault and subsequent flood as the Mississippi changed course had left a challenging mix of artifacts. With the unearthing of the Anomalies this site became fully funded by the Department of the Interior and fully protected by Federal law. However, the stadium owners retained above-surface rights and engineered a parking garage above the site, reverberant with concrete, creating the noisiest dig Marisol had ever worked.

Thank God for ear-buds.

Marisol rounded a concrete pillar and approached the gate. On the other side of the fence, lit by blue LED of underground parking, sat her sister's decrepit Plymouth. Her sister Rosa stood next to it, pressing its fob repeatedly and singing "Marisol! Marisol!"

"¡Ay, vengo!" Marisol called as she neared the gate. Rosa had such a stunning voice, but she only used it these days to annoy her relatives. Marisol secretly rejoiced at the annoyance. If only Carlos were still around to annoy her also.

"I tried to phone you," Rosa said. "You didn't pick up."

"Did you?" Marisol pulled the phone from the thigh pocket of her cargo pants. "The signal down here sucks." As she watched the screen flashed and a phrase of Mariachi music played as each of four missed calls registered upon it.

"Dios mio, Marisol, still with the Mariachi?"

She swiped her key card through the lock. "Sorry. I like old stuff. ¿Quieres entrar?"

"Sí. I need to show you what I made for you for this year's parade at Escuela Guadalupe!" She dove into the car and brought forth a garment bag overstuffed with feathers and ribbons stained blue by the LED. "You're going to love this!" She squinted at the washed out colors. "Do you have any real light around here?"

"I have full spectrum in my office. Come with me. Coffee?"

"¡Sí, siempre! Where is your friend Dr. Whitehorse?"

"Dr. Whitehorse has run off to get married. The students have their mid-terms; I am alone until the eighth."

Marisol's office was a small yurt that enclosed light, warmth and electronics while remaining close to the chill earthen trenches of the dig. Marisol pulled a flap aside and invited her sister to enter. She measured some beans into a burr grinder while Rosa unwrapped her latest creation.

Marisol looked it over. The body was a poncho banded with feathers of three colors: red, black and blue. It sported a collar of ribbons and marigolds. Its head, built to set upon a wearer's shoulders and tower over the wearer's real head, was skeletal, vertebrae leading up to a long beaked skullpainted with flowers and flourishes. Long, glittering eyelashes lined empty eye sockets. "Hmm. A giant chicken?"

"Not a chicken, a condor. *El Condor de los Muertos.*"

"Condors have curved beaks. It's a stork."

Rosa pouted. "It's too late to change it now. You will have to use your imagination. The kids won't care."

"I can help with that." Marisol wakened her nettablet and searched the University databases for point clouds of a condor skull. "We'll print a replica of a real skull in bone-colored resin. It'll take a half hour or so." She sent a file to her 3D printer driver, adjusted the dimensions and started the printer.

"Fine! If it will make you happy." Rosa draped the body over her head and adjusted the shoulder piece. She opened its wings; stark bare bones, twelve feet across, touched both sides of the office yurt. Black ribbons stiffened with wire hung down as pinions. It leaned toward Marisol menacingly, "If I say I am *El Condor*, who are you to argue?"

"*¡Disculpe, Señor!* You are certainly *El Condor* if you say so." Marisol poured coffee into cups.

El Condor closed its wings and leaned back. Rosa wriggled out from beneath its body. "Try it on."

Marisol draped the poncho over her own shoulders, settled the shoulder piece, and grasped the wands that controlled the wings. She waved them tentatively, peering through the fabric that covered her eyes. Surprisingly, she saw fairly well through the screen-like fabric. Not surprising really; her sister knew her materials even if she did not know her condor beak anatomy. "The kids will love it." Marisol waved the wings with more drama. She felt like a youngster in a school play. "*¡Soy El Condor! El Condor* with a stork-beak!"

Rosa did not respond. Marisol twisted her body to look at her sister. Rosa stood rapt, staring into her cupped hands. "Is this the Anomaly?" She held a pale blue speckled artifact, the size and nearly the shape of a swan's egg, but flattened on one side and impressed with a shallow geometric pattern.

Marisol's eyebrows rose. "What the heck? I distinctly remember boxing that up to take to Wash U. Where did you find it?"

"Right by the sugar bowl. It looked like a big egg—it has a texture like eggshell, but it has this raised pattern on it."

"Oh. I see. This is the printed copy." Marisol released the wands that controlled the wing bones and tucked them within the arm openings. She withdrew a small plastic tub from a rack of shallow drawers. A layer of bubble-wrap lined the tub. "Set it in here. Molly—Dr. Whitehorse—took the original to the University on her way out of town. This is for reference. But you shouldn't be handling it; it's made of complex materials, not just resin."

"Is the original really extraterrestrial?" Rosa set the object in the tub as gently as if it were in fact a fragile egg.

"It is anomalous. I can't speculate as to its origins. This is the Lesser Anomaly—we call it Little Nom. It tests to between 500 to 1000 years old. But its composition is nearly identical to the Greater Anomaly." Marisol tapped her nettablet and scrolled to an image. "This one. We call it Big Nom. This shows the convex wall of the object and the carving or molding that matches the Great Anomaly we found at Teotihuacan."

"Called Great Big Nom?"

Marisol grinned. "Just Nom. It was the first one found. Look. All have a veneer of calcium carbonate, but inside, an advanced ceramic. Scans show an alignment of crystals that suggest piezoelectric circuitry. Yet Big Nom tests at almost three thousand years, and the one at Teotihuacan over five thousand years—older than the strata in which it was found."

Rosa swiped the screen with a finger to reveal more images, her eyes wide with excitement.

Marisol picked up a flashlight. "Come on, I'll show you."

"I thought it was top secret?"

"Restricted, not top secret. If it were top secret there would be dogs and security guards and not just a cheap fence keeping people out. We're required to clear any articles for publication through the Department of the Interior before submission, that's all. Besides, I trust you. You're good with secrets. You've kept Carlos's secret all these years."

"True. Wikipedia still lists him as Carlita." They giggled together for a moment. Marisol gave the flashlight and plastic tub to Rosa to carry, then settled the Condor/Stork headpiece firmly on her shoulders and bent to manipulate the long-necked costume through the office flap.

Rosa giggled some more. "You are going out with the costume?"

"I'm practicing for the parade next week. I have to get used to walking with this. Who will see? The dead?" Marisol welcomed Rosa's laughter as much as her singing.

They left the office yurt glowing like a *luminaria* behind them and headed toward the darker depths of the dig. Marisol paused to switch on an array of spot lights mounted on racks that brightened the earthen trenches. She waved the wing-wands about and tried to march with dignity, if not grace, as *El Condor*. Concrete rumbled as vehicles drove above them.

They wended down a wide trench that opened onto several side digs where glowing plastic stakes arranged in grids marked human remains in sandy basins. Marisol halted and tucked the wing wands into the poncho. "We need to climb down into a narrower trench here. I had better set *El Condor* aside." She removed the shoulder piece and set it carefully upon a tool rack next to one of the burial pits, draping the poncho over the handles of shovels and picks to keep it from the dust.

Rosa shone the beam of the flashlight over the dead. "What a beautiful *ofrenda* we could make here!" She plucked some of the marigolds from the collar of the costume and placed them gently in the eye sockets of several of the skulls.

Marisol pursed her lips. "Those are printed copies, you know. The actual remains have already been removed to the University. These are teaching aids."

"I don't care! They are beautiful *sin embargo*. Marisol! You are such *un aguafiestas.* "

Marisol felt bad. "I'm sorry. Look. There to the left, still half buried. Those are real, we're still working on them."

Rosa took more marigolds and placed them on the genuine dead. "*El Condor* won't mind if I give them his flowers. These are his people. *El Condor de los Muertos ama a sus muertos.*" She sang a brief lullaby over them.

They left *El Condor* standing guard over his dead, and continued into a narrower trench.

At the edge of the dig was a section of a dome, around which a deeper trench had been dug to expose its equator, though the top and back of it were still imbedded in earth. Marisol switched on surrounding racks of spotlights. They climbed down into the deeper trench where Rosa shone the flashlight on the pale blue-speckled surface of Big Nom.

Marisol pointed out some key features. "Look at the molding at the top. See those beasts? At first we interpreted them as deer. But look, toes! Molly thinks they might be Eohippus, prehistoric horses of the Americas."

"There's a guy holding someone's head," Rosa directed the flashlight to highlight the detail. "And there's leaves—or feathers, maybe—growing from it."

Marisol gestured toward the bottom. "The images gradually lose detail—they become only patterns of dots, like Braille, or the holes in the punch cards of archaic computers."

Rosa compared Little Nom in the tub to the surface of Big Nom.

She focused the flashlight on part of the pattern on the lower right of the dome. "What does this pattern mean?"

"Perhaps a maker's mark."

"I wonder...the pattern here is sunken, and on there it is raised. Do they fit together?" She picked up the artifact and placed its pattern against its match on the dome.

Marisol bit her lip. *Careful! You shouldn't be handling that!* She kept the voice of *el aguafiestas* to herself.

Within the egg-shaped artifact, small bursts of light flashed. Rosa withdrew her hand. Little Nom remained fixed in place. The lights within flashed randomly like lightning obscured by clouds in a faraway storm.

Upon Big Nom's wall a thin line of red light grew from its connection with the egg, moving in an arc to a point where it split into three lines, and then into many, until the surface of the dome was wrapped with a web of red lines.

An elliptical hole opened with a snick, like a distorted camera shutter. The sisters stepped back against the wall of the trench behind them. "*Madre de Dios,*" Rosa breathed.

"*Ay,* maybe we boxed up the wrong one," Marisol muttered.

Rosa played the beam of the flashlight over the contents of the dome. Human remains lay stacked on what looked like bunks and on the tiled floor. A large shallow basin stood in the center holding more remains.

"A tomb!" Marisol said. "Look at the position of the remains—they lay as if placed ritualistically rather than fallen naturally."

"They are not bones. They have skin!"

"Mummified rather than decayed. Because of the protection of the dome. Wonderful!"

"They are in pieces!"

"A sacrificial chamber?" Marisol dragged one of the light racks closer. She swiveled the lamps to point into Big Nom. A dimly seen frieze on the back wall depicted vine-wrapped demons holding aloft body parts that bled jewels.

But Rosa drew away.

Marisol turned to her sister. "Are you okay?"

Rosa didn't answer.

"Do these remains bother you? The others didn't."

"No," said Rosa. "No...*pero*...was this done by extraterrestrials?"

Marisol frowned. "What? Extraterrestrials? Who knows? This is the first time one of the Noms has been opened. We must scan this chamber and then analyze its contents." Marisol peered eagerly into the shadowed opening. "The 3D laser is in the office. It wouldn't take much to set it up.

Let's go get it."

Rosa nodded and followed. In the office, she poured coffee for herself and sipped it as Marisol grabbed the lidar box, unplugged it from its charger and booted it up.

"¡Mire, Marisol, *El Condor's* skull is done! *Ay*, he looks scary for kids."

"With glitter and eyelashes he will be perfect. ¡*No hay que preocuparse!* Grab the nettablet. Will you take photos as I scan? Take lots. The more the better." Marisol shouldered the lidar and tripod.

Marisol set up the tripod just outside the opening of the dome and clamped the 3D box upon it. She adjusted its lenses and filters. A red vertical beam flickered across the space. On one of the box's monitors, a point cloud accumulated as green pixels. Rosa murmured about extraterrestrials but Marisol paid no heed: Once the chamber had been fully scanned and photographed, objects could be catalogued, removed and analyzed...and then they could speculate.

Rosa raised the tablet, turning it from side to side as she took photos. She lowered the tablet and raised her flashlight. She shone it upon a figure in the center basin, shadowed by its neighbor. "Marisol? Isn't that...isn't that Dr. Whitehorse?"

Marisol looked in Rosa's beam to see her colleague's face, tilted sideways, framed by a tulle veil with white ribbon, pearls and violets. It stared with half closed, sightless eyes. A thin line of dark red ran from the corner of its mouth. "Molly?" she grabbed the flashlight from Rosa's grasp and shone it fully upon the body. Head and trunk—its arms were gone. "That can't be her..." She directed the light to illuminate others that reclined within the basin. Some had only paper thin flesh stretched over skeletal faces, dead thousands of years; others had flesh that sagged, and some had flesh barely changed. Molly, her lipstick still red, her mascara fresh, looked as if she had died only this morning.

Marisol's eyes blurred. "She is supposed to be on her honeymoon..." Suddenly dizzy, she dropped the flashlight, reached out and leaned upon the scanner. It toppled and fell into the opening.

Rosa caught and steadied her. "This is bad. We should call the police!" She pulled Marisol away from the opening. She led her from the trench toward the office.

A figure was silhouetted upon the glowing wall of the yurt. Rosa halted, then pushed Marisol back a pace. "Who is that?"

They stood silently, frozen, until Marisol whispered, "Only Molly and I have key cards."

The flap of the office opened. A backlit figure stood and spoke. "Dr. Salvia? Is that you?"

The familiar voice surprised Marisol. "Molly?"

"*No es* Molly!" Rosa placed the tablet with the photo of dead Molly in Marisol's hand. "It is a trick. Run!" Rosa disappeared into the shadows. The rack of spotlights that illuminated the trench went off. Only the blue LEDs overhead shone, and the glowstick grids marking the burial digs.

The figure spoke in Molly's voice. "Oh, Dr. Salvia, I'm glad you're here. I'm looking for the Lesser Anomaly. Do you have it?"

Marisol looked from the staring face in the photograph to the backlit figure by the office; dead Molly to her imposter. Confusion coalesced into anger—an anger like that which smoldered beneath strata of grief ever since Carlos's murder.

The garage overhead rumbled.

The figure spoke. "Do you have it? You wouldn't have taken it, would you? You know you shouldn't handle it." A quick, dim line of light flashed from its throat. "Help me look for it."

Marisol darted into a shadow and ducked into a crevice formed by rebar-laden chunks of the ruined stadium, where students often retreated to do one of the myriad things that students did not want to be seen doing. She pulled the phone from her pocket. "*Llamar al a policía,*" she told it. "No signal found," it answered.

She squinted through one of the cracks at the stranger who pretended to be Molly. Though it was similar to Molly, the legs were a little too short—the forearms a little too bulky—something odd about the head—She wedged her nettablet into the crack and took a photo, then spread it with her fingers to see it more clearly. The lighting was bad, but it did show some form of gadgetry attached to the figure's collar and arms.

"Dr. Salvia? Where are you?" Another quick, dim line of light flashed from its throat, like the lidar Marisol used to scan her sites. Marisol was confident that no lidar would find her among the concrete. But the color of the light changed from silver to indigo. Perhaps it sought some other frequency; infrared most likely. Marisol left the crevice and flitted to another spot where old concrete met new, a spot where echoes reverberated in strange ways, and were heard as coming from unexpected directions; a spot beloved by upperclassmen who hid there to spook freshmen.

"Who are you?" called Marisol. The words echoed from a hundred concrete angles. "What are you? You're not Molly. I saw Molly. What did you do to her?"

Another quick, dim line of silver light flashed from its throat. "You shouldn't have handled the artifact. It's not made for you. You should have left it alone."

"Is that why you killed Molly? Because she handled the artifact?"

The dim line ceased. The brighter beam of a headlamp switched on. "Dr. Molly Whitehorse. She was an exemplary person. She was inventive, beautiful, and highly respected. Exemplary in many ways."

"Then why is she dead?"

"The exemplary make poor servants. They inspire others in unpredictable ways. Standard operating procedure mandates we clear away such people whenever we find them." The figure took a few slow steps from the office. "I'm only here to calibrate the equipment. Collection must continue. It's for the good of the future."

Marisol's hands grew cold. The cold of dread that arose in her heart warred with the heat of anger that rose from her gut. "Collection of what? Corpses?"

"Before they are corpses. We boost the economy of the future by taking laborers from the past."

"Laborers—you mean slaves!"

"The registration is out of spec. Things must be set right. Dr. Salvia, the artifact?"

Rosa's voice whispered from the nearby shadows, "Marisol, run!" The whisper echoed from the concrete overhead, repeating right by Marisol's ear, distorted into a faint echo of Carlos's voice. *Run!* The echoes continued, faint and overlapping as if the shadows themselves whispered.

"Is someone with you, Dr. Salvia?" asked Molly's impersonator. Its scanning light shifted to cover a wider area.

"Stay away from my sister," growled Marisol beneath her breath. Her beautiful, inventive sister. She ran from the echo spot, creeping half-bent behind racks of darkened lights. This thing who took Molly and threatened Rosa—she must stop it. The tool rack near the burial pit—there were sharp iron shovels there, and picks. They could serve as weapons.

Not-Molly followed. "Dr. Salvia? Is that you?" The beam swayed as it approached, its bearer limping along the wider trench.

Marisol darted past the burial pit, past the *ofrenda* of decorated dead to the rack of tools. She crouched behind it.

The beam scanned the pit and fell upon the figure *El Condor*. *El Condor* rose, stood upright and turned toward the light. It raised its long bony wings and shook them. The stiff black ribbons on its wings rattled like a shaman's gourd. Its glittered stork-head had been replaced by the bare oversized condor skull, the great eye-sockets empty and shadowed.

"Who are you?" asked Not-Molly.

"Soy El Condor de los Muertos," the theatrical voice proclaimed. *"Estos*

163

son mis muertos. These are my dead. What do you want here?"

The beam played over the costume. "I have heard of things like you. I did not know your kind were still active." The beam turned and searched the skeletal remains in the pit. "These have potential. When did they die...seven, maybe eight centuries ago? Were they sacrificed? Executed?"

"Not important. They are dead now. They are mine now."

"Once the equipment is calibrated we will find them before they are slaughtered. The condemned, collected right before execution, make very good laborers."

El Condor rattled its wings. "Leave them be. *Son míos.* Go take what is yours. There is still blood within the great dome. Look and see."

"No living blood."

"*¡Vea usted mismo!* Look and see."

A flicker came from the dome. Not-Molly straightened and shifted the beam toward the path to Big Nom. "Dr. Salvia? Is that you?" It turned away from *El Condor* and continued into the narrower trench.

Marisol lifted a heavy pick from the tool rack. Its wooden handle felt smooth and familiar in her grip. She looked for Rosa in the meager light, but saw only that *El Condor* already lay on the ground empty. The faintest of voices sounded in her ear, "Go to the dome." The whisper echoed like a swish of trapped wind—it was impossible to tell in which shadow it originated. "If it goes in, trap it there."

"*Sí.*" Marisol crept toward the dome, her quiet footfalls masked by screeches and rumbles from wheels overhead. She followed Not-Molly into the deeper trench, studying its shape, its movement: almost human, but for the gadgetry buckled to its coveralls. It limped as it walked. It paused, bending to adjust a brace on its knee. It's injured, Marisol thought. She remembered the kick-boxing classes that Molly took; she probably clocked it a good one before she succumbed. A wave of regret arose that Molly had not prevailed. A renewed flame of anger displaced it—This thing must be stopped, sealed away in its own structure, for Molly's justice, for Rosa's protection. She flexed her grip upon the smooth wooden handle and crept forward a step.

It switched off its headlamp and turned its face toward Big Nom. The faint flicker of Little Nom's storms and the red web engulfing the dome glowed chaotically. Not-Molly straightened and hurried forward. "Dr. Salvia, don't touch anything! The signal must be modulated." It climbed into the trench at the dome's equator and peered into the opening. "Dr. Salvia?" But it did not go in. Instead it stood to the side. With one hand it manipulated a gadget on its opposite arm and waved its device-laden forearm in front of Little Nom. The flashes within the egg-shape synchronized into a steady, urgent pulse.

The pick handle in Marisol's grip balanced itself, lost its heaviness, became warm and light and ready. She could swing it easily if she had to. She had always been so careful in the past, watchful of the safety of her students and of her finds when working with such tools. Precision was a necessary specialty. She eased forward as the creature manipulated the machinery on its forearms.

From the dome a voice sang out:

"Ay, mi corazón..."

The thing turned toward the sound. There at the dome's opening stood Molly; the real Molly, the dead one. Her stained gown spread to fill the opening. Her wedding veil framed her head like a cloud. Her eyes stared lifeless, but a drop of fresh blood streaked her cheek like a tear.

"Ah, my heart!
*Siento que mi corazón
es de dos corazónes,
un centenar,
un mil mil mil mil..."*

This was the song Carlita, cousin Carlos, used to sing, his soulful solo introduction to *Las Catrinas'* hit song *Uno Por Cada*. The voice however was Rosa's. It was perfect, as heart-stopping as Carlita's had been. "I feel my heart is two hearts, a hundred, a thousand..."

The creature stared transfixed. "Molly Whitehorse! How is it possible? More beautiful than ever!"

*"Uno por cada caricia
que deseo de ti,
uno por cada,
un mil mil mil mil..."*

Dead Molly opened bony arms toward the creature. "One for each caress that I desire from you..."

It stepped through the opening toward her. She backed smoothly before it. It followed her deeper into the dome.

Marisol crept forward. She heard a sudden crash, a wail, and then Rosa sprang from the dome. Marisol grabbed Little Nom from the wall. Its heat seared her hand; she dropped it with a cry. The opening snicked shut. The red web slowly dimmed.

Rosa joined her and turned to look at the dome, breathing heavily. Blood seeped from a slash in her hand.

Marisol stared at her sister. "What did you do? Molly—"

"I made a puppet. Molly on a tripod. Sorry. I had to! That thing...it kept calling your name. Did you call the police?"

"I tried. There's no signal. We have to go up by the gate."

The dome snicked open and the thing that was not Molly came out. Its gadgetry whirred. Orange light snaked from its devices to gather and whiten around the scanner at its throat. It turned toward the sisters.

Marisol stepped in front of Rosa. *"Huye!"* She held the pick before her.

It raised a hand to its throat. Marisol lunged with the pick, aiming for its game knee. It dodged and lashed out with a blow to Marisol's elbow. She spun backward; the pick was knocked from her grasp. She fell against the earth of the trench, but immediately rolled and found her feet.

Rosa scooped up Little Nom and hurled it at the thing's luminous throat. The artifact struck the brightening scanner with a splintering sound. Not-Molly staggered. The whirring stopped. The orange lines retreated, fading.

"¡Vamos!" cried Rosa.

They ran along the trenches. Rosa knocked over racks of spot lights and tools into the path behind them. They rushed up the ramp to the fence that separated the site from the parking garage. Marisol pulled the phone from her pocket. Here at the gate the signal lines shone vigorously. *"Llamar al a policía,"* she told it. "There is an intruder at the stadium dig." Her voice shook as she gave the address.

"Response time eleven minutes," responded the phone.

From the dig scraping sounded as the creature dragged the racks aside.

The gate to the fence was locked. Marisol searched her pockets. "I don't have the key card. I must have left it in the office!"

"Can't you use your thumbprint or something?"

"When our next grant gets approved we will!"

They stared at each other.

They turned and ran to the office. Marisol spun frantically around the space. *"¿Dónde está? ¿Dónde está?"*

"Aquí, by the coffee grinder!" Rosa held up the key card. Marisol grabbed it and they ran from the office.

Not-Molly came into sight from the trench. It saw the sisters. It pressed one of the gadgets on its arm. Orange lines snaked over its limbs.

Behind it, from the direction of the burial pits, a voice rang out:

"Ay, mi corazón...."

Carlita's voice: breathy, passionate; soulful cousin Carlos as Marisol had heard him many hundreds of times, both before and after his death. Yet she had never heard him so resonant. The song echoed against the concrete as though sung by hundreds.

The thing paused, listening. Its eyes widened.

"Siento que mi corazón

166

es de dos corazónes..."

Rosa clutched Marisol's arm. *"Carlita! ¿Qué en el nombre de Dios?"*

"It must be my tablet," whispered Marisol. "My playlist, *sí?"*

"Un centenar,
un mil mil mil mil..."

The creature raised its hands to its head. "How is it possible? Are there others?" It looked from the sisters to the direction of the magnificent voice. The next phrase offered a subtle catch in the breath, a throb of yearning in the voice:

"Uno por cada caricia
que deseo de ti..."

Not-Molly shambled back toward the sound of singing.

Marisol felt tears in her eyes. *"¡Ay, Carlos! Te bendiga."*

The sisters ran up the ramp to the gate, where Marisol swiped the key card with trembling hands. Carlita's voice soared louder and louder, leaping against the concrete overhead.

"Uno por cada,
un mil mil mil mil..."

As they climbed into the Plymouth, the air burst with thumping bass, trumpet fanfare and wild guitars. The car windows rattled with the volume of it. Rosa's tires squealed as she gunned the car through the bowels of the parking garage to the entrance at the street, just in time to meet the flashing lights of the police.

The sisters waited safely at the police station until the officers returned.

The sergeant brought them into her private office. They sat in chairs of well-worn brown leatherette before a glass covered desk. The sergeant frowned at an image on her hand-held for a moment before turning it for the sisters to see. "Is this the intruder you saw?"

The image showed a figure lying supine in the deeper trench, its head and neck bent at an impossible angle.

"Yes. That's the one. But what happened to it?"

The sergeant drummed a finger on her desk. "Am I correct that this, ah, perpetrator has something to do with the Anomaly?"

"Yes, I am certain of it!" said Marisol. "It killed Dr. Whitehorse!"

"I'm sorry, Dr. Salvia, but the Department of the Interior has instructed us not to pursue investigations regarding the Anomaly. We've contacted them and they are partnering with the FBI to send a team out. When they arrive they will do what needs to be done regarding Dr. Whitehorse."

"But what happened? Is it dead? How did it get killed?" demanded Rosa.

"The suspect seems to have fallen and broken its neck. The coroner is examining the body and will give the report to investigators. They will be in touch shortly. Until then they've asked that you do not speak of the incident to others."

Rosa leaned forward and placed a hand on the edge of the desk. "It was an extraterrestrial!"

Marisol straightened in her chair. "No, no. It was a being from the future! It talked about taking slaves from the past to use in the future. You heard it."

"I only heard it calling your name, using Dr. Whitehorse's voice."

"When it talked to *El Condor*, remember?"

"What?" Rosa's eyebrows rose. "Why would it talk to *El Condor*?"

"Because...you..." Marisol grew confused. Had her sister become so absorbed in her role that she had forgotten she had played it? Trauma did strange things to people.

The sergeant shook her head. "We can't speculate. When the investigators get here they will consider all the evidence and will find an answer, I'm sure."

They left the sergeant's office. An officer brought an armload of possessions. "Here are the things you described."

Rosa gathered up the bedraggled form of her costume. Its feathers had crumpled. Its long neck had snapped in half. It was absent its skull and one of its long wing-bones.

"What happened to *El Condor*?" said Marisol. "He looks like he's been trampled! The parade is next week—will there be time to repair him?"

Rosa shrugged. "If his neck is shorter, and he is missing a few feathers, who will know?"

"Here is your nettablet, Doctor," said the officer. "We've sent an image of its internal memory to the investigators. You can have it back now."

Marisol took it from him and brushed the dirt from its cover.

"I don't see how those *pequeñito* speakers could have made such loud music," said Rosa.

"I must have dropped it near the concrete beams, where the acoustics amplified it."

"I guess that was it—or that we were so frightened it sounded louder than it was!" Rosa gazed into her face. "You look so tired. Your poor hand all blistered, your arm all swollen—Do you want me to stay until Tia Nora gets here to take you to the clinic?"

"No, go ahead. I'll be fine. You must see to *El Condor*."

Rosa left, and Marisol waited quietly for her ride. She opened the

cover of her tablet. A smashed marigold rested on the darkened screen—
it must have dropped from *El Condor*. She looked at her dim reflection
and then smiled. She pulled the jack of the ear-buds from their input.
"Carlos? Was it you after all? You are a week early, *chica. Pero gracias*."

MOUNDVILLE REVISITED

BY LOUISE HERRING-JONES

THE GREAT SOUTHERN TRAIN FROM PHILADELPHIA slowed to a stop at Birmingham's Union Station. Among several observant first-class passengers, a trim woman with smooth skin and dark, but graying, hair gazed at a colossal statue reclining in pieces beside the tracks. Harriet Knorr watched from her enclosed cabin, protected by closed windows from the murky plume and cinders billowing from the smokestack of the steam engine pulling the train. Her fashionably waved hair remained in perfect order, her traveling suit starched and unwrinkled.

The statue had not fared as well. Sandaled feet, legs, torso, arms, hands, and head rusted in the humid air. The giant's slowly oxidizing hammer pointed west toward Harriet's final destination, a city of ancient mounds. Her new employer Clarence Moore, a retired Philadelphia paper company tycoon, directed excavations near the Black Warrior River during this eleventh month of a second year of discoveries, having begun his Alabama work in 1905.

Harriet sighed, reflecting on the dismal condition of the statue and wondering about the state of the antiquities to be found in her new job. "Look on my works, ye mighty, and despair," she quoted.

"Excuse me, Ma'am," drawled the conductor as he opened the door to her compartment. An enormous blond moustache and mutton-chop sideburns dwarfed his reddened face. "Ticket, please," he said through the thicket of whiskers.

She held out the strip of notched cardstock. "What is that by the tracks?"

"Vulcan, back home from the 1904 St. Louis World's Fair. It won first prize for metallurgy." He punched another hole in her ticket. "Traveling on to Moundville today?"

"That's correct." She returned the ticket to her valise. "Why was the Vulcan left here?"

"Returned after the fair closed, about a year ago. They'll move him somewhere permanent soon enough." The conductor closed the door.

Harriet shook her head at Southern lassitude. Appreciating efficiency and deploring its absence, she had trained and worked as a nurse for years. Her contract to the Army during the war in Cuba, spent

171

with blood up to her elbows in surgical wards, had enforced her resolve to work hard and strive for order, essential values men often chose to ignore.

Leaving a magnificent statue in ruins annoyed her. Women like her patron and mentor Sara Yorke Stevenson lectured about modern archaeology and struggled to preserve and archive artifacts discovered. Aside from a few wives, it was a rare woman who worked in the field alongside her male colleagues. Harriet intended to correct that gap in her gender's relative progress. After all, saving the great works of mankind might take a woman's governance.

The door opened again. The conductor stood in the narrow aisle. His nostrils flared and his whiskers bristled with the hot air of heavy breathing and unrighteous indignation. "You're moving to the colored car."

An ebony-skinned porter swept into her first-class compartment and removed her trunk.

"Wait, I don't want to change cars," Harriet said. "My father is white."

"And your mother?"

"My mother was mulatto."

"The one-drop rule applies," the conductor said. "If you have even one drop of Negro blood, you are colored and cannot mix with white folks. That's the law in Alabama."

The conductor reached for her valise. She clutched the bag to her chest. "The railroad must afford me equal accommodations."

"No, only what our customs dictate." He lowered his voice. "Don't pout at me. A lady in the dining car reported you. No colored folk allowed in first class. You will either move to a car with others of your own kind or get off the train. Your choice. I can't stand here all day."

She nodded. He held out two coins. "Your refund from first-class to coach fare." She opened her gloved hand and he dropped the silver quarters onto her palm.

She pushed back a lock of curly salt-and-pepper tinged hair that had strayed from beneath her hat. Harriet wondered if she had been identified as colored due to her inherited from her mother's African and Creek Indian ancestors mixed with the pale Pennsylvania "Dutch," actually German, heritage of her father and his kin. But she had learned not to argue when the color line imposed itself firmly, dividing her life into clear shades of black and white without any compromising gray.

Harriet swept out the door with the dignity of a New England-educated nurse and a veteran of the recent war. She said nothing more but vowed silently that these Southern bigots would not delay her access to the excavations.

Harriet reached the Moundville station as the sun slipped beneath the horizon. Her cousin Joel Prince and his adolescent daughter Beulah waited on the modest platform. On her last childhood visit to the town, Joel had worn a boy's short pants and ran barefoot through cotton fields he worked with his parents. Beulah was not born until 1894, the year the town's name was changed from 'Carthage' to 'Moundville' in recognition of the mounds of unknown origin sited in those same cotton fields on the town's periphery. Joel now stood over six feet tall. His daughter bloomed on the verge of young womanhood.

She waved vigorously as Harriet stepped down from the train. Joel wore washed-out overalls and a stained white shirt that had seen better days. Beulah's gingham dress was so faded that it appeared to be a colorless gray. A shapeless bonnet had slipped back from her cornrow-braided hair but remained tied at the neck.

Harriet struggled to straighten her hat and smooth her mangled curls. Coal ash and cinders blown through the opened windows of the coach car had turned her petrolatum hair ointment into dirty goo.

Joel lifted her trunk to his massive shoulders, crossed by overall straps, while Beulah greeted her with open arms. "Cousin Harriet, how wonderful it is to meet you. You are a sight for sore eyes."

"I had hoped to make a better appearance when we met." Harriet straightened her suit jacket and leaned over to hug Beulah, holding her valise behind the girl's back. "I've never traveled in a railway car with open windows before."

"Welcome to Alabama," said Joel. He led the way to a mule-drawn wagon. He lifted the trunk onto the wagon's wooden bed and helped Harriet onto the plank seat. He and Beulah hopped up and sat on either side, with Harriet squeezed into the middle with the valise clutched on her lap.

"What happened to the depot?" Harriet asked. "It seemed much larger before. Or have I just grown up?"

Joel faced Harriet. He appraised her in a toe-to-head assessment. His inspection made her feel uncomfortable, especially given their close relationship as second cousins and his status as a widower.

"You have certainly grown, Harriet, but you are right. The depot is much smaller. The tornado ripped the old building apart." He paused and chewed his lip. "Remember, I wrote to you when my wife was killed?"

"How terrible," Harriet said.

Beulah looked up, tears in her eyes. "I will never forget the day my mother died. January 22, 1904."

Joel reached over Harriet to pat his daughter on the shoulder. "None of us will ever forget. Hush, now, my Beulah, my beauty. Let's not cry in front of our guest when she's just arrived. We can all visit Mama's grave after Sunday service and pay our respects."

"I would like that," Harriet said.

Joel nodded. "The tornado destroyed the old depot and most of the buildings in town. A whole lot of homes and cabins are gone, too." He pointed to foliage along the railroad tracks. "It twisted those trees like they was matchsticks. Stripped them naked but didn't kill them. Growing back now."

He gave Beulah's arm a final pat. "That's what we have to do, too. Grow back."

Beulah dried her eyes and cheered up quickly as excitable youngsters sometimes do. With keen interest, she told Harriet about Clarence Moore's and his companion Dr. Milo Miller's arrival in The Gopher. They had tied the stern-wheeler at a makeshift dock on the Black Warrior River, just below the bluff where the mounds were located.

"He sent one of his diggers to the house this morning. They want to see you tonight, no matter how late you get in."

Harriet fidgeted with her hat ribbons. "I can't meet them on their boat, not alone."

"You have us," Joel replied. "Beulah's been dying to see inside that fancy steamboat of his."

He tapped the reins to the mule's back. The wagon jolted forward. Beulah smiled. She clasped her newfound cousin's arm, leaning against her and chatting about excavations the previous year.

The mile-long journey in the bumpy wagon passed quickly. Not far from the station, they crossed over the same railroad track on which she had traveled. A field road led them through stripped and dying cotton plants to a bluff overlooking the river. The lanterns of The Gopher reflected brightly on the dark waters below them.

"Just think on it. Daddy's worked for years plowing and picking Mr. Prince's cotton, but you'll be mixing with him and those Yankee gentlemen, just like you were white folks." Beulah pulled up her bonnet and hopped down from the wagon. Harriet waited until Joel helped her down from the rig.

"Mr. Moore is my employer and we're both from Philadelphia," Harriet said, countering the girl's naïve presumption. "This is not a social call."

"All the same, it's got folks around her talking about how well you've done for yourself up North," Beulah said. "Makes me want to leave home and get some more book learning." She smiled, but Joel grabbed her arm.

"Don't you dare think about leaving. Life wouldn't be the same without you."

He turned to Harriet. "Don't you be giving her any uppity ideas. Don't want my baby girl ending up stranded in a big city with nowhere to go but a good-time house."

Harriet blushed at the reference to a a brothel. "Please, that is not a fit subject for her young ears or for mixed company," she said. "Beulah would never do such a thing and more education would be good for her."

Joel shook his head but said no more on the issue. "Your trunk will be fine up here with the mule, too heavy to haul off, but I wouldn't leave your bag if you've got money or papers in it. You've been holding it mighty tight the whole ride through."

"I can carry it. Would you assist me to the water's edge?"

They walked side-by-side, Joel steadying her as they descended the bluff although she managed well in her laced, low-heeled boots. Beulah scampered before them, as agile as a young doe in spite of her long skirt.

As they neared The Gopher, two men came out on the upper deck and leaned over the railing. Both wore light-colored suits, with loosened ties, and had the graying hair and beards of middle-age. The smaller man displayed a luxurious moustache. One of his eyelids drooped. He raised his hand in salute. Dark liquor shimmered within the crystal glass he held aloft.

"Miss Knorr, delighted to make your acquaintance."

Harriet planted her feet on the even ground alongside the boat's lower deck. "Mr. Moore?"

"Clarence Bloomfield Moore of Philadelphia and owner of The Gopher. This rather taciturn gentleman is Dr. Milo G. Miller, my boon companion, secretary, physician, and surveyor." Milo nodded but did not speak.

Harriet smiled. "Permission to come aboard, sir, with my cousins Joel Prince and Beulah."

"Permission granted," Clarence said.

They stepped onto the deck and ascended the staircase to the upper level. Clarence offered deck chairs and refreshment. All sat, but declined drinks, Harriet alluding to Beulah's young age and the lateness of the hour. "Have you injured your eye, Mr. Moore? I'd be happy to look at it for you."

"Thank you, but it's an old tennis injury. Nothing to worry about, just slumps when I'm tired or frustrated."

Harriet nodded, wondering if Clarence was tired, frustrated, or both. "Why did you wish to see me tonight?" she asked.

"Your services may not be needed after all," Milo replied. "We've placed a number of trial holes on Mound Q, the main reason we are back at Moundville, but none have produced any burials."

"No burials, no skeletons. No skeletons, no artifacts," Clarence added.

"I've come all this way," Harriet said, opening her valise. "I have my recommendation letter from Mrs. Stevenson and my record of service during the recent war in Cuba."

"I'm certainly not suggesting that I renege on my contract with you or the promised payment," Clarence added, "but without skeletons to excavate and reassemble, I have nothing for you to do."

"I had so hoped to perform work in the field," Harriet said, closing her satchel.

"And so you shall, if we find some graves." Clarence turned to Joel. "Haven't I seen you working in Mr. Prince's field, picking cotton and driving a wagon?"

"Yes, sir."

"I've had no luck talking to any of the farm hands," Clarence said, "and neither has Dr. Miller." He looked at Harriet and held up his glass, his index finger pointing at her and his eyelid sagging so low he appeared to wink. "Do you think you might have more luck?"

"I'll see what I can do," Harriet said, trying to ignore Joel's subtle head shaking and his mouthed "no."

Beulah asked to see the parlor and their hosts escorted them into the onboard residence. The lavish furniture and pleated drapes looked more suitable for a public office in Philadelphia: velvet, gold-fringed, the drapes tied back with matching tasseled strands. Beulah, an expert seamstress in spite of her youth, studied the draperies to capture their shape for copying.

Harriet said her good-byes, promising to return on the morrow with any news of burial sites. They walked up the bluff path to the wagon.

"Harriet, didn't you see my signal?" Joel asked. "We done told them there's nothing more here, but they came back anyhow."

Harriet tossed her valise onto the plank seat and faced her cousin. "Why do you want to stop their work?"

"A man, Captain somebody, has been coming around to the sharecropper cabins, says he'll pay hard cash for any arrowheads or old pots we find."

"I wouldn't trust a grave robber who promises you'll get a fair price," Harriet said. "If Moore will pay you and your friends to help dig, would you trade the mere chance of selling a stolen artifact for honest, paid work? Moore donates his finds to museums around the country where anyone can see and study them. Children like your Beulah can learn something instead of stuffing priceless antiquities away in private collections."

Joel's forehead wrinkled. "Don't know that I understand everything you're saying, but I'm nothing if I'm not an honest man. I won't help a thief. What do we do?"

"Do you know where there are Indian graves that aren't on the mounds? Moore's Natural Sciences Academy reports show that he dug on most of the mounds and some of the grounds below. He worked here in the spring and couldn't explore all the fields because they were planted in cotton. Do you know what areas he did *not* excavate when he visited last year?"

Beulah frowned. "I picked cotton after he dug here before. He kept mostly to the mounds."

"Why weren't you in school?" Harriet asked.

"They let school out for cotton picking, but I'm thirteen now. That's too old for school."

"We'll talk about that later," Harriet said. "Joel, what do you remember?"

"I don't think he dug close to the mound farthest from the river. There are trenches on each side of it. The ground is heavy and hard to plow, but it's rich, black dirt with some clay." Joel paused. "Sometimes the plow turns up arrowheads, sometimes bones."

"Bones mean burials," Harriet said, paraphrasing Clarence. Is there anyone local who dowses for water? Maybe they could find graves."

"I don't go along with that hoodoo business," Joel said. "The Primitive Baptist Church goes by the *King James Bible*, 'Thou shall not suffer a witch to live.'"

"No, no," Harriet stammered, "No witch killings, please."

"Just saying."

"I think it's best we drop the dowsing idea. Will you bring me back tomorrow and show where we might find some burials?"

"You think Moore will pay us?"

"We'll be sure of it before you show him the burial grounds."

"Let's get home," Beulah said. "I'm so hungry I could eat this here mule. I made cornbread and purple-hulled field peas for dinner."

"Sounds better than eating your good mule," Harriet said. "We'll need lunch tomorrow, too."

"I'll pack a basket if you'll let me come along. Please, Daddy, can I come, too?"

"Only if you feed the chickens first."

"Sure enough," Harriet replied for her.

Joel chuckled. "Now that's the Harriet I remember. You can sure enough take the girl out of the country, but you can't take the country out of the girl."

With the wagon fully loaded with lunch baskets, shovels and neighbors, Joel brought Harriet, Beulah, and four burly friends back to the fields early the next morning. The men walked over the ground between the trenches, kicking up dirt and talking about items found in the past. They dug a few shallow holes and sent Beulah for Clarence and Milo when they found bones and pot shards. Clarence hired the men as extra local experts to aid his own crew. He also gave Beulah a position as Harriet's assistant.

Two weeks and many trial holes later, the crew had established excavations in a rectangular strip 172 feet long and over 45 feet broad at its widest point, all between the trenches identified by Joel and surveyed by Milo. Clarence personally supervised the work, walking among the diggers and making extensive notes of skeletons and artifacts revealed.

Joel worked in an area close enough to Harriet that she could hear him speak. "Except for my cousin's quick thinking, we wouldn't have had any work at all after the cotton picking," he said to his friends. She smiled and smoothed her hair back where it had escaped the rows that Beulah had braided in. Sweat dripped from her forehead and dampened her cotton blouse and the waistband of her skirt, both also stained with streaks of dirt and clay. Beulah had hastily sewn the outfit for Harriet to wear when the month of November had broken records for its warm weather. The girl dressed the same, bore the same muddy stains, and imitated Harriet's every move, even pronouncing some words, like "skool" for "school," with a distinct Pennsylvanian accent.

The two women, old and much younger, worked beside Milo. At his direction, Beulah drew diagrams of each set of bones found. Her general education might have been cut short, but her skills as a seamstress transferred readily into drawing skeletal and artifact diagrams.

Harriet's work was hands-on, within the excavations, just as she had hoped it would be. Trusting her nurse's skilled judgment and guided by Milo's experience, she separated one set of bones from another and adults' remains from those of children's. Her gloved hands, coated with dirt and red clay, straightened bones that had been disturbed by other burials. The ancient residents had interred their dead side-by-side as well as stacked layer upon layer. Separating individual skeletons presented a continuous puzzle which Harriet relished solving. Beulah recorded the results in her drawings.

"Dr. Miller, have you seen very many bones like this?" Harriet held up a femur marked by irregular erosions along the length of the bone.

"Miss Knorr, put on an extra pair of gloves. If I'm not mistaken, that pitting is a sign of syphilis. I doubt there is much risk of infection but better safe than sorry." He held up a tibia with a distinct periosteal node along its crest. "Did you encounter the disease during the war?"

Harriet dropped the femur as if it had grown hot. "We saw more cases than we expected to find. The men called it the 'Spanish disease.'" She pulled on a second pair of thick cotton gloves, yanking the ends down as far up her arm as they would stretch. "What do you want to do with these?" She gingerly picked up the femur and set it aside.

"Since the Army treats syphilis, let's send them to their doctors. If Clarence is right and these remains are pre-Columbian, they will support my theory that the disease began in the New World."

"Fascinating," Harriet said. She sorted through bones, looking for necrosis and other signs of syphilis. "Even with the risk, I'd rather sort through remains than lose yellow fever patients."

Milo looked up at her. "I understand completely. At least these poor souls are already dead."

"Oh, my goodness, look at this," Harriet said. She brushed away dirt and held up a round talisman as wide as her palm for Milo to inspect. Tiny indentations and lines dotted and decorated the disc in an irregular pattern.

"That's a shell gorget. Where did you find it?"

"Between these two skulls, the adult and an infant," Harriet said.

"Quite a find," Milo said. "Let's sketch it and get it back in place. Did you mark where you found it."

"Yes, I already have."

He handed the artifact to Beulah. "Be very careful and be sure to copy any holes as well as etchings."

"Happily," Beulah said. She drew a quick sketch of the gorget.

Harriet watched over her shoulder. "It appears to be intentionally carved that way. A rather stylized design, maybe a serpent of some sort or several snakes?"

When Beulah finished her rough drawing, Milo replaced the gorget in the exact spot Harriet had marked within the excavated grave. He left in search of Clarence and his camera. The two women rested in the shade as the shadows lengthened and the shade of trees at the edge of the field finally reached their spot near the resettled artifact.

Late in the afternoon a week later, Harriet and Beulah drank from teacups as the gentlemen saluted Clarence's successes with jiggers of gold medal-winning Jack Daniel's Old No. 7 whiskey. A tanned man with handlebar moustaches and long hair joined them for the evening. Self-proclaimed "Captain" C. W. Riggs dressed in tasseled buckskins and Western-style high-heeled riding boots. Joel snarled at the pretentious dealer whenever he approached the display of grave goods including palettes, pots, pipes, ear plugs, gorgets, and teardrop pendants. Some were plain but as many others were decorated in distinct Moundville styles, the rattlesnake and other animal designs, an eye in a hand, and interchanging bones and skulls, among other more abstract patterns. The antiquities awaited further photography and academic inspection, spread upon a plaid tablecloth Beulah had provided.

"Really, my old friend, you should allow me to sell these trinkets on commission," said Riggs. "They would draw good prices from well-endowed collectors."

"I don't need the money and museums welcome my contributions." Clarence drank from the upper shot of his jigger. "I prefer to become a part of history rather than sell it to the highest bidder."

"How noble," Riggs replied. He picked up the gorget Harriet had found, now thoroughly cleaned. "This one is interesting, but badly damaged. Look at the holes across its face. Why don't I sell it for you?" He closed his large hand around the artifact.

Harriet lunged across the room and pried the gorget from the man's fist. "You are not taking this to sell." She pointed to the winding bend etched and perforated into the talisman. "These are not damaged but quite intentional. The etchings are clearly a snake motif. These holes match the stars in the constellation Scorpius. It's only visible on the southern horizon in early evening during the summer. The local Creeks call it the 'Great Serpent.' She gently tapped a slightly larger hole at the top of the inter-looping image. "The star Antares is the Serpent's eye."

"Are you taking lessons in archaeology from a woman?" Riggs asked, turning to Clarence. "And a colored woman at that?"

"Don't presume to talk down to my staff. I daresay Miss Knorr has better academic credentials than you and certainly a commendable record of public service. She probably saw Scorpius while nursing our soldiers in Cuba although she is too humble to admit it." Clarence dropped his jigger on a table. He lifted the bottle of fine Tennessee whiskey as if to pour another shot but set it down, also. "I daresay she's seen more war than you have, *Captain*."

180

Riggs stepped forward and Joel emerged from the shadows. Clarence held up his hand, stopping him before he did anything that could warrant Riggs's lawful defense against a "colored" man under the Jim Crow laws.

But Clarence's deep mustachioed frown and drooping eyelid also gave him a menacing look. "Riggs, why you are no more than a tomb thief in buckskins. Since we have no further business to discuss and I'd hate to see any of my artifacts go missing, I suggest you leave, *now*."

"*I never*. Defending a Negress against a white man." Riggs shoved his jigger against the nearest table and stalked out of the parlor, down the steps, and off the steamboat.

"Dr. Miller, if Riggs comes back and touches anything, you have my permission to shoot him."

Clarence turned to Harriet. "Intriguing theory, Miss Knorr. I wrote in my field notes that this piece is 'highly stylized.' Do you think describing it as bearing a 'conventionalized serpent design' would be more appropriate?"

The first December frost covered the ground when Clarence and Milo said farewell to Harriet, Joel, Beulah, and the other local workers.

"I leave the restoration in your capable hands, Miss Knorr, but I'm sure your cousins could oversee the final work," Clarence said, gazing at Harriet. "I value your judgment and would have you accompany us to Crystal River."

"I have promised to help Beulah prepare for her matriculation at the Normal School in Huntsville. Dr. Miller's example has inspired her to become a teacher." Harriet gripped the girl's hand and Beulah graced Clarence with one of her inimitable smiles. "As much as I would like to do more field work, a lady must think of her reputation. I couldn't possibly steam all the way to Florida with you two gentlemen, not without a chaperone."

"I quite understand," Clarence said, extending his hand toward Harriet.

Harriet took Clarence's hand in her own and firmly shook it. "Please give my regards to Mrs. Stevenson."

"You won't be returning to Philadelphia?" asked Milo.

"Not right away. I'll stay here with Beulah and Mr. Prince, perhaps explore my own origins. We may visit the Vulcan statue when it's finally fitted together in Birmingham." She lowered her voice. "And make sure that Captain Riggs does not return."

Joel nodded and smiled, admitting his joint role as a guardian of the mound city.

Beulah clapped her hands when The Gopher's steam whistle blew. The gentlemen archaeologists steamed away to Crystal River and their next excavation.

After Clarence's and Milo's departure and pursuant to their final instructions, the local diggers carefully refilled the graves excavated at Moundville. The soft soils uncovered would not wash away. Clarence's team had uncovered 174 graves in the area between the trenches. Except for the bones sent to the Army's doctors for study, the ancient dead rested again beneath the dark earth their bodies had enriched.

ENCANTADO

BY MICAH HYATT

MORENA'S LIGHT SWEPT ACROSS the river bottom, hardly penetrating the murky brown water. The temperature was a cold contrast to the Venezuelan summer heat topside, but she was too absorbed in her work to notice. She raked her fingertips through the sediment, searching for the angular thing she thought she'd seen jutting from the mud.

What was it? Another spearhead? A potsherd?

The Arawak were known for their pottery, but this would be the first potsherd the expedition had found. Unlike a spearhead, which could have been dropped by traveling hunters, a potsherd might mean there had been a settlement nearby. Morena knew her father would be elated. A pleasant daydream began to play in her mind where her discovery single-handedly saved his expedition's funding.

Something large and pale darted towards Morena out of the murk, jolting her from her thoughts. Before she could react, the thing slammed into her and tore her light from its shoulder-mount.

Morena bit down hard on her rebreather's mouthpiece, trying not panic as the muddy darkness fell over her. Dizziness came before she realized how hard she was breathing.

Calm down Morena, she told herself. *It's probably just a fish.*

There were crocodiles in the Orinoco, but they were extremely rare—a fact she tried her best to remember. She thought of swimming for the surface, the vague hint of brightness above, but then the object she was looking for would be lost for certain.

Instead, she swallowed her fear and swam back down to the muck, fanning her arms out. The diving light could not have gone far. It weighed too much to drift.

Morena's heart leaped when her fingertips traced the light's familiar shape; she snatched it up and tried toggling it back on. To her relief, the light still worked. Its shaky beam cut through the opaque brownness, illuminating motes of organic debris that fell like snow from above.

Morena saw the thing returning for her.

It was a man-sized river dolphin, a boto, sleek and pale-bellied, with a large hump on its back. It circled her with playful curiosity in its eyes. Morena smiled broadly and reached out her hand. The dolphin nudged her fingers with its beak, then twisted upside down, did a loop, and looked back as if to see if she was impressed.

Yes, you are quite handsome, Boto, Morena thought, *but I have no time for play*.

She dove back to the river bottom, trying to find the exact spot she'd seen the artifact. The boto followed, gliding along beside her. When she raked her hands through the mud, the boto mimicked her, poking around with its beak. But eventually it grew bored and swam off.

After thirty minutes of searching without success, Morena cursed. Her air was nearly gone. She lingered as long as she could, still hoping to be the one to save her father's expedition. But whatever she thought she had seen was lost to the mud. Sighing, she righted herself and kicked for the surface.

The boto decided she was interesting again. It returned, sliding itself between Morena's legs, doing corkscrews around her. Then it nuzzled her in the ribs, hard. Morena turned back to scold it, and a glint of gold caught her eye.

In the boto's beak was a gold ring. Morena gasped, reaching for it, but the boto drew back, bobbing up and down as if to say, First, we play!

The boto swam up. Morena chased.

The water brightened, became clearer, warmer, and the current stronger. Now Morena could see the bottom of her father's houseboat, and the boto waiting for her in its shadow.

She swam close, and the boto circled her, weaving, brushing up against her body. She tried to take the ring, but it was too fast for her, and seemed to enjoy the game. They twined together, like a dance, until Morena was exhausted.

The boto stopped an arm's length away, looking very satisfied.

Hesitantly, Morena reached out her hand. The boto did not pull away this time; it opened its beak just as her fingers touched the ring, as if gifting it to her. Morena would have laughed if the respirator were not in her mouth. She nodded to the boto in thanks, and it seemed to understand, because it began to frolic beneath the waves.

She wondered what treasure she had clutched in her fist. Given to her by a boto, like some kind of fairytale.

Morena's head broke the surface just aft of the houseboat. The sun had begun to set while she was below, and the waves were like liquid rubies.

Jim, her boyfriend, stood shirtless on deck. He was yelling something, waving his hand and pointing at the water. Morena felt the boto against her legs again. She pulled the respirator out of her mouth and laughed.

Jim ran to the edge of the boat with one of the long wooden poles they used to push off from shore. He looked terrified, yelling, "-ark! -ena! -ark!"

Shark, Morena realized. He thinks the boto is a shark. Jim was an American and he knew nothing about the river or its ecology. He was terrified of water and barely knew how to swim. They'd met in college, and Morena had only brought him along on this expedition so he could finally meet her dad. She was beginning to think it was a mistake.

Jim thrust the pole into the water, trying to keep the boto away from her. "Stop it, Jim!" she yelled. "It's ok!"

But he either couldn't hear or didn't believe her. He actually managed to hit the boto with the pole. The impact was solid; Jim lost his balance and fell forwards, overboard.

Morena swam to him and threw her arm around his neck, trying to stop his manic thrashing. He pulled her under, and she gulped a mouthful of river water. *Idiot!* She was too worn out for this.

A life-preserver splashed into the water near Morena, and Jim practically fought her for it. She looked up to see's her father's dark form blocking out the sun, holding the life-preserver's rope, pulling them in.

It was like a metaphor. A frieze that explained everything about her life. Father looming above, his disappointment evident in his furrowed brow, and Jim pulling her under.

Morena's father was a tenured archeologist at the Universidade de Brasília. He'd been born in a favela, a shanty town made of plywood and cardboard. But now he was a respected professor. Morena had tried to follow in his footsteps, but recent...occurrences had made her think it unlikely she would succeed.

Five minutes later, Morena and Jim crawled onto the deck. Jim flopped down on a pile of rope. Rodrigo, Morena's father, stood over him, yelling "Shark! Shark!", slapping his knee and laughing.

"I didn't think you saw it," Jim said, still gasping.

"There aren't any sharks in this river," Morena said, too furious to even look at him. "It was a boto."

"Boto?"

Morena stood up and started pulling off her dive gear. "A river dolphin. They're harmless. I can't believe you hit him."

Rodrigo stopped mocking Jim and grew serious. "Que fragmento?" he asked, looking at Morena with hopeful eyes. She shook her head.

"Pah!"

"I found something else though."

She opened her hand and showed him the golden ring. She could instantly see it was not some wedding band dropped by an unlucky tourist. The metal was dented, imperfect, and slightly verdigrised, which indicated an amalgam of copper.

Rodrigo took it from her and held it up to the dying sunlight. He whistled.

Morena grinned. "El Dorado?"

Rodrigo shook his head. "Devaneios." Daydreams.

"Legend puts it not far from here," Morena says. "Lake Parime is only twenty kilometers away, and the city was built on its banks. This river would have been a tributary. We should look for more."

"Pah! E lixo." It's rubbish.

Jim came over to see what was so interesting. His blonde hair was slicked back, and his skin glistened. He was too beautiful. Right now, Morena hated him.

"We should stay here another day," Morena said, taking the ring back from her father. "I want to see if I can find more."

"E lixo," Rodrigo said. He pointed towards the stern of the ship. "Upriver. Fragmento."

"If we stay here, maybe we will find something better," Morena said with a grin.

Rodrigo laughed and shook his head.

"What did you find?" Jim asked.

Morena grit her teeth, opened her hand, and showed him the ring.

"Oh, wow! Is that gold?"

Morena nodded curtly.

"Vaminos, Boto," Rodrigo said, pushing Jim's shoulder. He pointed to the cabin. "Adults talking. Go make supper, eh?"

Jim looked hurt.

"Leave him alone, papa."

Rodrigo turned his head and spat over the railing. In portuguese he said, "Por que? Esse peixe é mais provável tornar-se um homem do que ele é."

That night in the cabin they ate a meal of beans and rice, and fish grilled over a bunsen burner. Morena argued with her father all through dinner. He wanted to move on, look for potsherds and other mundanities. But a big find, Morena argued, something flashy that inferred the possibility of a real city of gold, would virtually guarantee his funding.

Morena begged him to stay where they were for just one more day. She could see her father's eyes light up when she talked about Sir Walter Raleigh, Pizarro, Von Hutten and Orellana, all of them searching for El Dorado, the city of gold. He was tempted. Just one more day, she urged.

He said, "If Raleigh didn't find it, what hope do we have?"

But in the end, he relented.

All through the conversation, Jim picked at his food, sullen and silent, as if he's wasn't listening. At the end of the meal, Rodrigo went to his bunk, leaving the two of them alone to clean up. Jim fumblingly tried to apologize for almost drowning her.

Later, Morena lay awake in her hammock, feeling the roll of the ship, listening to her father snore. Jim crept through the cabin to kneel beside her in the dark.

"Your father," Jim whispered. "He said a fish is more of a man than me."

"Your portuguese is getting better."

"This isn't working out, is it? He hates me."

Morena sighed. "He doesn't hate you. He barely even knows you."

"Then why would he say that?"

"It's a story. A Brazilian myth. He was trying to be clever."

To make Jim feel better, Morena told him the story of the boto.

In the legend the boto was an encantado, an enchanted being with the ability to change shapes at whim. She told him of how the boto swam along the river, looking for villages, listening for music and the laughter of girls. How the boto crawled onto the shore and used his magic to become a beautiful man, so beautiful no woman could keep her heart from being stolen. How he sought out lonely young women to take out on a night of drinking and dancing and debauchery. But he never stayed, the boto, always returning to the river before dawn.

When Morena began to tell how amazonian women who find themselves unexpectedly with child always blame it on the boto, the story hit too close to home. Morena fell abruptly silent.

It was a hard silence, and Morena was thankful for the creak of the houseboat and her father's snoring.

After a long while, Jim said, "I won't leave." He leaned in and tried to kiss her.

Morena pulled away. She's was not ready to be a mother, and when she thought about it she almost wanted to scream. How could she finish her degree and care for a baby? How could she have been so stupid?

"Do you still want me to talk to your dad?" Jim asked.

"I don't want to have to tell you to do everything," Morena snapped. *Be a man,* she caught herself starting to say, but bit it off.

The smell of frying fish and bananas woke Morena. Rodrigo and Jim were already up, and she watched them through slitted eyes. They seem to be getting along alright.

Jim brought a plate to her bunk, along with a cup of instant coffee. "Your dad has been telling me about El Dorado."

"Really? In english?"

Jim scratched the back of his neck. "Some, but he's been surprisingly helpful with my Portuguese."

"What did you expect? He teaches at University."

A loud thud caused both of them to turn their heads towards the deck. Roberto had just severed a fish's head with a machete. His bearded face grinned through the doorway at them as he tossed the bloody hunk into the river.

"Ok," Morena said. "I admit he can be intimidating. What did he say about El Dorado?"

"I asked him if the legends really put the city only twenty kilometers away. He told me about Lake Parime. El Dorado was supposed to have been built on its bank. The Tukano and the Piratapuias tribes called it the 'lake of milk.' But explorers searched for the lake for years without finding anything, and so no one believed that the lake existed."

Morena put a bit of fried banana in her mouth. "Not bad for a PolySci major. Go on."

"Well, back in the nineties a couple of geologists did a survey upriver from here. They found evidence of a massive lake exactly where Lake Parime was supposed to be. Their conclusion was that tectonic shifting had caused the lake to drain away a couple hundred years ago. So I asked him, if the lake turned out to be real, how come no one has found the city of gold yet?"

"I bet he said that there was no city of gold. That it was only a story to drive white men into the jungles to be eaten by the snakes and crocodiles and mosquitos."

"Something like that."

Rodrigo swaggered into the cabin. "Hola, lovebirds," he said. "I'm going ashore. No funny business while I'm away, eh?"

Morena frowned at her father. "I was hoping to dive."

"Do it when I get back. It's Saturday. I have to call the Universidade to make my report. Or— " he kissed his knuckles. "—goodbye funding." He gave her a wink, then shambled off. A moment later, Morena heard the dinghy splash down into the water.

"He can't make his reports from the boat?" Jim asked.

"Poor cell reception, but there's a phone in the village. He'll be gone for a couple of hours."

The sudden longing in Jim's eyes made Morena feel a bit nauseous. She drained her coffee, set her plate aside, and went out onto the deck. After briefly checking to make sure her father was out of sight, she began putting on her wetsuit.

"You're going down?" he asked incredulously.

"Yup. We're only gonna be here today. I want to make the most of it."

"What if something goes wrong? I don't think you should dive without your dad here."

Morena tapped a small black box with an led screen that was sewn onto the wrist of her suit. "Distress beacon. Sends out a sonar ping. There's another on my father's suit. If anything happens, he'll be able to find me before my air runs out."

Jim clenched his jaw. "You don't just have yourself to worry about, you know."

"Don't," Morena warned, pulling up her zipper.

It was good to be alone, with the only conversation taking place between heart and her lungs.

Underwater Morena could think clearly. If Jim didn't tell her father about the pregnancy, she would have to, and Rodrigo would know Jim was not man enough to do it himself.

It would end the relationship. That she was certain of. Regardless, she was keeping the baby. But she thought she would like it if they could make it work.

Morena swam down into the murk. She had no plan. An archeologist should go about their work systematically, but then again, she had little hope of finding any actual evidence of El Dorado. Her father was right—the ring she'd found meant nothing. Jewelry of that kind had been worn by every tribe in the area. But it was a nice dream, and she thought about it as she sank towards the bottom to gaze at the muck, looking for a good area to work.

She was near enough to the shoreline that she could see a few sunken trees, their dead limbs reaching out to snag her like great pale fingers. These she stayed well clear of. In addition to the dangers of being snagged, they could be the home of some poisonous water snakes.

She'd brought a tool with her this time, a small rake with very close set teeth. When she found a broad patch of mud, she worked the ground with it like a gardner, sifting through the sediment for the detritus of a dead civilization. She raked until her back began to ache. But there was nothing, and as time passed, she became disheartened. Patience was important for an archeologist to have, her father always said, but today she had none. So she gave up, and went for a swim.

In the murk it was difficult to tell which direction she was headed. She knew she should surface to get her bearings, but she did not want to go up. There were too many problems in the world above. So she swam on, wishing the boto from yesterday would come and play with her. Dolphins were better company than men.

She lost herself in the water, fantasizing that she found the ruins of El Dorado. Her father was so proud of her that when she told him she was pregnant, he did not even mind. What greater success could she ever have? Finishing her degree meant nothing next to uncovering the legendary city of gold.

Abruptly, the current shifted, and Morena felt it pulling her off to the side. While she was daydreaming, the river had grown shallow.

She saw the reason the current had changed. She was near the river wall, and in it was an opening—a yawning, dark mouth in the rock.

Morena swam close and shined her light in. The water was clearer inside. There was a long underwater tunnel full of jagged rocks about as wide as a small car and as tall as a man.

She thought it looked safe enough to at least take a peek. Curiosity dragged her in like an undertow.

Was she the first person to have ever seen the inside of this cave? She wondered how it was formed, entertaining theories that involve volcanoes. But she was no geologist, and no archaeologist yet either. This work study with her father was part of her junior year. She wondered if he would give her a pass once he learned he was going to be a grandfather.

The tunnel went on, took a sharp right and then turned downwards where it widened suddenly into a large cavern.

On a field trip in grade school, Morena and her class traveled to the city of Sete Logos to see the Gruta Rei do Mato, the Cave of the Forest King. She remembered being in awe of the stalagmites, rising like the pillars of a cathedral, and feeling that she had entered some kind of holy place. She remembered imagining that she could almost see the ghosts of the bandits who had taken refuge in the caves, and that they were watching her from the afterlife. This cavern was like that, but on a much larger scale.

The water in the cavern was clear and very cool. Sunlight could not reach here, and without her shoulder-light it would have been black as pitch. The thought frightened her, but she did not turn back.

Swimming up to the ceiling, she weaved her body between stalagmites, playing like a boto. It was interesting that there were stalagmites, she thought, because it meant this cave must have originally formed above water. Then something caused the water level to rise in the river and flooded it.

As she explored along the walls, she passed a narrow crack in the rock, and in it she saw something moving.

Morena circled around and shined her light into the crack. About ten feet away, she spied a jumble of debris, as if the crack had partially caved in. Something was stuck beneath the rocks, waving slowly. *Some kind of vegetable matter?* she thought. *A dead fish?* It lured Morena closer. The crack was just wide enough for her to fit through. She squeezed inside to get a better look, pulling herself along the walls with her hands.

It almost looked like a scrap of cloth, she thought. A little further in and she began to see shades of brown and white mixed in among the rubble, and she became almost certain she was looking at bones.

Careful not to let her rebreather's tanks bang against the stones above, Morena crawled to the end of the crack.

The waving thing was a strap of leather, nearly disintegrated. Morena's heart skipped a beat. Yes, those were bones, crushed beneath the pile of stones. She briefly considered if it would be safe to try and pick some of the stones away. It probably wasn't, but she did anyway, removing them one by one and setting them aside like a game of Jenga.

Beneath the rocks she uncovered a crushed human ribcage, partially clothed in leather. And then she found gold. A buckle of some kind, probably for a belt.

Caution forgotten, Morena quickly cleared more stones. She found fragments of a skull, gold noserings and earrings and a little golden knife. It was growing hard to see, but she kept at it, and was rewarded with a fractured femur and some ancient shell beads.

A theory formed in her head as she worked—What if El Dorado sank with Lake Parime?

What if it, when the lake drained, the city built on its shores had collapsed and been swallowed by the earth? The debris would have been sucked down, perhaps into an underground river, where they could have been swept along to be collected here and in other undiscovered caves.

The fading light began to agitate her, but Morena stayed at it, recovering everything she thought she could carry.

Then, with a sudden, horrible clarity, Morena realized why the light was fading.

In her hurry to get away from Jim, she had forgotten to swap her dive light's battery out for a new one.

Morena left her treasures where they lay and started backing out of the crack. However, it was slow going, crawling backwards, and she couldn't turn her head far enough to see over her rebreather's tanks and ensure they didn't bump into the jutting rocks.

By the time she was back into the cavern, the light was almost dead. She swam towards where she thought the tunnel to the surface was and found only the cave wall.

Morena stopped with her hands pressed against the wall and tried to remain calm. She checked her air gauge and saw that she had over an hour's worth left.

Feeling with her fingertips, Morena worked her way along the wall. *If I'm calm and methodical like papa taught me, I'll make it out,* she told herself.

The light only lasted a few minutes longer. She inched sideways, searching. Darkness enveloped her, and it felt like being buried alive. She began to tremble uncontrollably. With every bump in the stone and every crevice, she prayed the wall would open up into the tunnel. For a while she tried to keep time by counting her breaths. But in her panic, she lost track, and if a hundred breaths passed or a thousand, she could not say.

In the dark, she began to see things. Her father's disappointed face. Jim, propped up on his elbows, smiling at her. A boto swimming with a ring in its mouth. Hypoxic illusions.

She tried to clear her head. It meant her oxygen was almost gone, and she was breathing too much carbon dioxide. When her movements became lethargic, she became certain she was going to die.

Then the wall gave away beneath her hands.

She pressed into the tunnel, relief flooding over her. She surged forwards, kicking for the surface, promising herself she would never do anything so stupid ever again. And found herself wedged in a narrow, familiar space.

The crack. She had circled the cavern and come back to the same crack.

Morena choked back a sob. She lost control of her breathing. Hyperventilating, she swam back into the cave and made one last desperate search, bumping into stalagmites, ripping her wetsuit and her hands on sharp rocks. Her muscles burned from exertion without oxygen. She fought unconsciousness, raging at her own idiocy for coming into this cave alone, and the anger sustained her for a few moments longer.

The passage from consciousness to unconsciousness was smooth. She let go of the wall and drifted in the dark. When the seizures started, she spat her mouthpiece out, sucked in water, and dreamed.

Of a city of gold, its buildings ablaze in the sunlight, towering over a lake of milk.

A father and mother and child were playing together on the sandy shore. The father stopped midway through the game and said goodbye. He turned and walked into the lake, transforming into boto, for he was secretly an encantado, a shapeshifter.

The mother yelled for him to come back, but the boto only leaped from the water, higher and higher, trying to impress them, before diving back down, never to be seen again.

But Morena saw him now. He had sought her out to play. The

encantado nuzzled her with its beak, and in that instant he was no longer a dolphin but a beautiful man.

In Morena's dream, Jim came to her in the dark and wrapped his arms around her. He drew her along through the tunnel, and they swam together. Sometimes he became a boto again, but never for long.

And Morena thought, if only you would stay a boto, then perhaps I could love you.

GATE OF SUN, GATE OF MOON

BY ALVARO ZINOS-AMARO

AWUNA DRIFTS FOR A PERFECT MOMENT beneath the memory-pool's soothing, lapping turquoise wavelets.

Then she shunts.

Her dive takes her two hundred thousand years into the past. A new world coalesces around her. Gone are the warm, gentle waters of the memory-pool, replaced by the bracing, choppy eddies of her host's mind. That mind belongs to one Myriam Medina, a noted twenty-first-century Argentinian archeologist working in Bolivia. Awuna's pattern adapts to Myriam, and Myriam's mind receives her. It's a feeling quite unlike any other. Awuna is *in*.

On with the mission. Time to observe. Time to assess these people's sense of historical continuity and report back to the Commission.

Time to make a decision about who will be resurrected and who will remain dead.

The sun shines off the waters of Lake Titicaca in shimmering golden sheets, dazzling Myriam despite her sunglasses.

Jose Quebrasco, an expert on Tiwanaku archaeoastronomy and about fifteen years Myriam's junior, places his hand on her shoulder, seemingly unbothered by the glare. "You okay?"

She doesn't respond.

He pinches her shoulder gently.

At last Myriam sighs, relinquishing the lake's spell. Or is the lake really to blame? Though the instant of reverie has passed, Myriam can't shake the feeling that she's different, somehow, from who she was a minute earlier. But it would be folly to try to explain this to Jose when she lacks the words to explain it to herself. "Yes," she says. She removes his hand from her shoulder firmly, but with appreciation. "I'm fine."

She and Jose are eating their sandwiches—vegetarian with hot *llajwa* sauce for her, *sándwich de chola*, or roast pork, for him—about half a mile from the lake's shore. Myriam's eyes scan the horizon, then move back inward, finally coming to rest on a huge slab of rectangular volcanic rock

195

a few hundred feet away. *Una piedra cansada*, she thinks. A tired rock. That's what they call these abandoned artifacts: centuries ago, the Tiwanaku extracted them from a peninsular quarry and shipped them across the lake in reed boats. Competing coca-fuelled Tiwanaku communities then dragged the stone slabs over the land, on wooden rollers perhaps, and used them to craft spectacular temples and pyramids. And yet the tribes' strength must have faltered at times, or perhaps the elements interfered, because some stones never made it to their destinations. They were simply abandoned, over a thousand years ago, left here in the open. Myriam has a strange thought then: *Y si soy yo como una de las piedras cansadas?* What if she's like one of those rocks? What if she was intended for a purpose she will never fulfill, stuck somewhere between her point of origin and her destination? *Estoy cansada*, she thinks.

Then the sense of internal change returns, like she's carrying a new inner weight. Myriam's bones seem to sag. Her whole being succumbs to a deep, rending tremor of exhaustion.

"You look a little pale," Jose says. "Maybe we should get out of the sun."

Myriam's skin is dark brown, years of tanning crevassed with the fine wrinkles that come from perpetually worrying about grant money. The sun has never bothered her before. But again the feeling of ponderousness swells inside her. "Maybe you're right," she says.

They rise, she unsteadily. Jose helps her back to the camp site, an old-fashioned cluster of tents, portable toilets and equipment lockers.

During the fifteen minute trek Myriam can't help but reflect that after six months here she has little to show. Perhaps it's time to finally admit that her ambition to explain the recurring symbols of Tiwanaku textiles in terms of astronomy will never be realized. The grant money is about to run out. Meanwhile, Alex Rivas' sensationalist rival project has been a resounding success. The media has sent three documentary crews, maybe more, to interview Alex and his team about their "groundbreaking" work on Tiwanaku drug rituals. Myriam and her team have received exactly zero visitors.

When they reach the tents Myriam leans close to Jose and says, "I've noticed some of my team members exchanging worried looks these last few days. Camila and Alejandro. Flavia, Javier, Moïsejr. They're wondering if I've lost it, aren't they? Wondering if this whole project has been a waste of everyone's time."

Even Jose, who is technically working for Alex now but on loan to Myriam for two more weeks, has expressed doubts about the project. It was a long time ago, back in its conceptual stage. At the time Myriam bulldozed through his concerns, hard-headed, stubborn. *Perhaps a psycho-*

linguistic approach may be more useful, he had suggested. *Someone with a background in linguistics and semiotics may be better suited to decode the textiles.* She thought he was wrong then, and she still does now. The textiles, she believes, can be deciphered by careful study of solstice and equinox rituals, by the analysis of star charts and an understanding of how the Tiwanaku mythologized the cosmos. Yet sometimes at night, when she has trouble sleeping and the only thing she hears is the wind soughing against her tent, Jose's voice comes back to haunt her. *Maybe I should have listened to him,* she thinks. Jose was once a student of Myriam's at the Universidad de Rosario, and she has come to rely on his truthfulness over the years, to involve him in her decisions. So why, then, didn't she heed his advice this time?

"How do you feel about what you've accomplished?" he asks.

She raises her head. "We've kept busy," she says. True, but not exactly meaningful. Sisyphus kept busy too, especially in later life. "I'll admit that we've fallen a little short of my ultimate goal. But it was ambitious. You know that."

Jose nods. "Yes, of course."

Her voice quakes a little. "What do you think?"

Jose straightens his backpack. His brown eyes are covered by fancy reflecting Ray-Ban sunglasses. His thin nose and short black hair, gelled and neatly parted to one side as is fashionable with the locals, make him look like a Hollywood movie star from the silent era. "I think," he says finally, "that you're an amazing archaeologist with an astonishing track record."

She laughs ironically. "Until now."

"I didn't say that."

"You didn't have to."

Myriam fumbles with her bag. Alex has gotten to Jose, she thinks in anger. Alex has coached him on political correctness, has told him, "Say it this way, not that way, and the media will like you more." He has instructed him to be guarded, wary. As she searches Jose's face for traces of the young, puppy-eyed student she once knew, she realizes that man is gone. Instead Jose has become a mirror: all she sees when she studies him is a reflection of herself. Perception is what matters to him now, not personality. While she and her team labor in the uncomfortable camp site, Jose joins Alex and his group at the hotel, traveling an hour by bus each night and then an hour again each morning, wasting precious time. He's grown soft. He's lost the raw passion that made them dirt diggers in the first place. "What are you saying?" she demands. "Cut the crap. Tell me what you *really* think."

"I think your assessment is accurate," Jose says. He shakes his head. "You haven't accomplished what you set out to. But it was a tall order. A lot of sharp minds have taken a crack at those Tiwanaku rags. I'm sure something else more reasonable will turn up."

Her teeth grate at the condescension of his words. Tiwanaku "rags"—the old Jose would never speak so callously of artfully preserved cloths over thirteen hundred years old, painstakingly dated through accelerator mass spectrometry and seriation. But they're merely commodities to him now, means to an end. And "something else more reasonable": meaning a more modest problem, one whose difficulty will match her limited capacity for ratiocination.

To hell with him.

"You're on *their* side now, aren't you, Jose? You have no faith, no confidence—"

Just then the heat from the midday sun seems to join forces with another, more ancestral heat rising up from the sun-baked earth, and Myriam finds herself caught in the middle, trapped in this collision of invisible, rippling energies.

They are high, she thinks, high above the rest of the world. The *altiplano* where she has labored for half a year now is at thirteen thousand feet above the sea. The elevation seems to catch up with her all at once. Her breath becomes shallow. The air is thin. She hears Jose cry out as though from a distance. *I'm here, at Tiwanaku*, she wants to say. *The stone at the center of the world.* But her lips don't move. She falls to her knees as the world loses its center. It spins around and around, until she's thrown clear into the void.

Awuna has decided to take Myriam back, riding her mind in the process. This is rash behavior, and Awuna should know better. She should be following protocol. But playing it safe won't earn her the title of full-fledged Preserver. No. She must take risks. Her evaluation is almost over. Like Myriam, she's running out of time. Awuna must prove to the Temporal Commission that she's more than simply an apt evaluator of the distant past. She must demonstrate that she's willing to assume the responsibility of bringing back one ancient civilization while relegating another to the oblivion of exclusion from the Catalogue. "*You*, come back," she'll say to one civilization, and from the dust they'll return, while another civilization remains in the dust. Not a job for everyone. Requires a certain amount of chutzpah.

Awuna wants Myriam to make the breakthrough, so that her tribe can be saved. *Maybe*, Awuna reasons, *if Myriam can see for herself how the Tiwanaku lived, she will understand.*

Maybe.

198

Myriam opens her eyes and at once feels that things are different. The moon is out and the stars are visible against a black sky. The air has a new quality to it, harsher, more bitter, carrying wisps of a powerful incense. And it's colder. A lot colder. She stands up, shivering. She hears chanting in the distance, a sporadic holler or two. Dim lights in the same place. She moves toward the spectacle, her heart stirred by faint but identifiable drum rhythms, by a heightening unison of frenzied voices.

As she stumbles in the night she tries to use moonlight to spot the man-made landmarks with which she's familiar. But they're gone. Alex's storage shed, where his team's fossil and pottery evidence is kept, apparently no longer exists. Her own encampment's tents have also disappeared. None of her people are around. Have they all succumbed to some sort of temporary insanity? Are they the ones responsible for the chanting? *Jose, where have you gone?* Myriam wonders. She regrets the earlier flaring of her temper, her petty rancor. *Have you joined them and given free reigns to your passion? I'd like to see that! Or perhaps you've rushed off in search of medical assistance, while I lie here hallucinating, having some kind of stroke or seizure.*

But Myriam's body seems to be functioning fine. The freezing wind carves runnels of goose-bumps across the exposed areas of her arms and legs, sending waves of chills through her skin. Her face twitches at the cold, her body shudders. Grinding her teeth, she pushes forward, enticed now more than anything by the promise of heat.

Soon Myriam realizes that she's headed toward the Kalasasaya. This is perhaps the greatest of all remaining Tiwanaku structures: a rectangular enclosure aligned with the cardinal directions, made of alternating tall stone columns and smaller rectangular blocks, with a central sunken court overlooked by the famous Gate of the Sun several steps above. This, she discovers, is the source of the commotion. A celebration of epic, stentorian proportions is underway.

They've all gone mad, Myriam thinks. *My team; Alex's team; all of them. They're out of their minds!*

But the dancing flames that sprout up from *mecheros*, the massive ceramic lamps, reveal something different. A throng of several thousand people is crammed into the Kalasasaya, a group much larger than that of both archaeological teams combined, even if local coca-munching *ayudantes* were included. And none of them look like the field archaeologists or academics Myriam knows. Their bodies are short and squat, an exaggerated version of modern-day Bolivians'; their faces, transfixed in various grimaces of ecstasy or terror, are rectangular, with short stubby noses and small ears. Some of their skulls, she notices, are u Don't they notice how different nnaturally long. It takes her breath away. Those heads must be the product of cranial stretching at an early age.

That hasn't been practiced in Bolvia for centuries.

Closer still, Myriam sees their excited muscles rippling under skin that glistens with fever sweat, as they stampede in concert to the drummers' pounding and the chanters' incantations. Many of their bodies and faces are dabbed in gaudy colors, the same paints that cover the stone faces protruding from the columns: bright reds, yellows, oranges, whites, browns. Some writhe with their eyes closed, lost in private universes—surely the result of hallucinogens in the food and in the smoke. *Chicha*, the common maize beer, is being passed around in copious quantities. Standing at the rim of the court now, Myriam makes out a plethora of objects, unremarkable except for the fact that she has never before seen them intact: ancient bowls, urns, vases, beakers with scalloped rim-edges, effigy jars, flat-bottomed bottles, tripod forms, *tabletas de rape*, or wooden snuff tablets, and the *sahumerios*, or incense burners, spewing veritable billows of intoxicants into the night. Some of the *lebrillos*, or jars, are short-bodied with large, out-flaring rims that are as disproportionate as those elongated skulls. There are snuff pipes aplenty, too, and everywhere the famous *keros*, the ceremonial beer-drinking vessels, being passed from person to person, sloshing *chicha* with every changing of hands.

Myriam ventures forward, entranced. No one seems to notice her. Don't they see how different she looks? How odd her clothes and features are? She climbs the steps until she is standing at one side of the central courtyard. Still no one shows any interest in her presence. She reaches her hand forward.

It passes, immaterial, through the undulating bodies inches beside her.

This must be a dream, she thinks. *I don't exist*. Or perhaps the god Viracocha, creator of the sun, moon, and stars—of time itself—has transported her to this place so that she may witness first-hand what the Tiwanaku were really like. *Why not?* she thinks. *If Viracocha fashioned time, then surely he can move a mere mortal like me through it*. But she has been rendered insubstantial in the bargain, wraith-like. She can see, but cannot be seen.

Poor Myriam, Awuna thinks. *She sees, but she does not see.*

Myriam lingers at the edge of the square, attempting to be practical. *Surely*, she reasons, *if I've been brought here it's for a purpose. What is she supposed to see or do?*

She studies the way the Tiwanaku dance, the patterns of their movements. She tries to memorize the sequence of drumbeats. Then two dancers, quite drunk, break off from the group and start kissing beside her, their limbs occasionally passing through her. After a few moments the woman pauses, says something, and the man laughs at her. He tilts his chin upward. They begin to speak again, but their passion has turned sour, into agitation. The fate of the world depends on this conversation, and by the looks of it the world is going to end. Myriam listens intently to their language. *That's it!* she realizes. Those quick guttural bursts of consonants, the staccato cascades of vowels—*no one else has ever heard the Tiwanaku speak*, she thinks. *They have left us no writing. This is the closest we will ever get to decoding their communication.* She reaches frantically for the notepad and pen in her pocket. Good! Both are still here with her. Younger team members have given her grief about using pen and paper more than once, glibly poking fun at her antiquated methods. "Why must we sleep in these uncomfortable tents? Why must you write on paper, instead of using an iPad?" For them half the thrill of their work is seeing the reactions of far-away friends and colleagues to their findings. They live in a world of instant gratification, powered by wi-fi, mingling in sprawling social media networks she doesn't understand, all of it floating in an invisible data cloud. Myriam feels vindicated by the realization than an iPad would probably be useless to her here. Who needs their cloud? She's *in* a cloud of her own right now; she's in the sky, over the rainbow, beyond the horizon of the known. Viracocha, or whoever has brought her here, is not taunting her. That she has a way of writing down what these two quarreling lovers are saying proves it. She writes down as many words as she can, scribbling furiously, using simple phonetic approximations. The lovers' row goes on for a few more minutes before it dissolves in an embrace. Myriam feels only vaguely guilty for wishing that the tiff would go on. But they are only whispering now, as they caress face and neck, and soon the man is fondling the woman's breasts. The woman closes her eyes and moans. Hand in hand, they trot down the steps, receding into nearby shadows, where Myriam is sure they will do more than caress and fondle.

The amorous display makes Myriam think about the last time she experienced passion of that type. She can't, at least not easily. And that's depressing. *A train straight to glumness central*, she thinks. Blinking the self-pity away, she refocuses on her surroundings. There's so much beauty here that her endorphins rush. If only she could capture what she's seeing—

Her fingers reach down into her left pocket. There it is! Her camera. Unbelievable. The gods must truly intend for her to be a pioneer, to document what no one else has been able to document.

She whips it out and starts snapping away, flash on maximum. She checks the first few electronic stills on the camera's screen to be sure the pictures are taking. They are, and crystal clear, too. *But what if they're erased later on,* she worries, *lost during the trip back?* So while she continues to click away like a demon she tries to absorb every detail of her surroundings mentally as well, as though by osmosis. She devises complex mnemonics to stash away strings of knowledge, like pearl necklaces. The faces of the animals carved into the vessels and effigies around her seem to come alive as she commits their every contour and shade to memory. Toothy jaguars, pumas, birds, abstract geometric elements and half-divine figures, they all glow with a secret inner life under the intensity of her regard. She smiles. From her notes and pictures and memories, she is sure, will be derived the findings of a lifetime.

After a while, her mind wearies of such an intense pitch. Little by little she starts to come down from her high, until the startling wondrousness of her environment becomes a normal, expected strangeness, like that of a hyper-realistic video game, but a video game nonetheless, something commonplace.

Her senses have been saturated by the goings on at the Gate of the Sun, so she wanders around until she reaches another treasured Tiwanaku structure, this one in the Kericala area, where few seem to dwell at present: the Gate of the Moon. The monument sits atop a three-tiered pyramid and is engraved in a style similar to the Gate of the Sun, with the same dizzying arrays of geometric symbols. *From the fourth period,* the scholar inside Myriam whispers, *400-800 AD; marvel at its impeccable condition.* In fact, from what she can tell in the moonlight, whose sheen the gate transforms into silver animal shapes, the stone looks so smooth, the carvings so sharp, it may as well have been erected yesterday.

Myriam breathes deeply, stilled and comforted by the discovery.

And yet the sense of well-being is precarious, brittle. Away from the crowds, the cold envelops Myriam once more, her breath freezing white puffs. She realizes she is alone. Here as much as in the present. The insight penetrates her core, numbing her.

No one will believe her when she returns to her time. Why should they? Her tale will be outlandish by any standards. She'll have proof in the pictures and scribbles. But some other explanation will be found for her "evidence." *The scrawls of a delusional woman,* they'll say. The sounds can't be checked against any other references, so how will she make her case? And the pictures will be even worse: *digitally created fantasies,* they'll claim, *disguised to look like photographs. Her project was a failure, and she grew desperate. She concocted the whole thing.* She wouldn't believe it herself, if she was one of them.

Awuna realizes what is happening to Myriam: Awuna's consciousness is beginning to destabilize her. It should not be so. It should take much longer for her surreptitious presence to have any effect whatever. But she's become the source of the undercurrents of self-doubt tugging at Myriam. Perhaps the stress of the jump, combined with her presence, has proved too great a burden. Or perhaps Myriam's mind was already in a more debilitated state than Awuna had realized.

No matter. She must take action before the damage becomes irreparable. Myriam can survive a few more minutes in the past, no more.

A girl, perhaps twelve years old, finds Myriam. Myriam is sure the girl will pass right through her, as all others from this era have done, but she's wrong. The girl stands a few feet away, staring *at* her with fixed black eyes. Just as Myriam asks how this is possible—an inconsistency inside an impossibility, she muses—the girl speaks. From her tone Myriam guesses the girl is asking her a question.

She has no idea how to respond. Even if she knew the Tiwanaku language, what would she tell a girl from this time? Myriam's intellect, her experience from decades out in the field, scrambles for answers, stirring up a dozen panicked, half-finished thoughts about rituals, food, storytelling.

The girl asks her question again. She is calm, poised. She points at Myriam, then at the sky, back at Myriam.

That's when Myriam realizes the real root of the problem. Time and culture are not the barriers preventing her from effective communication; it is her own insecurity, stemming from her lack of experience with children and the bizarreness of her situation. *Tranquila*, Myriam tells herself. *Be calm, like the girl.*

"It's a beautiful night," Myriam says. She stares up at the moon.

The girl nods, then points in the general direction of Lake Titicaca. She trembles. Fear? Anticipation?

Myriam studies the girl for any signs that she may be considered special, part of a privileged caste. If she is, she may be bound for the *Iñaq Uyu*, or Temple of the Moon, on Lake Titicaca's *Isla de la Luna*: a sacred moon observation center where the *nustas*, the virgins of the sun, are chosen. Perhaps tonight's festivities signal the end of one chapter of the girl's life, and another will begin when the sun rises. If only Myriam could stay here longer and find out...

The girl smiles, sings for a moment, then walks back toward the Gate of the Sun.

The experience fills Myriam's mind with strange thoughts. She ponders the scope of her immersion in this time. If she's really here, in the seventh or eighth century AD, as she's surmised, what is her permitted level of interaction with the local environment? The temperature is affecting her, so she is not thermodynamically isolated. Clearly, too, she can smell. Which means that molecules are entering her body through her nose. Can she eat? Can she drink? What about the touch of physical objects? If she damages an effigy jar, will it irrevocably alter ensuing centuries?

She wishes there was a way to truly bleed through, to touch these people. She feels like they would understand her. They would instinctively respond to what drives her. They share her thirst for the ineffable, the transcendent. Isn't that why she was drawn to their culture in the first place? Myriam wants in this moment, more than anything, to become one with the dancers and the love-makers and the farmers and the priests of the Gate of the Sun.

She longs for connection. She wants to leave her smallness behind.

There, Awuna thinks. *There it is.* Just in the instants preceding the return jump, Myriam has experienced a flicker of understanding.

Too little too late, but it's better than nothing.

The heavens above Myriam peel back to reveal a tunnel in the sky. Pinpricks of starlight framing the tunnel's edges become lances that tumble together to form a bridge of light, one that rushes down at her from the vastness and lifts her up off the ground, flings her forward, rushing up into the cosmic wilderness. . .

Light flickers.

Pain.

Myriam moans.

She twists her body away from the brightness. A shaft of sunlight is poking through her tent flaps.

The magnitude of her headache makes it difficult to recall anything about the previous night. Did she get drunk? She's not a heavy drinker, and doesn't remember doing so, and has none of the symptoms she'd expect if this was a hangover—no thirst, shakiness, rapid heartbeat. She gets up slowly, checks her face in a mirror. Eyes look fine. She staggers outside, pain lingering in her temples. The sun, high in the sky, causes her to squint, exacerbating her discomfort. Then too she's embarrassed, because she's not used to sleeping this late into the morning.

Jose comes running up to her. "There you are!"

She rubs her face. "Yes, I'm here. Where else would I be?"

He's about to say something, stops himself. "Don't tell me you don't remember? You got sick yesterday, during our lunch. I brought you to your tent. You fell down. Alejandro, your ethnobotanist, looked after you for a while. You had a fever. He left after his dinner. I came back to see how you were doing and you weren't here."

The shooting pains are finally starting to dissipate. Myriam feels like her brain has been twisted into a pretzel and she's only now unfolding it. Memories from last night flood back, bringing both confusion and tremendous relief. Myriam's hands touch her pockets, where she can feel the bulge of the notebook and pen, the camera. The proof is right there. But one look at Jose tells her this isn't a good time to debut her extraordinary story. "I must have been stretching my legs," she says instead.

"In the freezing cold, without your jacket? It was inside the tent when I dropped by last night. And this morning you still weren't back."

"I'm not sick," Myriam says. "Feel my forehead."

Jose does so. "Okay. So where *were* you? I was worried."

Despite everything that's happened between them, Myriam grins. "Thank you," she says. "Really. It was a weird night. Can you give me a few minutes to get my head together?"

Jose looks disconcerted. "Sure," he says. "Then maybe you can address the team. They got a little nervous when you didn't show up for breakfast this morning."

Myriam can understand why: they probably thought she bailed. But the last thing she wants to do is talk to the group now, offer pat reassurances that she's all right, that the project is proceeding apace. For starters, she probably *isn't* all right. She believes that she travelled back in time thirteen hundred years last night. Doesn't that make her crazy, psychotic? And the project isn't moving forward. This week she'll probably get the news that there's no more money.

Yet no good will come of admitting defeat publicly. If she does, her career will effectively be over. Who else would want to work with her? Word spreads fast in such a small field. And some still resent her, simply because she's a woman and archaeology's history is male-dominated. Schliemann, Pitt Rivers, Petrie, Evans, Carter—a boy's club. Her role models are different: Kathleen Kenyon, Harriet Hawes, Maria Reiche, Dolores Piperno. South American male chauvinism minimizes their accomplishments, as it will hers. She must be twice as diligent, twice as impressive with her work, as the men, just to level the playing field. If she quits now Alex will come swooping in, with his boyish good looks, his white teeth and jutting square jaw, and take over, misrepresenting her work, lying to the media, spinning a dramatic yarn about Myriam's "breakdown" while he promises to rescue her research from the brink of disaster.

No, that won't do.

Myriam's resolve strengthens. She reviews her notes, the pictures in her camera. Her trip last night was not a dream. She really did go back. She spent time among the Tiwanaku. She experienced one of their seasonal celebrations. That changes everything. The world doesn't need to know what she's been through. It's only important that *she* know it's true. That's all that matters.

For now, she'll speak to the group. She'll feign a smile. She'll sound convincing. Then she'll request an extension of the grant. It can be done. She'll be persuasive. She'll enlist Jose's help.

"I'm ready," she tells Jose, who has been pretending not to hover by her tent while he hovers by her tent.

After I'm done with this meeting, Myriam thinks, *I'll head to the Kalasasaya. I'll stand below the face of the staff god carved into the Gate of the Sun, and I will talk to him.*

And perhaps he will reply.

In that moment something seems to rise up from her. She feels lighter.

Renewed.

Awuna's primary Time Commission evaluator and once-mentor, Sefaraya, arrives right on schedule, floating up towards her in the memory-pool. Without preamble, Sefaraya diffuses her thoughts into Awuna's mind. "Have you made your choice?"

"I have," Awuna sends back.

Sefaraya absorbs Awuna's relevant memories. "I see you have performed your investigation in an unusual way. You allowed one of the twenty-first-century humans to directly observe the culture they were studying. Why?"

"I felt like I owed it to them."

"To whom?"

"The twenty-first-century humans."

Sefaraya pauses. "We do not owe them anything. They were. Now they are no more. A simple state of affairs. Time inters all except us, and we unearth only those whom we see fit to unearth. Being chosen for our Catalogue is a privilege, not a right; never forget it."

"Of course."

"What, then, did the woman learn from her immersion among the Tiwanaku?"

Awuna feels the pressure of the evaluator's question. It is Awuna's frame of mind, her ability to narrate the past and defend her choices, that is being tested. "Not very much," she admits. "It *was* an intense personal experience for her—as might be expected. But she wasn't able to share it with her tribe. She remained isolated. She failed to understand the importance of the Tiwanaku's collective connection with their own past. Her tribe, the twenty-first century humans, remained largely disconnected from *its* past. Only a few specialists like herself had any inkling of what preceded their civilization. Ignorance was common, temporal knowledge scarce."

"And so what are we to make of her failure? Of her people's failure?"

"We judge the merit of past civilizations not by their artistic, military or scientific accomplishments," Awuna recites, following the venerated formula, "but rather by the depth of their temporal continuity. Despite all the excavations and analyses, and even the rare gift I afforded the archaeologist, the twenty-first-century humans failed to learn that the Tiwanaku's most profound trait was embracing their history *as a group.* Myriam's people remained prisoners of the belief that their time was somehow privileged, distinct from that of their ancestors'. They did something worse than renounce their history; they ignored it. My choice is therefore clear."

"Your argument is a compelling one," Sefaraya declares. "But what of the objection that Myriam may not be representative of her people? There were billions of those beings, after all, compared to perhaps only half a million Tiwanaku."

"Myriam was one of their best, trained in the past," Awuna counters, sidestepping the trap. "If *she* could not understand, what chance is there that the majority ever would?"

"Very well. Let it be noted, for the record, that while you pursued your study, a myriad of other Time Commission members performed a similar evaluation of the twenty-first-century humans, immersing themselves in hundreds of other cities and years. They agree with your decision, and I find no further objections to your argument."

"The Tiwanaku shall therefore be restored and brought into the Catalogue," Awuna announces, concluding the formalities. "And the twenty-first century humans will remain a memory, trapped in the amber of time."

Sefaraya expresses her concurrence chemically. "Congratulations," she sends. "You are now one of us. You are a Preserver."

Awuna gives herself little time to celebrate. There is one final matter to attend to.

The twenty-first-century humans will remain extinct, yes. But not *all* of them. With her new abilities Awuna can, discretely, send one of them back; fling one individual's consciousness on a one-way trip to a body and time and people where it will truly belong, and from which it will be resurrected by Awuna's own kin two thousand centuries later. None of her peers will notice such a tiny move. They are too busy investigating a million other cultures during a million other times.

A small gift for the assistance she unwittingly provided, Awuna tells herself. It would be inappropriate for a Preserver to admit anything more, even to herself.

Myriam wakes to find herself in a strange body, a young girl playing with her hair, singing songs of the Gate of the Sun and the Gate of the Moon, and of the great lake atop the stone at the center of the world.

Acknowledgments

Foreword © 2015 by Nisi Shawl
Introduction © 2015 by Eric T. Reynolds
Cover Her Corpse with a Feathered Cape © 2015 by Jennifer Crow
The Ball Game © 2015 by Kaolin Imago Fire
The Alux's Cave © 2015 by Jamie Lackey
The Red Queen © 2015 by Gerri Leen
One Village © 2015 Neil O'Donnell
Would Olympus Fall © 2015 Lou Antonelli
Searching for Peace © 2015 Rob Darnell
The First Time © 2015 by Tammy A. Branom
This Love Remains © 2015 by Rebecca L. Brown
The Seam of Life and Death © 2015 by Vannessa McClelland
To Touch the Past © 2015 by Memory Scarlett
The Spaceman's Tomb © 2015 Sarah Frost
The Delver © 2015 by Ransom Noble
Uno Por Por Cada © 2015 by M.C. Chambers
Moundville Revisited © 2015 by Amy L. Herring
Encantado © 2015 by Micah Hyatt
Gate of Sun, Gate of Moon © 2015 by Alvaro Zinos-Amaro